THE TWISTED BOOK OF SHADOWS

Edited by

Christopher Golden
&
James A. Moore

Introduction by

Linda D. Addison

With assistance from

Rachel Autumn Deering
Lee Thomas
KL Pereira
Nadia Bulkin
&
Linda Nagle

Twisted Publishing
An imprint of Haverhill House Publishing

The editors would like to dedicate *The Twisted Book of Shadows* in memory of **Charles L. Grant**.

Cover design & setup by Dyer Wilk

978-1-949140-15-6 Hardcover
978-1-949140-09-5 Trade Paperback
978-1-949140-14-9 Leather Bound Ltd ed.

For more information, address:

Twisted Publishing
Haverhill House Publishing LLC
643 E Broadway
Haverhill MA 01830-2420
www.haverhillhouse.com

The Twisted Book of Shadows

Acknowledgments

The editors would like to thank the contributors, of course, but also every other author who submitted a story to The Twisted Book of Shadows and waited patiently for our reply. We owe our gratitude to all the people who contributed money to the crowdfunding that financed this book and made certain that we could pay the authors a professional rate for their work, as well as to everyone who posted about our call for submissions, particularly in traditionally marginalized writing communities. Our thanks to our publisher, John M. McIlveen, to everyone on the Twisted Publishing team, and to the indefatigable Matt Bechtel, who not only ran the crowdfunding effort but played traffic cop for all 700 plus submissions, making sure we had no idea who had written which stories until we had already accepted or rejected them. Finally, massive thanks to our editorial committee—those authors who waded with us through hundreds of stories, searching for the best of the best. KL Pereira, Nadia Bulkin, and Lamar Giles read some of the submissions, and we're grateful to them. Linda D. Addison, Rachel Autumn Deering, and Lee Thomas read every single story that came in, and for that extraordinary effort, we're eternally indebted. Finally...thanks to you, every one of you who purchased this book, supporting short horror fiction and horror anthologies and new and emerging writers. Thank you so much.

TABLE OF CONTENTS

INTRODUCTION: SHAKEN AND STIRRED

Linda D. Addison

Everything created by humans begins as an idea. The editors of this anthology wanted to create a professional paying opportunity for authors and have submissions open to anyone. No slots were reserved for established authors, and no personal invitations were distributed. They hoped to introduce lesser-known writers to the horror community, as has been done in the past with other anthologies.

As a result of the discussion of how to make this as inclusive as possible, they put together a diverse editorial committee of writers and editors (I was one of them) charged with reading the stories sent as blind submissions. The call for work was distributed as widely as possible. I hope other editors will take notice of this approach of creating editorial readers of different cultural, etc. backgrounds. In this way, writing that may contain more expansive human elements, but is still well-written, will be published.

The window for submissions was one month; the shortest month of the year, February.

A wonderful thing happened —hundreds of stories were submitted. A daunting thing happened —hundreds of stories were submitted. How to go from seven hundred stories to the nineteen in this book was the challenge. The selection criteria used: well-written, twisted, shadowy stories. The hope was that an open call would bring in stories with characters and by authors more representative of the world.

As one of the readers, I can tell you that many more than nineteen stories grabbed my attention. I'm relieved I didn't have to make the final decisions. How that was done is worth talking to the editors about, but I imagine there were some heart-breaking conversations involved. My job (and the job of each member of the editorial committee) was to pass the editors our individual lists of the stories we recommended. There was no limit to how many stories we could select, and I can tell you, my list was a long one.

Although I've been writing short fiction for many years, I learned a lot from having to read so many submissions in a brief period. There's a short list of the lessons I will carry with me; I include them at the end of this introduction.

Once the decisions were made, I sat down to read the book you have in your hands without editorial pressure. Even though I had seen these stories before, with the hundreds of submissions, they were brand new to my reader's mind. New and darkly twisted. Some of the stories made me want to turn on more lights, others made my heart ache, and each and every one stands strong.

The editors' vision of creating an anthology of excellent stories from familiar and lesser-known authors, with characters and storylines reflecting an interesting mix of humanity, worked out beautifully.

I've edited a horror anthology that was open to story lines without one specific theme (ex. *Killer Dogs from New Jersey*, which I made up, but feel free to use it). It was interesting to look at the anthology after it had been set and see the common themes that presented themselves. What patterns surface, I believe, are echoes of the real-life shadows in the human condition.

There are stories with love, loss, and/or surviving death and demons through romantic, sibling, and parental attachments. There is a fair amount of family dynamics with flawed parents, resulting in nightmarish scenarios. Some loved ones are called back from the dead to soothe a grieving parent or lover; other times there are dangerous attachments in the shattered, razor stories of siblings torturing/testing each other and their parents. The family themes made these very unsettling (in a good way).

Of course, there are demons, ghosts, and the undead in the mix, but in unpredictable, edgy ways. There are creatures like dogs, cats, flies, coyotes, wolves, and grubs and unexpected ones: chickens (yes, chickens!), rabbits, chipmunks, horses, sparrows, octopuses —with some fungus thrown in for good measure.

There's been discussion in the horror community over the years about work that is a mix of horror and science fiction. I was delighted to read the stories with portals to other dimensions, strange alternate futures, and lost extraterrestrials (some who wanted human sacrifices, others survived by creating symbiotic relationships with physically/psychologically damaged humans).

Each story left me chilled and deeply appreciative of the author's imagination. Each tale, from start to finish, reflects a different facet of human desire/fear/greed/loss/sacrifice, told so well that I sat and let my reactions marinate before reading the next. Now it's your turn to enjoy (in that way readers of horror find joy in being disturbed) these twisted pieces of shadow!

p.s. What I've learned from reading hundreds of stories:

- make the genre (ex. horror) clear from beginning
- the first page matters, write with energy
- keep the energy high
- keep flashbacks short/tight
- make the approach to an old storyline unique
- make endings consistent/not rushed
- even a good style/voice needs all the above.

Linda D. Addison, award-winning author of ***"How to Recognize a Demon Has Become Your Friend"*** and *HWA Lifetime Achievement Award* winner.

The Pale Mouth

Melissa Swensen

The bacon was too crispy. And she'd scorched the coffee. It was obvious in the way he shook the newspaper. She wondered how he'd express his displeasure when they stopped printing the paper next month and every household was issued electronic readers.

In the other room the TV blared cartoons. The kids giggled along. For a moment, the sound blurred into the harsh kitchen light and Layla had to grip the sink to steady herself. Her skin prickled. Her eyes hurt. God, they hurt. Mac's sweet, abundant aftershave clashed with the acrid burnt coffee and threatened to give her a headache. There were seven naked bulbs in the kitchen, the mandated amount for the room's square footage, and the light felt like a branding iron on her eyes. No one else ever seemed to be bothered, but for Layla the days were a raw nerve licked by an endless flame. She pressed her fingers against her eyelids. A rare moment of relief.

A mouth appeared in the oily darkness; framed by colorless lips, it moved against the inside of her mind. An ashen face formed around the pale slit in the black, eyes glinting like quicksilver from their own light. Layla saw a hand reaching for her.

It flickered.

Something beeped, and kept beeping and beeping. The newspaper banged against the table, rattling dishes. Layla covered her ears. The sound of the alarm ripped like hot iron through her skull. Mac had his back to her. She whirled around to the cabinet next to the sink and yanked it open. Lightbulbs of various sizes and wattages filled the cupboard from top to bottom. She grabbed the one she needed and tossed it across the kitchen to him. They looked at each other briefly. Layla smelled the children lingering at the edge of the room, their sugar and sweat. She didn't look, instead she covered her ears again and fought the urge to close her eyes, letting the glaring light burn itself onto her sensitive retinas as punishment; they burned. Everything burned. Mac had the new bulb out of its packaging and held it next to the old one as he unscrewed it with quick, precise movements. Layla fought back the frisson of laughter that welled up in her throat. The old bulb fell into Mac's grip; the room dimmed slightly. The new lightbulb tightened in its grooves and the beeping stopped. Layla's ears felt cottony. The kids stood in the doorway, looking up at Mac with their cow eyes.

"Go back to your cartoons, kids. Nothing to worry about." He said it quietly so they'd know he was angry with Mommy. They turned around without a glance in her direction. In the family room the TV's volume went up. It wasn't necessary, though; Mac never yelled. Layla ached to close her eyes as she walked over to the new bulb. She entered the reset code on the timer and the new ‘hours remaining’ flickered onto the digital readout. 480 hours. Twenty days.

“It’s just one light,” she said, against his silence.

“One today, one tomorrow. What if three or four went out at once?” He was clearing dishes off the table. Doing her job to remind her she wasn’t.

“You know that isn’t possible. The failsafes…” she trailed off. He didn’t know as well as she did that each light burned for an exact amount of time and that those times were staggered. They would never all go out at once, not unless she replaced all seven in the room at the same time with bulbs of the same lifespan. But if she did that, the signal each lamp sent back to the County would show it, and they’d send techs out within thirty minutes to ‘correct her mistake’. It wasn’t possible to live in darkness; every room was lit just like this one, and there was protocol upon protocol for her to follow to keep it that way. Layla spent hours every week checking, monitoring, and changing the bulbs. And then she logged all her actions into her data account on the County’s website so they could monitor her. Darkness could not happen. She watched Mac. His back was tensed as he stood over the kitchen sink.

“I guess it’s not you that’ll get taken into the dark if you let the lights go out.” His voice was a hot shaft of sunlight spat out against her dysfunction. She closed her eyes.

One second, two, three.

The pale mouth-

Open.

The monsters that came out of the dark took children, usually babies, but sometimes the older ones, too. It had been two years since the last abduction. A toddler had accidentally been locked in a toy chest. All they'd left behind were its eyes. Now all chests and trunks had to be registered and fitted with lights or destroyed and replaced with clear plastic bins. The trunk lights were monitored wirelessly. Everything was monitored. It wasn't as dangerous as it used to be when she and Mac were young, but that was because of Layla and all the other Primaries.

"It was an accident, that's all, Mac."

"You're the Primary. The first line of defense."

"I know what I am." She smelled his fear. It trickled down his back in a wet rivulet. She closed her eyes. The pale mouth was quick this time, right by her ear. But the light on the other side of her eyelids acted like static. She felt a hand on her shoulder. She hadn't heard him walk over to her; the pale voice could do that. Blind her and deafen her. Tempt her to the darkness she craved. Even if she didn't know why she craved it. Or why she was drawn to the creature.

"You have to be more careful, Layla."

She nodded. He kissed her cheek and left for work. They were on Winter Schedule, the doors had unlocked precisely at 7:15, sunrise. She let her eyes fall closed again. Ten, fifteen seconds. *The pale mouth rasped, and she shivered. It had been haunting her mind for two weeks and every time she closed her eyes the voice got clearer. She wanted to understand.*

The kids were screaming. Layla opened her eyes and winced at the pain. In the family room, she switched off the TV.

"You know the rules. If you fight over cartoons, no one watches anything. Go get dressed for school. The bus will be here in twenty minutes." Ethan, the youngest, groaned and fell backwards onto the carpet.

"Are you going to double check all the lights today?" He stretched like a kitten. Amanda, just a year older, tugged on his foot.

"She's the Primary, that's what she does everyday." She tickled her brother's toes.

"But she'll do it special today, right Mom?" Ethan said through giggles.

"Of course I will. I'll triple check." Layla felt her chest tighten. "Now go get ready for school." The kids raced off up the stairs to their rooms. Layla pictured them with no eyes, blood oozing from dark, hollow sockets. Forever dark. They both had Mac's eyes anyway.

Layla ate dinner in silence. The kids were chatting to their father about the day. It was cloudy and had snowed. Headlamps had been required all day. The kids loved them and strutted around like adventurers. Their father had been less enthused; the headlamps seemed ridiculous in an accountant's office. Hypocrite, Layla thought. She had been stuck in the house all day. Primaries maintained the light and needed to avoid any injuries bad weather might cause. They were only allowed out on stormy days to knock the snow off easily accessible exterior lights. Government crews took care of everything else. She had triple checked, as promised, all the bulbs and the wiring as well. There were no switches in the house since the lights were not allowed to be turned off. The wiring was maintained by the County, but at Primary training she'd learned how to check it and spot potential problems. She was even trained to do minor repairs as long as they were approved by the County, and providing she posted before and after pictures on the website. Despite her longing for the darkness she imagined fell like thick syrup outside, and despite what Mac thought, she could never kill her family. The County had too many failsafes.

"Mommy!" It was Ethan's little boy squeak that pulled her from the abyss she wished would swallow her.

"Yes, Honey?"

"We got a new hamster at school. The old one died last week." He shoved the last bite of his mashed potatoes in his mouth while he talked.

"I'm sorry, that must have been sad." Layla smiled at the glob of food that fell from his chin as his face grew serious.

"It bit me once."

"Well, then good riddance."

"Layla, honestly." Mac shook his head at her, that same fire from earlier flaring in his eyes. Layla blinked, slowly.

"Anyone want chocolate silk pie?"

"You made pie?" Mac raised his eyebrows. Layla saw nothing but suspicion pooled underneath them.

"Yes, I made pie."

"That's wonderful. Thank you, Dear."

Layla got up and opened the fridge. The light wasn't on. She let out a nipped squeal.

"What is it?" Mac was collecting dirty dishes. Layla slammed the door shut.

"Defective light, the meter still reads 104 hours remaining." She avoided Mac's eyes; she didn't want to see the suspicion in them. She couldn't control defects.

"Here's my headlamp, Mom," Amanda said, flinging it across the table.

"Thank you, Sweetheart." She snatched it out of the air by the strap and pulled a fresh bulb from the drawer next to the fridge. Pulling the lamp over the crown of her head, she opened the door again. Pale fingers emerged from the dark maw at the back of the fridge and curled around the milk jug. Layla bit her lip as translucent claws shot out from its fingertips. The thing's hand gripped the jug, puncturing the tough plastic. Behind her, as a muffled chuckle rustled in the gaping darkness, Mac distracted the children with talk of weekend plans. The creature walked its fingers forward, revealing a hand just like a human's. The claws retracted as it reached a bowl of oranges and closed around the thick-skinned fruit. Someone moved behind her and Layla switched the headlamp on. From the darkness came a gurgled cry and the hand pulled back, still holding the orange. A voice hissed, "Bad girl." The hand was visibly blistered as it retreated to the shadows at the edges of the headlamp's light. Layla covered her mouth with one hand and unscrewed the faulty bulb with the other, trembling one. The new bulb flooded the fridge with sixty blinding watts. The punctures in the milk jug gaped. She'd have to have a fresh gallon delivered in the morning. She closed her eyes for a second and the pale mouth was there, a hard edge to its usual subtle smile. "Bad," it whispered. Layla opened her eyes and grabbed the pie, slamming the fridge door shut behind her. She turned. Her family smiled at her.

"The pie looks amazing, Hon."

"Thanks Mommy," the kids said in unison.

"I'll have to report the faulty bulb tonight," she said, absently dishing out pie. The knife scraped the bottom of the glass plate and Layla shivered, feeling those claws raking her skin.

That night, as Layla and Mac made love under the nine lights mandated for their master bedroom, she closed her eyes to hear the pale mouth call her bad. She was a bad girl, it said, as Mac laid kisses along her neck.

Her dreams were writhing flashes of light in the dark. Voices called to her as claws and teeth nipped and picked at her flesh, drawing blood, but never really hurting. Their cold caresses raised gooseflesh on her hot skin and made her insides burn. She awoke haunted and exhausted.

She had forgotten to mention the faulty bulb the night before, and forgot it again in her morning report. She had to make excuses when a County rep called to ask why the fridge counter had been reset early. There would be a small fine if she forgot again.

"Nothing is more important than the job of the Primary. You'll be replaced after three mistakes. Do you understand that, Mrs. Hughes? Children are too precious a resource to be left in incompetent hands."

"Yes, of course." Layla had her eyes closed throughout the entire conversation. *The static was clearing. The pale mouth said words like 'touch' and 'forgiven'. Layla watched it move against the black, its lips full and pale pink, its tongue flicking delicately between two rows of sharp, jagged teeth.* She didn't close her eyes the rest of the day.

When darkness fell and Mac was asleep, she tiptoed to the front of the house and unlatched the safety curtain secured over the front window. She barely remembered the night and wondered at the inky black darkness; how soft it must be. She ran cold fingers over her arm. Her skin was dry and flaky and tender. She pulled the heavy, thick curtain back, but no darkness crouched behind it. Beyond her porch light, waist-high lamps lit the path to the sidewalk. The lights continued along the sidewalk up and down the street, streetlamps towering over the treeless neighborhood and lights blazing at regular intervals along the roofline of her house and all the others on the block. Faint patches and pools of shadow lay here and there, but the pools were void of life. Fat winter snowflakes blossomed in the lights.

She dropped the safety shade and secured it to the windowsill. It was odd that the shades were removable at all; the doors and windows locked automatically at curfew and unlocked at dawn. She fell into a rocker in the front room and closed her eyes. It wasn't dark enough. She pressed a chenille throw pillow to her face. The pale mouth appeared.

"Not the way," it whispered. Layla dropped the pillow and rubbed her eyes. She went back to bed. The searing LED light burned her skin until she pulled the covers up over her head. She dreamt of claws and pale kisses.

Morning came with a phone call. Surveillance cameras had caught her peeking out the window after curfew. One more infraction and she'd be removed from the home and replaced. At the detention center, she'd expect no trial; her infractions were well documented, and she'd be charged with criminal neglect. A judge would determine the length of her sentence, but it would be a minimum of three years while she was re-trained. Layla listened, and said she thought she had heard a scream.

"Then you should have called the police. There's nothing you can do about a scream outside, Mrs. Hughes. I'm required to inform you that a message of concern has been sent to your Secondary, Mac Hughes."

"Of course," Layla said. She slammed the phone into its cradle before the woman could say goodbye.

She made her rounds, replacing one bulb in the hall bathroom and one in Ethan's room before she tugged on her coat and went out into the snow. The big, wet flakes had come down fast the night before and now the snow clung to her boots as she high-stepped through it. A blazing sun hung in the sky above the glistening, white landscape and burned tears into her eyes. In the corner of the backyard crouched an old shed with peeling paint and a sunken roof. It was useless and the County had it scheduled for demolition in the spring, but until then, it had to be lit, so it had to be checked.

Inside, white shafts of sunlight streamed in from gaps in the roof, paling the three yellow bulbs hanging from the center beam. Layla inhaled the faint smell of rot suspended by the cold and exhaled expectation; her breath curled around her like pale fingers. A stepladder leaned against the wall by the door and she dragged it over to the lights. The first lightbulb had 382 hours remaining, the second 240, and the third, 144. She marked the hours on her clipboard and closed her eyes, she hadn't closed them yet that day.

"Come out of the light." The mouth smiled, pale pink lips pulling back against teeth like broken glass. Claws brushed her cheek. Blood hummed through her veins. Snow fell in wet clumps from the trees. A rat burrowed through the snow. Layla felt the heaviness of light crushing the shed, bearing down on her. "Come out of the light."

Open.

In the corner of the shed, under a blanket, there was an old trunk that only Layla knew about. She'd never opened it, but it seemed big enough for her to squeeze into. The darkness curled inside would receive her, and that would be the end. Or the beginning. She was surprised by how willing she was to give her eyes for a dark new life. The rusted hinges resisted her numb-fingered grip and the lid only gaped at her, tempting. She leaned into the chest and the hinges gave with a pop, snapping from the trunk and sending the lid and Layla crashing to the floor. Light flooded the empty box. She kicked it, its ancient leather crumbling, and it gave way, leaving a hole. She closed her eyes.

"I tried," she told the pale mouth.

"Try again," it ordered.

Mac called on her cellphone while she sat on the cold shed floor. He wondered if their family meant anything at all to her. Why, if he loved her and the kids loved her, didn't she love them back? She did. She said so. Being a Primary was a big responsibility, maybe it was getting to her.

"That must be it," she said. Mac agreed to help her get through it. The County man had already assigned her a therapist. Had told him that therapy could erase her previous infractions if she took it seriously and allowed the therapist to report her progress to the County. She would, of course. She was an open book. He loved her again. He hung up. Layla wondered if she could explain to the therapist that the pale mouth said things she understood best with her body. That it left her dream-scars she felt even in the brightest daylight. That she could smell her children coming and hear flies buzzing in adjacent rooms. She trudged inside. The darkness tracked her like a cat; it was never there when she turned and looked.

Inside, she opened the dishwasher and reached in to grab a clean bowl. A crimson drop of blood slid down the smooth curve of the glass. Then another followed it. Layla pulled her hand back; smudged red fingerprints marred the sky-blue pottery. Had she cut herself in the shed? She leaned over the sink and inspected her fingers. Blood welled at all her fingertips on both hands. She turned the faucet on and rinsed, sucking in a breath as the water stung. With the blood rinsed away she could see hard, clear points emerging from her fingertips, splitting the soft flesh just beneath her fingernails. She pictured the punctured milk jug still sitting in the fridge and vomited into the sink, blood and bile curling down the drain as the hard, sharp points pushed further out of her fingers. A curved, serrated edge appeared at the raw, bloody margin of her skin. Her body trembled despite her efforts to contain it. She closed her eyes. *The pale mouth smiled wide. "Good girl," it said.* Layla lost control and an animal scream escaped her, a ragged howling that eased the pain for a few seconds. But only a few.

It took an hour for the claws to grow to an inch in length. Her hands were numb from the cold water she'd kept running over them and they shook as she scrubbed the blood from the toothed edge. Her body felt unfamiliar, like a secret. It took her an hour to figure out how to retract them with ease like the creature in the fridge. An hour of clearing her mind and thinking of taking things back. But when she did, there were red, swollen slits at each fingertip. How would she hide them? She finished the dishes, the hot, soapy water stinging her skin, and by the end, she was crying.

Layla had gloves on when Mac came home from work.

The kids were at the table doing their homework.

"What's this about?" He said, taking her gloved hand in his, and squeezing. She tried not to flinch.

"My hands are really dry, I think from the cold today. On the internet it said to put lotion on and then wear gloves." She watched him, watched his eyes; they were somewhere else. He handed her a note.

"The name of the therapist. I've already scheduled an appointment for you, the details are written there. As the Secondary, it's my job to keep you in line. And I haven't been, I guess. But that will change. From now on," he pulled her close, "I will be there for you every second."

"Thanks," she muttered into his shoulder.

"Now take those ridiculous gloves off. Your hands are fine."

"No, they're too dry."

"Layla, you are my Primary, I have been too soft on you. Now do as I say and take them off." He pulled at the gloves. Layla didn't fight him. Claws had to be good for something. The gloves slipped off and Mac caressed her hands, turning them over and kissing her palms.

"They feel soft to me," he said. He didn't see the puffy red slits hiding the claws. Layla closed her eyes, the pale mouth smiling at her. When she opened her eyes, Mac was watching her.

"What are you thinking about? You have the cutest quirk to your mouth right now."

"Oh, nothing. Just kissing, I guess."

"Kissing, huh?" He winked and walked to the fridge, to find the light was burnt out again. "Report this immediately." He slammed the door and walked out of the kitchen; the children gathered their books and followed him. Layla was left alone with the dark fridge. She grabbed the new lightbulb and opened the door. A face met hers. Human, but so pale. She recognized the mouth.

"Good girl," it said. She reached out to the creature in the fridge and touched its cold, smooth face. "Come," it said. Layla set the new lightbulb on the counter and closed the fridge door. She walked to the living room. Mac looked up at her from his laptop.

"Go directly to the computer and report that lightbulb." His brow was set firm and he stank of fear. Layla leapt at him, her claws raking his throat. Blood gushed from his neck as he gurgled for help. His wide eyes seemed to search her face, his perfect eyes that never burned in the light. She took them, scraping them out of their sockets with a clawed forefinger. He deserved that. A cranberry scented candle burned on the end table, so she set him on fire. Let him be consumed by painful light. She retreated, shielding her eyes as the fire spread, holding her ears against the shrieking.

The children, she'd almost forgotten their candied scents over the reek of burning flesh. Layla regarded them. They might survive.

She turned and ran to the hall closet. Inside, two bright lights greeted her. She put her hands up and grabbed the bulbs, for once reveling in the burn. Then she let her claws out. The bulbs exploded; the light went out. A hand reached out for her and Layla took it.

CAKE

M.M. De Voe

Your cake knife is missing. One of the boys has taken it, no doubt.

The boys are dark, with mischievous brown eyes and brown curly hair. They look like their father whether scowling or blank. They are miniature versions of him with scraped knees, bruised elbows, brimming with lies. They look nothing like you.

Well...

Maybe around the eyes, when they laugh.

Your daughter is a miraculous blonde, unlike anyone else in the family. Tiny fat Buddha sitting on the kitchen floor. Straw-like tufts of impossibly white hair, blue eyes. Nude, but for the diaper. You swish a finger through the cold, cloudy dishwater, unwilling to get too wet, unwilling to finish your most hated chore, wanting that knife so you can carve yourself a hefty slice of her birthday cake as a treat to reward yourself for getting through another family breakfast.

She examines your feet just outside the spill of

morning sunlight. Pokes at your red-painted toenails until you pull away from the tickle. She seems intent on finding your weaknesses, exploiting them.

Turn away from her to search the rest of the counter. You want that pink, frothy cake. Lift off the cover. Inhale the cloud of sugar. There's her name and the fat number 1 in thick buttery frosting. Cake after breakfast? Why not. Who's watching? Anyway, you baked it—-why shouldn't you eat it whenever you want?

Where's that knife?

Use the cleaver. Hack off a big chunk of pink frosted fluff. Turn back, mouth full of cake, to offer little Sarah a piece, and find her holding a handful of her own straight, white hair in her little plum-sized fist. The hair is not connected to her scalp, and it's tipped in red. The baby's pudgy face is smeared across her pudgy face. It takes a moment even to register that this is blood, because she's not crying. Not making a sound. Just staring curiously at the red-tipped hair. Looking at your toes. What is glinting near her other hand?

The cake knife.

Swoop down and snatch it from the floor.

She is staring in wonder at the tiny red fingerprint she's left on the linoleum. The cat is sniffing at the mark; testing the blood-tipped wisps of hair with a paw.

Okay, it's bad. Not as bad as when Nicholas stabbed Benedict through the hand with a letter opener. Not as bad as when they tied their baby sister to her crib and set the whole thing on fire. But bad. Still, she's not hurt enough to cry. It looks worse than it is. But oh god, the baby, the baby!

Sarah grins when she sees you've noticed her, reaching her hands above her dark-streaked head to show she wants to be carried. Her scalp is oozing blood, but there's no bone showing. Recall from experience that head wounds bleed profusely, but often look worse than they are. Breathe. Red-tipped hair drifts to the floor from her outstretched palm. Did they try to cut her hair with the cake knife? To scalp her?

"Boys! Boys!"

No answer. Perhaps a soft click of Legos in that part of the apartment. A footstep. Your attention returns to the baby, who is still reaching for you.

"Up! Up!" she demands.

A thin streak of red dribbles past her tiny ear and drips from her chin onto her pink overalls. The cat sniffs at the blood, tastes it. Sarah makes a beeline for the family pet, but you scoop the baby into your arms.

"None of that. We have to take you to the doctor, little one. What happened here, sweetie? Show Mommy. Let me see your boo-boo. Yucky, huh? But it's okay; it's just a tiny scratch. You'll be fine. Did your brothers do this? Who gave you the knife, sweetie?"

She smiles widely. Shows off her four new teeth. Coos "am ma ma ma am." Leaves a red smear on your favorite blouse.

You shout towards the den with its eternally closed door: *Watch the boys. I'm taking Sarah to the clinic.*

Strap her into the car seat as she stares with those huge blue eyes welling with betrayal.

Dr. Chandler examines her, fusses over her teeth, slaps her bottom, and sends her home with a little ointment.

Instead of cleaning up, the boys have used their sister's blood to draw a sigil on the wall.

"It's a protection one, mom. Not a bad one."

Bang on the den door: *Didn't you hear me say watch the boys? What part didn't you understand?*

No response.

"Nicholas. Benedict. Clean this mess right away."

They sigh. They whine. They claim it wasn't their fault. They slink away, knowing that if they fitfully return to their Legos, to their trains, you will do their work for them. Put the baby on the floor and roll up your sleeves.

It's always you, cleaning up the mess.

Fifteen minutes later, the walls are pristine, the floor shines, but the house has gone silent except for a strange scraping sound.

Run.

Find the baby playing with the cleaver. It's too heavy for her to pick up by the handle; she is dragging it along behind her by the red ribbon from which it usually hangs. The silver blade shines in the late-morning light, its edge still covered in pink frosting. Luckily all her fingers still seem to be attached. The cleaver makes a clanking, clattering sound behind her as she drags it from the kitchen linoleum and onto the tiles in the hallway.

"How'd you get that?"

The scraping sound of metal-on-tile chills your skin.

Glance at the shadows hoping to see Benedict. He's a hider. No time to really search. Give up. Sarah only learned to walk three weeks ago and is still prone to falling down.

"Akka-poo" she says, smiling. The fresh scab shows dark against her pale scalp. She plunks down on her diapered bottom and notices the fluff of frosting on the cleaver's blade. She opens her mouth for a little taste. Leans forward to the edge, pink tongue eagerly outstretched.

"No, honey. Not safe."

Pry the ribbon from her hand. Don't show the anxiety you feel. She screams as if you've taken her binky. Fights. Kicks. It is as if the cleaver is working against you. Wince as the blade slices into your palm. The handle seems heavy in your hands. She is okay. She is okay. Who gave this to her? Which of the boys did this? When mothers get mad, they have superhuman strength, and you are getting very mad. Conquer that cleaver and brandish it overhead. Ignore the cut on your palm. The cat hides behind a curtain. Sarah totters off after the cat. Let them go.

Bang on the door of the den with the dull edge of the kitchen utensil. No answer. *Could really use some help out here!* No response. *Hey! Come out and give me a hand!*

Nothing. Typical.

Head reeling from a mix of anger drawn from the situation and relief at having averted disaster, brandish the cleaver over your older son.

"Did you give this to your sister?" Nicholas, at eight,

has just begun to realize that this tiny baby might steal everything of value from him. Don't put it past him to set up an accident. "Tell me or I cut your head off."

"Come on. No way, Mom," he shrugs. "Knives are not for babies. I know that." He clearly hasn't budged from the Lego set. What is he building? A mausoleum? He never flinches. Move on to his brother.

"Benedict? Explain how Sarah got this."

Banshees are quieter. Wailing, screaming shrieking denials. "You are so stupid! You hate me! I would *never!*" Dark hair flying. Hold up your palms to fend off this onslaught of noises honed on the playground. He could shatter crystal with those screams.

The den door remains closed. Hack it with the cleaver. Take satisfaction in the deep *thunk* as the metal slashes into the wood. Leave a gouge. Stroke it lovingly.

No response.

Return the cleaver to its high hook in the kitchen. Pour a cup of tea. Relax.

"Mom! Sarah's standing on the windowsill!"

Clatter of cup returned hastily to saucer. Run into the dining room. At the top of a makeshift staircase: chairs, a large crate, a stepstool, a few books…the baby is holding on to the window and waving back at Nicholas.

"Hi!" she says.

Choke back fear. The window is open. It's never open. You live on the 8th floor. Sarah holds her tiny bare foot out over the edge, as if to test the water.

"Honey. Sarah. Not safe. Hold on, mommy's coming."

Wade through the sea of tin soldiers dumped out on the floor like caltrops.

"This isn't funny, Nicholas."

A cold breeze billows the curtains into the room. Sarah sways with surprise and her fingers tighten on the painted sill. She pivots on a heel, a move she often makes before losing her balance. Run to snatch her. She burrows her face through your long red hair and into your neck and bites.

"Ow! No biting, Sarah! That hurt!" A metal spoon hits you in the back of the head. Put her down on the floor. Nicholas is laughing. The baby runs off after the cat.

"Time out for you, Nicholas. Go to your room. This isn't funny; Sarah could have been very hurt. She might have been killed. Honestly. She can barely walk. What were you thinking?"

"She likes to climb," he shrugs. "She wouldn't have fallen."

Close the window and point to his bedroom.

"I didn't open the window, Mom. She did that herself."

Point.

"I didn't do the spoon either."

Point.

"Fine. I'm going. But it's not fair."

An endless string of raps on the door of the den finally elicits a low growl. Finally. *Hey! They take after you, you know. They'd love it if you came out once in a while.* Nothing. So much for communication.

The front door is open. Don't panic. Try to suppress the images of Sarah ready to fall down the stairs, plummet down the elevator shaft, what have you. Dash out of the apartment to check on her. The door clicks softly shut, locking you out.

"You're so stupid, Mom," Benedict's other voice, his loving one, comes from the neighbor's shadowy stoop. That boy can hide.

"Don't use playground language in the house."

"We're not in the house, Mom."

"What are you doing out here?"

"Sarah tricked me, same as you."

"What are you talking about?"

"Sarah locked us out."

"Sarah can't reach the door handle. Don't tell stories."

"You never believe me, Mom. She really did."

"How. You tell me how a baby can unlock and open a door. Tell me. Go ahead."

Benedict falls silent. Glares. Crosses his skinny arms across his chest; the picture of an angry kindergartener copying his mother's moves.

Think about it. Wonder a little. Put together various little scenarios: the way the plastic binky falls to the floor all the time but the spoons never do. The way she loves your noisy keys and can get them from any bag. The way she looks so longingly at that cleaver when you chop the vegetables...or at the cat's metal license and shiny metal nametag on the silver-studded collar. *Wellington Cat.* Brand-new. Happy birthday, Cat.

A mother's instinct moves faster than her brain. Pound the door. Shout. Ring the metallic bell, which of course doesn't work. Of course. Collect yourself. Catch enough breath to tell your five-year old: "Benedict. Run down to Mr. Dan's office, you know the one? Run down there and get him. Third floor. Tell him to bring the extra key. Do you remember our apartment number? Can you manage? Can you do that without me, Benedict? It's really important. Can you do it?"

"Sure, Mom." He goes to the elevator, where he is absolutely forbidden to go alone. He stands as tall as he can and presses the down arrow. He soberly watches until the light goes green. The bell pings. He turns when the elevator doors open. "I can handle it, Mom. Don't worry."

Inside the apartment, there is a crash. The baby screams. Then another crash. More screaming. Pound the door. "Sarah! Let mommy in! Sarah! Please! Honey! Unlock the door! Nicholas?" Nicholas will never hear you. If there is a God, your oldest son is safe in his room, in an unwarranted time-out, probably wearing earphones while playing a video game. And what's new about screams and crashes, anyway? This sort of thing happens all the time.

There is a long silence.

Then Sarah giggles.

"Sarah?" Keep that voice cheerful as you can. "Honey? Can you let mommy in? Sweetie? Unlock the door, okay?"

She can't understand you. She's only one. Twelve months yesterday. She can barely walk. She has a three-word vocabulary. You hear a scrape as — can it be? —

the knife rack slides across the stone kitchen counter and crashes to the floor. She can move metal, that girl. All kids have a talent. Sarah's little hands clap: just picture how happy she is with her work. "Sarah! Let mommy in."

"Kitty! Hi!"

Kitty? Sarah uses that word for any furry creature. Maybe she is after Wellington. Maybe she's just playing with her stuffed animals. Maybe.

The super shows up with the extra key. "Hey, sorry Mrs. Hawks," he says, slurring his sibilants. "I was just…you know…watching the game." He reeks of patchouli, and a lethargic smile twitches at the corners of his mouth. Snatch the keys from him and enjoy his expression of surprise. Benedict hovers, waiting to hear you tell him you're proud of him. An ungodly scream of animal agony from inside the apartment keeps you from doing so. The sound cuts off. Sarah giggles.

"Kitty." Sarah sounds happy. "Aka-bobo. Bo."

The right key on a ring of 72 is hard to find, even if you're not panicking and frustrated. Look harder. Find it, fit it in, turn it. Hear the click of the heavy bolt. Open the door.

Happy red handprints. Little red footprints tottering off to the kitchen. Entrails.

No fur.

"Sarah?"

It has to be the cat. They always start with the family pet. You can't teach them — pets — they have to move FAST to keep away from these kids. This cat lasted a long time. Longer than the hamster by far. Teething babies, wow. They just grab anything. Smirk a bit, thinking of the catastrophe *that* was.

"Nicholas?"

He will be pissed. He loved that cat. But Sarah can defend herself against her brothers. That much is clear. She has a gift.

Kids. No two are alike.

But what a mess.

"Nicholas! Time out's over! Nick? Honey?"

Walk to his bedroom. The door is closed. The sign, written in marker, "no girls allowed," is curling up at the corners. Pause with your hand on the doorknob. Whisper his name, a question.

No answer. Do not open the door.

Jump when a child's small hand touches your arm. It is Benedict. He is shaking his head. Sad. He is holding something in his hands. It is dripping. It belongs to his brother. Belonged.

Cover your mouth. Turn. Run.

Bang on the den door. *Just once would you help me watch these monsters?* Nothing. Silence.

MIDNIGHT SUN

Andrew Bourelle

The snow is melting in Kaktovik. The ground is soft enough to dig the grave, and the mortician removes Alignak's mother from storage so that she can be buried. Alignak is the only person to attend the funeral. He shovels the dirt in himself.

He takes his backpack and grandfather's rifle and sets off. The streets are muddy. Dogs drink from brown puddles. People are out performing spring repairs. One man is on his roof, patching holes. Another leans inside his truck, working with a wrench, his flannel shirt rolled to the elbows.

He stops at the dock and observes a plane fly in over the edge of the Beaufort Sea, dropping and then touching down in an explosion of white foamy water. A white man in a shirt and tie and big rubber boots steps out. He zips up his coat even though the locals are shedding theirs.

Alignak stands in the back of the crowd. The people have come to see the commotion. The white man stands behind a podium. Another white man films him. The brown faces watch emotionlessly. The man with the tie around his neck says he is the representative of the tribal council, here on behalf of all the Alaskan tribes.

"Good news, my friends," the man says. "The agreement has finally happened. The Company is going to expand its pipeline. Your oil compensation allowance will go up fifty dollars per person."

Murmurs spread through the audience. Alignak can't tell if the reactions are positive or negative.

He walks away from the crowd and toward the wilderness. He says goodbye to no one. He plans never to return.

Alignak is the last of his tribe. When he dies, his bloodline dies with him. Like a stream through millennia drying to a trickle, soon his ancestry will be an empty creek bed.

He crosses the vast tundra. The mosses and lichen are soft and spongy from the thawing layer of soil above the permafrost. Rivulets crisscross the land, and geese and shorebirds float in the cold water. Among the larger streams, sedges cling to the banks. In the distance, the mountains of the Brooks Range stand like sentinels, black but snow-capped in shining white.

Days pass. The pipeline stands in front of him, elevated by stilts. Two feet wide and made of weather-dulled steel, the pipeline stretches as far as he can see in either direction, like a giant metallic serpent. A potholed dirt road runs parallel. In the distance, a moose walks next to the pipe, eating grasses. The moose moves on. The land is silence.

Mosquitoes flourish. A snowy owl with ghost-white wings swoops from the sky and picks up a mouse in its talons. A fox plays with her kits. A swan and her cygnets swim in a pond created by the melting snow. In the distance, toward the ocean, a lone grizzly bear lumbers through the shallows of a delta.

Alignak comes across the skeleton of a wolf, its sun-bleached ribs rising out of the grass. He kneels and finds the skull, easily distinguishable from a dog: the long, extended muzzle, the wide forehead, the size and shape of the teeth—the canines thick and strong.

His ancestors lived among the wolves. The stories spoke of something called the Ritual of the Moon, where the men and women ran with the wolves under the full moon. The wolves were not pets but equals. His people thought of the moon as a great gray wolf, and when they made a kill, they made an offering to the wolves as a gift to the god of the moon.

These are the tales Alignak heard growing up. He tried to ask his mother about the wolves as she was dying—was there any truth to the stories?—but she had lost her ability to speak.

The days grow longer. Still a month from the summer

solstice, the sun stops setting. Instead, each night, it dips toward the horizon, moves parallel to it, and then rises again. The sun won't set again for three months. Each night, the moon shares the sky with the sun. Alignak sleeps when he is tired or when he finds a dry spot. But sometimes it's nine o'clock at night, sometimes nine in the morning. It doesn't matter when he rests; night never brings darkness.

In the winter, the sun will rise only for a few hours, then only for a few minutes, and then not at all. The land will be dark for a month, with temperatures far below zero. Ice will cover the plain, and the earth will be indistinguishable from the frozen sea. Alignak doesn't expect to survive the winter.

He watches the sunlit nights and thinks about death. When his tribe becomes extinct, the world will not notice.

A Jeep drives through the tundra, splashing through puddles and digging thick ruts in the soil. He stands and watches. He thinks they won't see him, but they turn in his direction. The Jeep smells of gasoline and cigarette smoke.

"Hey, buddy," says the driver.

He wears a gray jumpsuit embroidered with the logo of the oil company. He holds a can of beer, as do the other two men inside. The driver has a lump under his bottom lip, and he smiles and spits tobacco juice out onto the wild grasses. It glistens like oil.

"What'cha doing out here, man?" the driver asks.

Alignak doesn't know how to answer. Living, he could say. Dying.

"Cat got your tongue?"

Alignak opens his mouth to speak. It's been weeks since he's heard his own voice, and the first syllables come out in a croak. He swallows, tries again. He asks the man what they are doing.

"We're a repair crew," the man says. He gestures to the man next to him and to the one in the back. "We'll be out and about most of the summer, fixing leaks or problems with the scaffolding. You out here by yourself?"

"I'm alone," Alignak says.

"Not taking pot shots at the pipeline with that rifle, are you?"

Alignak ignores the question. "Why aren't you on the road?" he asks.

"Takes too long," says the driver. "All them turns. Easier just to cut through."

When they're driving away, the man tosses an empty beer can out the window.

When the caribou come, they come in thousands. A vast herd that covers the tundra. They avoid Alignak, veering around him like water running around a stone in a river. They are on all sides, in every direction, males and females, bending their long necks to pull up grasses. They chew, with mouths like horses', and bend and eat more. Their antlers are in velvet, growing back from the winter's shedding.

The females calve, and Alignak watches the mothers lick afterbirth from the newborns.

He reaches the Brooks Range and, in two days, ascends nine thousand feet to a peak. He stands in the snow, soft and slushy and peppered with dirt. He looks all around, toward the mountains and over the plain. He sees the caribou, thick over the valley. Clouds sail through the breeze like white whales floating on an invisible current, lower in elevation than he is, casting dark shadows across the tundra. Over the ocean, he can see the glaciated ice and the broken bergs that float around it.

A bald eagle perches on a tree below, its body like a mountain, black except for a white, snow-capped skull. It lifts into the air and drops down, gliding over the land. The valley is green and vast, decorated with marshes and estuaries. The pipelines—zigzagging with mechanical angles—cut through the tundra like incisions.

Descending the mountain, he sees a wolf sneaking from the foothills into the plain. He follows and watches. He is quiet. Uphill and upwind, Alignak's odor is hidden, but he knows wolves can hear better than they can smell. The wolf is gray and thin, ragged in its shedding coat. It is big, even for a male, nearly five feet long and three feet tall at the shoulder, with a heavily muscled neck. It walks with confidence and stealth.

In the valley, a caribou with two calves drinks from a deep stream. They do not see the wolf coming. When it pounces on one of the calves, the mother and sibling run. It wrestles the calf down in the water, its jaws locked on the animal's neck as it thrashes. The water churns and froths until the animal stops fighting. The water settles, and the wolf drags the calf to shore, leaving a plume of red in the water. The wolf dissects the caribou with its claws and teeth, and then carries a slab of meat back toward the mountains.

The wolf makes the trip again, tearing off a chunk of the carcass and returning into the mountains. Alignak watches from the shade of a spruce tree.

The wolf travels to and from the kill, carrying large pieces of meat each time, until finally it returns no more. Alignak takes this as the cue to leave his hiding place, and he descends from the foothills into the valley. The sun is high and the moon is absent, and he walks with no direction.

Days later, he sees the Jeep parked along a section of pipe. He turns the other direction to avoid the oilmen. But later in the night, with the orange sun and pale moon sharing the sky, he hears gunshots far in the distance. He tries to sleep but can't. He walks in the direction of the shots. By late morning, he sees the Jeep driving east. He intersects its tire marks and backtracks its trail.

He finds the wolf carcass next to the cold ash of their

campfire. It's been decapitated and skinned. Its feet and tail have been taken with the fur. Without the pelt, the animal seems much smaller. The ridges of the ribcage are punctured with two bullet holes. The meat around the holes is congealed and dark red.

The moon is full and fat on the horizon, pale against the blue sky. Alignak pulls his clothes off and stands naked on the tundra. The air is cool. He runs through the grasses and smells the scents of the wild country. He laps water from the streams. He chases a ground squirrel and lunges on it. He breaks its neck with his hands.

He carries the squirrel to the mountains. He can see the blood trail left behind by the wolf. He enters a forest of spruce and birch. In a dense thicket, he spots the she-wolf. She stares at him through the fingers of branches. Her eyes are yellow and cautious and beautiful. He approaches, and she bares her teeth. A low growl rises from her, a sound that seems to come not from her mouth but from deep inside her.

He shows her the dead squirrel then slowly kneels to set it on the ground. He backs away, head low. Once out of the thicket, he runs toward the ocean, wishing it were dark so he could see the moonlight reflected in its waters.

When he wakes, he is naked, lying near the shore. Far out in the water, among the ice floes, a polar bear swims and its cub follows. Alignak wades into the water up to his waist and watches the salmon swim around him. The muscles in his legs feel like they are being crushed by the cold. He drops down and dunks himself, and then stands up, gasping. He shakes his long hair and walks to the shore. His cold skin glows in the warmer air. He walks in search of his clothes, his limbs tingling.

He rests the day in a poplar grove in the foothills. A cool breeze comes from the Arctic. He thinks about last night and convinces himself it was a dream. But the moon rises again, one day past full and still rich with power. He can't see its rays in the sunlight, but he can feel them on his body. He sheds his clothes and howls at the sky. In the distance, he hears the she-wolf howl with him. He sniffs the air and listens, and lets instinct take him. He chases down a marten and bites its neck and shakes it until it stops moving.

The she-wolf is waiting. Her body is still tense, but her eyes are different: hopeful and expectant. He ducks his head and drops the marten. He backs away, and she takes it and walks deeper into the thicket to her den.

When Alignak wakes from the dream that isn't a dream, his face and forearms are caked in rusty blood.

He sees the Jeep parked by the poplar grove where his clothes and backpack should be. The men stand around, smoking and drinking. The man he spoke to before has a chew in his lip again, and Alignak can smell it from twenty feet away. The others—one with a shaved head, the other with an unkempt beard—are playing the game of stretch with a sheath-knife, each taking turns throwing it into the soil. The driver is going through Alignak's backpack.

Alignak approaches, and the driver stands up hurriedly. "We wondered what happened to you," he says. "You okay, man?"

Alignak stands before them, naked.

The man with the shaved head says, "We thought we saw a man running around in the nude last night, barking like a dog. Thought we were seeing things. Guess we weren't."

Alignak says nothing, and the silence makes the men uncomfortable.

"Well," the driver says, "when we saw your stuff here, we just wanted to make sure you was okay."

Alignak thinks for a moment that maybe he's forgotten how to speak their language. "I am okay," he says, and then he adds, "I am happy."

The men laugh.

The driver says, "To each his own."

Each day when the moon rises, he feels the change. He removes his clothes and runs through the vast plain, hunting. He offers his kills to the she-wolf, who grows to expect him. But as the moon wanes, he feels the call less and less. When the new moon arrives, he worries for the wolf and her pups, but he can't hunt for them. Whatever came over him with the full moon, stops when it's gone.

But enough time has passed; the pups have grown enough to leave the den. The she-wolf and her two pups wander out from the foothills and into the tundra. He watches from the crest of a small hill. Each pup is gangly and thin, with stick-like legs and paws they will grow into. One is dark gray and the other light gray. The she-wolf is both, fading from a dark hue on her back to white on her belly and legs. Her dark tail is flecked with white. The coat looks sleek and soft.

The pups want to play. They roll on their backs, kicking their feet. The she-wolf wrestles with them. But when it's time to be serious, they heed her body language. She creeps through the tundra toward caribou in the distance. She carries her head at the level of her shoulders except when she raises it to listen. Her ears twitch at every sound. The pups watch her with respect.

Some of the caribou notice her and bound off, but a few stay. She eyes a lone calf, and when she chases it, she pounces with less brute strength than the male wolf had used—but more skill and dexterity. When the caribou is dead, she begins pulling its viscera out with her teeth, and her pups come in to feed.

When the moon starts to show itself again, growing from a crescent sliver to a waxing gibbous, Alignak hikes down into the meadow where the wolves are playing. The she-wolf sees him coming and approaches, keeping herself between him and the pups. He removes his shirt and then his jeans. He stands before her and then kneels in the grass. The soil is moist on his palms and knees. He lets her approach.

He can see intelligence behind her yellow eyes. And he can see something else: a fraternity of ancestry, recognized by her just as he recognizes it. Their lineages have a primal connection.

As the days go by, the moon changes to a fat oval, and each day, he feels its call more powerfully. He follows the wolves, or they follow him—he isn't sure which. Like any migrating animal, their trail is determined as much by instinct as conscious choice.

The she-wolf brings down an elk fawn, and she and her pups feed on it. When they finish, she approaches Alignak and walks back and forth, coming toward him and then back to the kill, until he realizes what she is trying to say. He approaches, and she backs off to let him feed. He kneels over the carcass and pulls at the meat with his teeth. The coppery taste of blood fills his mouth, and he buries his face in the animal.

When he is finished, sitting logy in the grass from overfeeding, the she-wolf approaches warily. He knows he would have no chance if she attacked, but he does not move. She comes within only a few feet. He holds his hand out and she nudges it with her muzzle. Then she begins to lick the blood from his fingers, her warm tongue wrapping around each digit. She comes closer and licks the blood from his beard and face. Her nose is cold and her breath is hot.

He hunts with them, learning from her alongside the pups. The way she stalks. The way she pounces. He kills several ground squirrels. He kills a fox. She lets him chase down a caribou calf. He tackles it and bites at its neck, but he can't get to the jugular through the hide, and it runs away. She shows no impatience, but he aches with the worry of disappointing her.

He plays with the pups, rolling in the grass. They climb over him, nipping at him playfully. They are growing larger and stronger, and soon they will be too strong to play games like this. He is on his back, pushing their advances away. He sits upright when he hears the engine of a vehicle. He scans the horizon, and the pups stop, sensing his concern. Alignak crouches to look and sees the Jeep rolling through the tundra in the distance. The she-wolf is there with him, watching. He rests his hands on her shoulders and gently nudges her downward. She complies and they lie together—mother, pups, Alignak—pressed against the tundra floor. When the Jeep is gone,

Alignak runs his hand through the she-wolf's soft fur.

The moon begins to wane again, and Alignak senses something different in himself and knows the wolves sense it too. They begin to distance themselves from him, and by the time the new moon comes, they have traveled ahead without him. He is far from his last campsite, where he left his backpack and supplies. He has no clothes. He waits in the tundra, alone. He is caught between two worlds. He longs for the moon to return him to the world where he wants to be.

Rains come, and he has no shelter. He finds a lone tree in the bend of a stream and crouches under it, hugging himself. Finally, he sleeps, curled on his side. When he wakes, a rainbow bridges the sky, thick and distinct, with each color distinguishable. He smiles and kneels at the stream to lap from the water. He stops, seeing his face. It is not the face he wants, nor the face he recognizes as his own.

When the moon is fattening again, he runs under the blue sky, following the scent of the wolf and her pups. His heart races with anticipation.

After a day of travel, he crouches in the grass, listening, smelling. The sun is at the edge of the horizon, but the moon is at its zenith. He speaks to the moon—not with his mouth but with his soul—and asks for direction.

Then he hears gunshots echoing across the plain.

He runs and runs, and when he sees the Jeep moving through the tundra in the distance, he heads in the direction it came from. When he gets close, he hears the pups' high-pitched cries. He finds them in a bed of blood-streaked moss. The she-wolf is dead. Her body is skinned and headless. The pups pace next to her, nudging her with their noses, yelping.

Alignak breathes in and out, in and out. His heart pounds, his muscles burn. He throws his head back and howls to the sky. Then he turns and runs, following the deep rut of tire tracks.

The men sit around a campfire under the midnight sun. He can hear their voices from far away. They crack open beer cans. They curse. They tell stories of women and bar fights.

Alignak uses the Jeep for cover and sneaks up on them. The man with the shaved head whittles a block of wood with a knife. The man with the beard eats potato chips from a bag. The driver pulls out a can of tobacco and packs it against the palm of his hand. Behind him, the rifle leans against the driver's side of the Jeep.

Alignak is eight feet away, crouched behind the tire on the other side. He smells beer and body odor and, from inside the Jeep, the strong scent of the she-wolf's blood and fur.

The driver stands and says, "I've got take a piss."

He turns and his eyes go wide when he sees Alignak coming at him. He knocks the man backward into the fire, and then he goes after the man with the knife. He pins the man's hand down before he can react, and clamps his teeth into the man's neck, finding the jugular. A torrent of blood erupts into his mouth. Alignak releases him. The man screams and writhes in the grass, one hand reaching into the air, fist opening and closing, the other grasping uselessly at the damage to his neck.

Alignak turns, hunched on all fours, blood streaming from his mouth. The driver is rolling away from the fire, trying to extinguish the blooms of flame on his jumpsuit. The other man is up and backing away, but he makes eye contact with Alignak and freezes, still holding the bag of chips. Alignak leaps over the fire onto him. They go down together into the grass, and Alignak claws at his face. His nails slice the man's skin, tearing red trenches like the tracks of the Jeep in the soft Alaskan tundra. The man shrieks, and Alignak bites a chunk out of his face. Then he bites off a hunk of ear. The man screams and squirms, and finally Alignak crushes the man's windpipe with his teeth.

The driver is on his hands and knees, looking at him. His jumpsuit smolders. Alignak, crouched, stares at the man. He snarls. He licks the blood from around his mouth. The man's eyes dart to the rifle, and Alignak lets out a long, guttural growl.

The man lunges for the gun.

He doesn't make it.

Alignak and the pups run across the plain, hunting and sleeping and moving by instinct. The moon rises and falls, wanes and waxes, but Alignak doesn't change back into what he used to be. The three of them live together through the summer. The pups grow larger and stronger. He knows that when winter comes, they will leave him and go on their own. Their coats will thicken to protect them from the month of darkness in the heart of winter and the cold that comes with it. Alignak knows he will not survive. He is not the same as them. He is something else. Just as the moon can share its night sky with the sun for only so long, his time with the wolves must one day come to an end.

The three of them sit in a meadow, smelling the scents on the breeze and listening to the sounds of the wilderness. The sun has been skirting the horizon for days now, and tonight Alignak watches as it finally sets. The sky is not fully dark, and the sunset will only last a few seconds. But the full moon is high, and the young wolves see the shimmer of moonlight on the plain for the first time. They howl to the great gray wolf, and Alignak howls with them.

Smeared Star in Your Hands

Sara Tantlinger

Three rabbits hung above Roksana Marinov's kitchen sink. Weak, but alive. She clutched the butcher knife, prepared to slit their throats and drain the blood while their hearts still beat. She bowed her head and murmured a prayer of hope that their blood would do as promised. After all, such promises had not come cheap.

Hair like dirty straw curtained her face as her lips moved in quiet rhythm. An early autumn breeze swept through the open window and into the small house. The air carried an electric scent that promised lightning. The evening sky sulked over the village's broken houses, and Sochi loomed in the distance. Other than the occasional groan of cattle, or yowls from stray cats, the silence in the village spoke of emptiness. The yellow larch trees near Roksana's garden sang soft tunes of falling needles as the wind drifted. Birds used to fill the branches with delicate melodies, but they had fled long ago. So many trees had been chopped down and sold. There were no more songs to hear. Roksana had not enough life in her to sing in place of the siskins and finches.

Not yet. She might sing again one day if everything went as the old woman vowed. Roksana swallowed. The rabbits twitched.

This *must* work. She gripped the knife handle and unknotted the first rabbit from its ties on the overhang. Footsteps padded behind her.

"You are still sure?" Demyan's voice rumbled in her ear. He wrapped his hands around her until his palms rested on her stomach.

She nodded. For six years she had pleaded, *Demyan, light of my soul, I want a child.* Her body craved to create life, but whenever she mentioned the word "baby," Demyan would fidget in his grandfather's old rocking chair and *squeak-creak-squeak* back and forth because they couldn't…*she* couldn't.

"Let us keep trying," she would plead.

"It is too painful, *zvezda moya.*" *My star,* he called her. *Roksana, my star.*

So, she kept her smile bright. She glowed like Venus in the sky beside the moon —what else could a star do but shine? She thought of summers with her father, when the village hosted fields of wheat, and the grains would dance in the golden sunbeams. Her young body had twirled along to the rhythm of the wind in the field and the song of cicadas. She collected fireflies in dusty jars, her prisoners twinkling inside the glass until she freed them, or until she reached her hand inside, scooped up the insects, and closed her fist tight.

"What do you want, malyutka, with the bugs?" her father had asked her, his little one.

"To hold something beautiful, Papa." And she would stare in awe at the smeared shimmer between her fingers.

Now the earth bristled, bald bumps of dirt replaced the wheat fields, and the fireflies rarely came. Why would life stay in an old village that opened its arms to the embrace of decay? Dead were the fireflies and birds and trees. Dead were the miscarriages she buried deep in her garden, but the cabbage had grown over. It was a sign for life, and she would try again.

Demyan hugged her tighter. "Will a baby from dark magic make you truly happy?"

"Our baby will be light," she whispered, and kept her eyes on the rabbits. "Full of stars."

He kissed her neck. "My little rabbit killer, how you please me." His voice lulled her like rain.

Demyan. Storm in my heart. "You will go through with it? Just as she said?"

"For you, *zvezda moya,* anything," he whispered into her ear. Goosebumps journeyed down her spine and arms. Roksana untied the rest of the rabbits and held each one over her empty womb before she stretched their necks over the bowl in the sink and cut them one by one, silencing their sharp screams. Blood pooled up in the bowl.

Demyan slid cool hands under the too-big sweater of his that she wore, and tugged it off her pale body. "Imagine it," he said. "*Zvyozdochka.*" *A little star.*

She turned around and her backside collided with the counter. He undressed her and lifted the bowl from the sink. She took his hand and led him to their bed.

"Are you ready?" he asked. Roksana nodded and lay still on her back. Demyan sat beside her, dipped his fingers in the blood, and outlined the curved symbols the witch had instructed him to draw on Roksana's body. After she was streaked with crimson, he set the bowl on the nightstand, kissed her face, her lips, and made love to her. The blood smeared against his body and Roksana remembered a time years ago when the trees had lived. She had climbed the branches higher and higher because they were full of krazulya pears, ripe and plump.

And Demyan, so handsome, would watch her long limbs climb as if she belonged to the trees, as if they called her home to the sky. He would say, "I am going to marry you, Roksana. When we are old enough, I will have you." And he did. She was lost to him, to those cognac eyes, that hair like a cover of night, and to the crooked smirk that promised love.

Such love stayed true; Roksana knew this, for soon after the ritual, her body changed and her stomach grew round. The first few months shifted between good and bad days, lack of sleep, and fierce cravings.

"What I would not give for pears. Krazulya pears," Roksana said one day, as drool pooled in her mouth at the thought.

"Weren't those on the list of things the witch forbade? They only grow in the cursed city now."

She sighed. "You are right. We would not want to ruin this." She spread her fingers over her warm stomach. "It does not matter. We wouldn't be able to afford any from the city. How my taste buds dance for them, though."

Roksana drifted back to her daydreams, but the

craving did not cease. The yearn for krazulya pears spiked into a need. The flesh of other fruit could not satisfy her, no matter how sweet or filled with juice.

"You must eat something," Demyan begged. "For yourself and for the baby, please."

Her stomach growled and hunger pains wracked through her gut. She clenched her jaw as if that could fight the ache. She'd had no appetite for three days now. Weakness overtook her. She shook her head at Demyan and closed her tired eyes to drift back to daydreams of old summers and ripe pears.

The next morning, Demyan disappeared before the sun rose. Roksana did not stir from her bed. The aches in her abdomen spiked like hundreds of curved needles scraping against her skin. She thirsted for the juice of the pears, for the hidden spice under their sweet skin. Oh, she could practically smell them.

She opened her eyes and Demyan appeared in the darkened bedroom. A bundle of pears was nestled between his arms. He must have ventured into the city, a horrid place left to wickedness, yet it shunned their little village.

"How did you get those?" Roksana's mouth watered. They could not have been cheap.

"It does not matter, my light. Anything for you."

The pears tasted even better than she remembered. She relished the nectar of each bite. The honeyed zest cooled her mouth as she chewed, and the remnants slid down her throat like water after the hottest afternoon. Happiness eased its way back into her body. The dark thoughts and hunger pains scattered, and even the bad dreams became less frequent, but her craving grew.

The pears disappeared much sooner than anticipated. A fierce wave of night terrors distressed Roksana. She blamed stress and hormones, the way her muscles ached and stretched as the baby grew. It pushed up her organs and twisted her insides.

Something was wrong inside her.

Near the final month of her pregnancy, Roksana struggled with morning sickness to the point of blood in her vomit, but she did not cry. Demyan tried, bless his heart, to cheer her, but the black cloud in her womb knew no love.

One day they decided on Feliks for a boy, Pasha for a girl, and Roksana almost remembered contentment. It faded quickly, like lost childhood. All she could imagine was a sexless alien inside her, a foreign germ that sucked away at her life. She often daydreamed of death, her own or the baby's, just so long as the hell inside her disappeared. Sometimes at night her stomach whispered strange words that turned her blood to an ice river.

Soon, her water broke, warm and sticky down her thighs. Demyan rushed her to the nearby village where the witch waited. Roksana was instructed to deliver the baby in the old woman's home. She was too poor for anything else.

Contractions came, furious in their pain, and Roksana howled as her stomach felt clawed apart from the inside. It was going to tear her up, rip away her organs, and make her burst into bloody ribbons. Dampness touched her thighs and blood's copper tang stung the air. Her lungs strained and every muscle burned.

The old woman pressed her ear against Roksana's belly, and her brow furrowed. "Stupid girl, you ate krazulya, now you pay. Pears bad, stolen pears worse. You break ritual's codes, you all suffer." She lifted her head and squinted gray eyes at Roksana.

"Baby sideways. Wrong. Cord prolapsed and heart rate down. Have to cut her out now." The woman's ancient face hardened, and she walked toward a high cabinet. Inside gleamed several sharp instruments, some knife-like and others curved like spoon handles.

Roksana's head swam, and when she closed her eyes, only shades of scarlet came to her. The whispers from her stomach grew louder. *Could no one else hear it?* Sweat beaded down from her forehead. "Just get it out of me."

The old woman grabbed Roksana's arm and antiseptic filled her nostrils. A quick jab followed. Blurred agony consumed Roksana. She faded in and out as her stomach was sawed open. Searing pain consumed her and she clung to it, then embraced a black oblivion.

When she woke, Demyan knelt by her side and grabbed her hand. "*Zvezda moya*," he whispered. Roksana's hands trembled as she lifted the torn quilt that covered her belly. Its swell had gone down, but a small mound of fat stared back at her. She didn't mind that. What she minded was the jagged series of stitches that trailed a long, angry red path across her lower abdomen. Nausea crawled up her throat and she sucked in air like a misplaced fish.

Nightmares returned, but in those dark dreams everyone else saw the baby how Roksana did. Beneath the pink skin lingered malice, curved and crooked. Maggots crawled through the baby's heart, which resembled a decayed krazulya pear.

Demyan did not acknowledge the wrongness of the child. He appeared in the bedroom doorway and held their crying baby. Roksana's heart cried along, not in yearning to hold her baby, but for it go away and be quiet.

Her nose crinkled at the sight of the flesh bundled up in a quilt. "What's wrong with it?"

Demyan's eyes flashed with hurt. "She's hungry. Don't you want to feed her?" He stepped closer, a smile crossing his tired face as he held his little star. His daughter.

"No," Roksana said. The thought of that thing's toothless gums latched onto her like a leech brought back the nausea.

Demyan's brow wrinkled and he sat beside her. "Why won't you hold her?"

A sour puff assaulted Roksana's nostrils. It came from the baby... an odor like rotten fruit. "She is wrong," Roksana said. "Don't you smell that?"

Demyan stared back and held the baby closer. "What are you talking about?" He shifted away. Roksana did not have the energy to argue. If he could not smell the rancid stench, then his every sense must be blinded by the monster in his arms.

The next morning, Roksana awoke rested, and her stomach growled in need. She took slow steps to the kitchen and prepared a cabbage stew. Demyan lit up to see her mobile once again and her heart sang at his happiness. He was so perfect in the kitchen light, standing beside her while not holding the swine.

"We must get Pasha baptized soon, now that you are feeling better," Demyan said. His faith had always been greater than her own.

She said nothing and sliced her kitchen knife into the onion on the counter. Demyan was her soul, but the baby was corrupted. How must she make him see the truth? She tried to explain what she saw. He called her unhinged, but a shadow covered his eyes. He hesitated.

"She is just…restless. That's why we must take her to the church. All will be well."

"You've seen something. You just won't admit it. Don't be blind." The sharpness of the onion caused her nostrils to flare. She cut to reveal the middle, and a mustardy rot stared up at her from the onion's center, from its very heart.

"You have become so cold, Roksana. I could place ice in your mouth and it would never melt." Demyan rushed out of the kitchen as the baby wailed from the other room. Roksana stabbed her knife through the corroded onion and swallowed down a scream.

No other child would ever exist in Roksana's womb. No life could grow in her again after being host to the creature that broke something so deep inside her. She savored the bitterness of her thoughts. The taste soured and curled against her tongue. She shivered when the revelation came to her, quick as death, about what she must do. It was too late to save the thing that had clawed itself out of her, but she could still save her husband.

Roksana killed her baby around three in the morning while the moon shone upon her garden. It was almost the time when demons came out to play. Perhaps they all watched her. Perhaps they protected her.

She was covered in dirt, her dead daughter in the ground by the larch trees, a little farther away than the miscarried babies beneath the cabbage. Her fingernails dug into the thick soil and she bent low to kiss the earth.

"I am sorry, little one, that I brought you into this world only to destroy you." She said goodbye to the thing under the dirt and turned back toward the house. She would look at Demyan and he would know. One look and he would hate her.

"Infanticide," Demyan whispered behind her, his mouth pressed against the top of her ear. He said it over and over until there was hardly a breath between each word.

"*Infanticide-infanticide-infanticide.*" His hands slid against her sides and he pulled her back. She stood silent, pressed against his body, wondering if he would strangle her.

What Demyan called *infanticide-infanticide-infanticide,* she simply called *mercy.* She had helped give life to the baby, helped it grow, and she had to be the one to uproot it.

"Take me to her."

In the numb hours of the morning, before the sun

rose, Roksana led him to the makeshift grave by the trees. He shone his lantern upon the small heap of upturned earth. Demyan fell to his knees and placed his hands over the mound of earth in the gentle way he had placed his hands on Roksana's once-round stomach.

"Pasha, Pasha, forgive me for not protecting you, *zvyozdochka*." He wept, and Roksana ached to hold him. Between tears he turned to her. "I think I hate you."

She opened her mouth to respond, to tell him she loved him anyway, but the mound of earth quivered over Pasha's grave.

The dirt spluttered as if coughed out of a grotesque mouth. A tiny pale hand shot forth from the heap, and Roksana screamed as Demyan jerked away from the soil.

"No, no," Roksana moaned. "I killed you!" She ran her hands through her hair and pulled tightly. Demyan crawled back toward the mound and she yelled for him to stop, but he reached forward and pulled on the little hand.

Like a demonic birth, the wicked child emerged from the earth.

If Roksana had thought Pasha ugly before, in her pink flesh, this thing was a mutant. It did not resemble a human child at all, but looked much like what Roksana had dreamt about.

Its bald head wobbled on top of a thin, warped body and crooked spine. The blue veins threatened to burst beneath the translucent skin. Serpent-like teeth replaced the once soft gums. It stood taller than the one-month-old infant Roksana had smothered softly before burying. The thing wore Pasha's white dress, but it was tattered. It walked, or at least attempted to. The thing staggered toward Roksana and held out pale, sticky arms.

Maggots. Some still crawled; the rest laid smashed against the thing's skin. The reek of rotten pears suffocated the air. The creature unlatched its dreadful mouth and let out a scream that made Roksana's flesh want to crawl off her skeleton.

Roksana grabbed Demyan by the arm and together they ran from the demon as it stumbled on unsteady legs toward them.

"Something went wrong, Demyan. Please believe me. The dark magic, the pears..." Roksana panted between words as they ran, but she needed him to understand.

"I don't know what to believe. We should've taken her to the Baptist. Now she is unholy in every sense." He shook his head. She knew he'd curse what he viewed as his own failure.

Roksana glanced behind and the creature was not in view of the moonlight trees that encircled her little home.

"Let us leave. Run away with me," she pleaded, and held Demyan's hands in her own.

"Where will we go?" His strong voice was just a whisper, but her heart leapt because he did not refuse her, did not tell her he hated her still.

"We'll spend the night in the old church just outside of town. The morning will bring light and we can return to take what we need from home, and then we shall be rid of this place." Dawn was mere hours away. Roksana hoped the creature would hide itself when the sun rose.

Demyan nodded and thunder rumbled. The sky opened and the unwelcome visitor of cold rain cascaded upon them. Roksana tightened her grip on Demyan's hand and led him quickly toward the uninhabited church where they settled for the remainder of the night.

"Why do you forgive me, Demyan?" she asked as they curled up against one another in their makeshift bed of quilts they'd stolen from a clothesline.

"Because we exist at the same time, and even in all your sins, *zvezda moya*, I could not stand my existence without you."

"You still love me?"

"As long as there are stars in the sky and blood in my veins, I love you." He kissed her forehead and fell asleep beside her.

She stroked his wild, dark hair until she drifted off.

She dreamt the creature followed them, but the rippling chills across her arms drew her awareness into a more lucid state. Rotting earth filled her nostrils, and she broke away from the mist of a clouded nightmare. This was no dream. This was more, and the child was here.

Pasha, with her maggot-smeared skin and ragged dress, stared up at her mother.

"You found us, *malyutka*." Roksana echoed her father's favorite phrase. She had a little one of her own now; a perverse, distorted little daughter.

It stared at her with those milky eyes, but Roksana was not afraid. She was tired. Pasha directed her eyes toward Demyan, her dear father, and limped toward him, arms outstretched.

"No, please, child. He is not for you, nor for me. He is too good for us."

The creature stopped and tilted its massive head. Its

arms were thin as spider legs.

"I don't regret your death, dear unholy child. But let us save each other now. My drekavac."

The creature held out its maggot-smeared hand to her. Roksana, from her place of dreams or wakefulness, moved toward the beast. She gazed at Demyan's beautiful, sleeping face and cursed her foolishness for everything she had ruined. "You will spare him if I go with you?"

The creature nodded.

"I love you, Demyan," Roksana whispered in his ear. He did not stir, but his hand grasped hers before she pulled away. "More than stars and blood, I love you, but I must do this. I owe it to our child. Live for me, for us."

The child shook, eager for the touch of its mother, for the one who would love it, even if such love must be forced. Roksana took a weary step toward her daughter. The child's skin glistened as if a fire were lit behind it. The voice of Roksana's father sounded in her head again.

What do you want, malyutka, with the bugs?

To hold something beautiful, Papa.

Her child was not beautiful. It was foul, but she would hold her all the same and she would love her because Roksana had once again reached her hand inside the jar and smashed the fireflies. Only this time, the crushed shimmer that emerged was this corrupted thing named Pasha, her little creature of shining darkness.

LIZA

Jeffrey B. Burton

How do you fill a void?

Do you spend your days like my wife Kathleen, sitting at the picnic table in the backyard with photo albums and valium? Or, like me, do you tramp about the house with no real purpose beyond the occasional refilling of your scotch glass with two fingers of single malt? That had become our waking hours in the weeks since the funeral for Sierra and the twins, the weeks since the car wreck. And as for sleep . . . what the hell is sleep?

Parents should never outlive their only child.

Or their grandchildren.

Kathleen had taken the steps up from the lower level and caught me gazing at the television screen as though it were turned on. She stepped in front of my chair. In her arms was a small black dog.

“She doesn’t have a collar.”

“Where did you find her?” I asked.

“She found me. She came up through the ravine, sat at my feet, and started licking at my fingers.”

"It's a neighbor's dog." I took a last sip of scotch. "We'd better start asking around so they don't worry."

And so we did, carrying the mutt door-to-door, first quizzing our immediate neighbors in case they knew the dog, and then working our way along the boulevard that sits on the opposite side of the sliver of woodland that shrouds our backyard. No luck. Then I drove us around the neighborhood, my wife in the passenger seat with her new friend on her lap. We searched for any signs on posts or fences mentioning lost pets. I drove to nearby grocery stores and, while Kathleen ran a hand down the dog's black mane, I slipped in to search bulletin boards for any notes on missing animals.

Finally, we drove to the closest veterinarian—Eastview Animal Clinic—to have them check and see if our new arrival had some sort of GPS microchip implanted in her neck or upper back. Again, no luck.

"She's a Pomeranian, right, doctor?" Kathleen asked.

"She has the general looks of a Pom, but her face is broader, with a more jutting mouth. And she's about five pounds heavier than your average Pomeranian. Some kind of mix, I think." The veterinarian, a young doctor named Patricia Strouts, held the dog out in front of her. I watched as a shadow of curiosity crawled across the vet's face. "She seems a little . . . *unique*. Would it be okay if I gave her a quick examination?"

"It's not our dog," I replied. Kathleen shot me a look and I knew what the conversation on the drive home would entail, but we'd spent the bulk of the afternoon searching for the elusive owner of our mystery dog and I wasn't about to double-down and shell out money for someone else's pet. "But I'll let the family know of your interest when we find them."

That night, we sat in front of the television, this time with it turned on, watching whatever sitcom the station served up. In my periphery I watched my wife pet the dog as it lay across her lap. It was the first time I'd seen Kathleen smile in what seemed an eternity.

"She looks frumpy and frilly," my wife said. "Kind of like Eliza Doolittle."

I stared at the dog, then back at Kathleen, and read between the lines. In every high school there's a star that carries the theater department for that year's class. Our Sierra was that star, and she'd earned the female lead in *My Fair Lady* her senior year.

"Eliza's a bit long for a dog's name," I said.

"Then we'll call her Liza."

As if in response, our little visitor glanced up at Kathleen.

Considering the backyard woods, we toyed with picking up an electric collar, but Liza rarely left our view, only long enough to dip into the tree line and take care of business. This was a windfall, as I had feared my life would now include scooping piles of waste into baggies, and I mouthed a silent thanks to Liza's previous owner who must have taught her where best to go. Liza also signaled to us whenever she had to step outside by standing in front of the sliding glass door and, once opened, she'd dart toward the ravine to make her daily deposits. She rarely touched her food, and made a continual mess tipping her water dish, but that was a meager price to pay for bringing a degree of energy back into the household. She lived on Kathleen's lap and the two of them went for long walks several times a day. The photo albums eventually worked their way back onto the bookshelves, laundry started being done, and Kathleen, a trained chef, began stirring about in the kitchen.

A week later, I returned to my accounting firm.

In my dream, I am asleep on my back in our king size. Liza is curved in a ball against me, snuggled in for the night. My hand is cupped against the fluff of her back and I sense a chill. Not ice; more like placing your palm against a window on a late October evening. I wake, and all is as it was in my dream—if it *was* a dream—but the sense of chill, of coldness, ebbs.

And Liza stares up at me.

The obituary showed up in the suburban weekly that magically appears in the newspaper box under our mailbox every Saturday afternoon. An elderly woman who lived several blocks north of our back ravine had passed away about the same time Liza appeared in our lives. I didn't show the obit to Kathleen but spent the weekend chewing over its implication.

I left work early Monday and, on the drive home, parked my car in front of the woman's address, which now sported a For Sale sign in the yard. The house was a block up from where Kathleen and I had abandoned our door-to-door quest for Liza's owner that first afternoon. I picked the house on the right, walked up, and rang the bell. A young woman with an armful of toddler answered the door. I explained how my wife and I were having difficulty locating the owner of a lost dog and asked if the pet could have belonged to her recently deceased neighbor.

"She's got a privacy fence that obscures her backyard," the young mother said, "but sometimes I could hear her talking back there. I knew she lived alone, so I guess I assumed she had a small dog or a cat."

"You never saw the animal?"

The woman shook her head. "We've only lived here a year. We tried reaching out to her when we moved in, but she didn't so much as open her screen door. She wasn't very *welcoming,* if you know what I mean. And we've had nothing to do with her since she screamed at the kids when their ball rolled into her yard."

"Sounds a little harsh."

"Shame how she died, though."

"How's that?"

"All alone. They didn't mention it in the paper, but she had a stroke and lay on the kitchen floor for almost two weeks before the mailman started asking questions about her overflowing mail. Poor woman had no friends or family checking in on her."

"I thought the obit mentioned a daughter."

"Her daughter lives out of state. I got to meet her for a second when she swung by with the realtor." The young mother glanced next door. "I feel so sad. The poor woman, lying there all alone until she . . . finally passed. We might have kept an eye on her had she been halfway civil." She looked back at me. "You know something? I hope that dog was hers. It could have worked its way out the backyard or gotten free when the paramedics and police were here."

I thanked the young mother and then checked with the house on the other side, but the neighbors there were of little help beyond confirming that the elderly woman had been an unpleasant recluse.

"About a fifteen-pound black Pomeranian mix," I spoke into the telephone. It was an awkward conversation, but I felt obliged to contact the woman's surviving daughter in case she was searching for her mother's missing pet.

"Mom and Dad picked up a dog like that from a kill shelter or somewhere after I left for college. Come to think of it, I haven't seen Pico—that's what my parents named the dog—since dad's funeral," the woman's daughter replied. "My husband Gene got a job in Atlanta and what with the kids and work and everything, we didn't visit much until toward the end. To be honest, we were *estranged*."

"I'm sorry to hear that."

"My parents didn't like Gene; wouldn't give him the time of day. They didn't want me to marry into the Jewish faith. They didn't even come to our wedding."

"That couldn't have been easy." It had been difficult enough tracking down the daughter's phone number, and I didn't wish to get sidetracked by their soap opera. "Do you think the dog—Pico—could have gotten out and run away?"

A moment of silence passed between us, like dead air on the radio.

"I think you misunderstood me, mister. Mom and Dad got Pico around the time I left for college," the woman on the other end of the phone said and chuckled. "I'm almost fifty."

Every spring, it was my habit to pull on the work boots, grab a rake and a fistful of lawn bags from the garage, and head into the back ravine to bag up any branches or tree limbs that had tumbled to the ground and which, over the season, could turn into a fire hazard. I'd let it go too long this year and was loading the fourth bag when it dawned on me what was missing. As a recent pet owner, the fear of stepping in a fresh pile and trailing it back into the house had crossed my mind, but it turned out not to be an issue. There were no piles of poo—fresh or not.

We'd had Liza for a month, and I assumed I'd be clearing the brush in a minefield of the little dog's waste. I hiked further into the ravine, thinking that the newest member of our family, with her Mensa-level IQ, was bright enough to ramble deep into the woods to relieve herself. But there was nothing for me to see. Still, Liza's a small dog, I reasoned, it wasn't like we owned a Saint Bernard. A rainstorm or two would melt any of her piles into the dirt. Hell, a dog Liza's size, her output was probably comparable to rabbit droppings.

Feeling a bit silly for going Ahab and the Whale over dog shit, I shrugged it off and finished loading eight bags of dried twigs and rotting branches, when I began noticing miniature pellets that were littered here and there. I squatted down and squinted, figuring I'd cracked the code of Liza's missing by-product, when it occurred to me what it was that I was examining. It wasn't rabbit droppings or those of a small dog. I picked up one of the little round pieces and held it a few inches from my eye to verify. Sure enough, I nodded my head; it was an undigested piece of dog food.

Liza sat mid-yard and watched as I carried the bags to the front of the house.

Was our little dog ill?

I didn't mention anything to Kathleen. There'd been enough despair in the household to last numerous lifetimes and the last thing we needed was to find out that the tiny light at the end of our tunnel was in reality another abyss. I began counting the number of food pellets I'd placed in her bowl and audit them at night. About half were missing so she was in fact eating, but was she keeping them down? I would hold Liza in my arms as I weighed myself on the bathroom scale, and she held even at fifteen pounds.

Concerned, I began noticing other things.

Like how I never caught her sleeping. She'd live on Kathleen's lap in the evenings as we watched mindless shows on television, lying prone as my wife scratched at her back, but whenever I'd peek over the top of her head I'd find her eyelids open as she gazed across the room before she'd inevitably pivot and peer back at me. As I advanced deeper into middle age, I found myself making a trip or two into the bathroom in the wee hours of the night. As in the night of my dream, Liza's always awake and like a school crossing guard, tracked my trek to and from the master bath.

We had floor-to-ceiling windows in the front family room, with a prime view of the cul-de-sac, where, years back, we'd sit and watch as Sierra and her friends played games, where more recently we'd watched as Sierra's children, our twin granddaughters, made snow angels last winter, and where the latest batch of neighbor kids were in full view—learning to ride bikes or skateboards, playing catch or tag, or whatnot. It was a view that would cause sensory overload in any animal.

Yet Liza never barked . . . not even once.

"We never did find the owner, Dr. Strouts," I said into the speakerphone in my office.

"That's too bad," the veterinarian replied. "I've thought a lot about that dog since you first brought her in."

"I guess we wound up *informally* adopting her. We named her Liza and my wife is head-over-heels in love with her, but Liza is..." I paused to collect my thoughts and continued, "I believe you used the word *unique* when you met her. And I called to ask *why* you chose that word?"

"Well, she's a beauty that one, a real charmer, but I remember looking into her eyes and . . . I know this sounds crazy, especially coming from a veterinarian, but it was like getting lost for a second, like when you were a little kid at a store, and you got separated from your mother for a second. Does that sound crazy?"

"Not at all, Doctor. Not at all," I said. "In fact, I'd like to take you up on your offer to examine Liza."

I checked in with the veterinarian's aide at the front desk and then took a seat in the reception area to wait for Dr. Strouts. Liza settled in at my feet. I felt bad about misleading Kathleen. I knew she'd insist on accompanying us to the animal clinic for the physical, so I told her that Liza and I were off on an errand and that it was a surprise. And I did plan on picking up chow mein from her favorite take-out on the way home, but I didn't want my wife to be in attendance as Dr. Strouts put my delusions to rest—delusions about an ageless dog that didn't eat or drink or bark or shit or sleep . . . and might not even be a dog at all.

I felt like an ass. This was no longer about a lost dog.

It was about a man closing in on retirement that had recently lost his only child and his only grandchildren in a horrible car crash and was now in the process of losing his mind.

Across from me, on the waiting room's tiled floor, a gray-and-black Rottweiler lay as motionless as a statue. A shaved patch above his right eye hinted at surgery. I tracked the leash from his collar upward to the hand of a round woman in an orange blouse. The dog's owner sat alone, quietly weeping, her free hand dabbing at red eyes with a Kleenex.

"Are you okay?" I asked.

"There's just nothing more they can do for Reilly," the woman said.

"I'm sorry to hear that."

"He's riddled with cancer and he's lost his sight in both eyes." The woman began to tremble. "But Reilly's been a good boy. Yes, Reilly's always been a good, good boy."

I nodded and stared at my feet, best to let the woman say her goodbyes without my interrupting. I looked down at Liza. Her eyes were fixed on the ailing Rottweiler. A minute passed, and then another, but Liza didn't turn away or blink. I followed her gaze across the dark tile and was surprised to see that Reilly had raised his head, his blind eyes somehow staring back at Liza. The Rottweiler's head shifted toward the corridor and a low snarl began to emanate from his throat.

"Mr. Garner."

I turned at the sound of my name. Dr. Strouts stood in the hallway, a smile upon her face.

"I'm ready to see Liza now."

"My God," Kathleen said, her jaw dropping. "What happened?"

I stood in the doorway, a numb look on my face as if it'd been injected with Novocain. I wore a green smock that the Eastview Animal Clinic had lying about because my dress shirt was ruined. My neck remained speckled with a misting of crimson, as I'd been too stunned to achieve a thorough cleansing. The leash fell from my hand and Liza ran to my wife.

"What happened?" Kathleen repeated.

I told her about the attack at the animal clinic. I told her about the Rottweiler diving for Dr. Strouts' throat, ripping at the young doctor's neck, snapping at her face. I told my wife about rushing forward, grasping at the dog's collar, grasping at a fistful of fur, and doing my best to yank the enraged creature off the veterinarian. I told her about the receptionist joining me, helping wrestle the monster backwards. I told her about veterinarians pouring out of other rooms, running to aid Dr. Strouts, stopping the bleeding, and saving the young woman's life in the minutes before the ambulance arrived.

But I didn't tell Kathleen everything.

I didn't tell her about the blood spray. I didn't tell her about the gap where the veterinarian's eye had been torn from its socket. I didn't tell Kathleen about the Rottweiler being on death's door a mere instant before the attack. I didn't tell her how the Rottweiler was blind or how the dog expired in my arms after the receptionist and I managed to pull him off Dr. Strouts as if the savagery of his exertion had extracted a fatal toll. I didn't tell her about the lady in orange sobbing and calling out to anyone who would listen that "Reilly has always been a good, good boy."

And I didn't tell Kathleen how I sat there on the floor after the ambulance sped away, chest dripping with Patricia Strouts' blood, and how I glanced over at Liza, who still sat at the foot of my chair and hadn't so much as moved a muscle during the entirety of the attack.

I didn't tell my wife how Liza stared back at me.

Kathleen, good sport that she was, sat up with me until midnight, until her eyes began to droop and she knew she needed sleep.

"Come to bed, hon," she said, and kissed my cheek. "Come to bed."

"I'll be up in a minute, Kath."

She scooped Liza up in her arms and headed for the staircase. I poured another two fingers of single malt and stared at my empty fireplace. An hour later I stood, picked up the fireplace poker, slipped out of my shoes, and headed up the stairs. I walked as quietly as possible down the hallway and slowly twisted the doorknob before pushing open the door. Light spilled in from the master bath, keeping the room from total darkness. There lay my lovely Kathleen, deep asleep, the picture of tranquility. Between the curve of my wife's neck and the slope of her pillow sat Liza, her gaze locked on mine.

We stared at one another for several seconds before Liza turned her face towards the side of Kathleen's throat, toward what might be the carotid artery. Liza then turned back to face me and opened her mouth as though in yawn. Even in the gloom I saw enough to marvel at how such a small dog could have such sharp teeth—incisors like razors, canines like spikes.

It wouldn't take much—the implication was unambiguous. It would not take much.

At that moment, I understood more than I cared to admit. That Liza might not be a dog had become abundantly clear. Which left me with a simple question, really . . . what was she? Something timeless, so it seemed, ethereal. Something that could do more—much more—than protect itself if threatened.

I slowly shut the door and spent a sleepless night on a family-room chair.

Time has passed . . . each day I question my sanity.

It has been a traumatic year and, as Kathleen continues to point out, I've been drinking too much. Kathleen is active again at church and plans to return, part-time, to teaching pastries, breads, and desserts at a culinary school not many miles away. She's able to speak of Sierra and the twins without a meltdown. She's come out the other side, as they say, and is likely praying that I'll soon find my bearings. And she's done all this while doting on Liza—her new best friend—the dog Kathleen claims *chose her*.

As for me, I live and let live. Nothing more I can do.

But as time passes, every now and then I'll feel the hair rise on the back of my neck, and I'll turn to Liza. There she sits, staring up at me as though we share a secret. And for a moment, like young Dr. Strouts had intuited, I feel like a little boy lost in a big department store. And I reflect on the secret Liza and I share.

Everything needs a home.

Everything.

The Birthing Pool

Eóin Murphy

A small cramp twisted Sarah's swollen belly. She winced and rubbed a hand over the tightened muscles. It faded, leaving behind a gnawing worry.

"You okay?"

Sarah nodded. "Aye, just a bit of wind again." She forced a burp and covered her mouth, smiling behind her cupped hand. "Pardon me."

The Passenger shifted, and another burp slipped out. Jim laughed, earning himself a slap on the arm.

"Not funny." she said.

"It's a bit funny." Jim glanced towards her, his grin growing wider. The passing streetlights reflected orange light from his glasses and hollowed out his cheekbones. Along with the smile, he looked like a malevolent imp.

"Be quiet and keep driving." She leaned back in the seat, enjoying a moment of relief from carrying ten pounds of baby and god knows how much of fluid. Sarah stroked the bump, pushing down the fear. The longer it took to labor, the better.

The car rattled a little as it went over one of the speed bumps that lined the way into the village like irritating guardians. She missed the jingle of the beads and the little bell of the blue elephant that had hung from the rear-view mirror, but Jim had taken it down when he had started to drive her car. She eyed the twisted knot of dried seaweed he had put in its place. For protection, he'd said. It was her car, but she decided to let it go. Not worth the drama, not at the minute.

The car drifted past the bigger houses that lined the outskirts of the village and down into Danog, a little peninsula that cut out into the North Sea. A perfect harbor that had appeared overnight a hundred-and-fifty years before after a great storm had ripped apart the headland and left a single finger of rock pointing out to sea.

They reached the seafront, the drab little houses of Danog giving way to the open expanse of the sea. Along the seafront, a mix of heavy-bellied fishing boats and elegant sailboats bobbed up and down on the waves, bound to the marina by lengths of rope. Block and tackle clinked against masts, the sound echoing across the quiet village.

A breakwater protected the marina, but the beach itself was exposed to the raw sea. The car glided past the beachfront, Sarah keeping her eyes from the rolling, white flecked waves as they broke on the black stone of the beach. She had never liked the sea, and the many walks along the beach that Sylvia had recommended ('babies love the sea air') hadn't helped. She had spotted things washed up that didn't seem to belong on Earth, let alone the seaside.

Sarah groaned.

Jim's head snapped towards her, eyes dropping to her belly, then to her face and back again.

"I was groaning at the sight of that, not this." She pointed at the shape looming out of the darkness, then down at her bump. "I don't know how many more of your aunt's classes I can put up with."

The car slowed and pulled into the car park. Jim took a moment or two to respond. She glanced at him as he spoke.

"Not too many more, I'd say." He said, his voice quiet.

She nodded and rubbed her belly. "Did she say why she changed it to Friday night?"

Jim shrugged. "I think it's something to do with the Festival tomorrow. She wanted to get the class out of the way first."

The car slowed as they neared their destination. Danog Community Centre hunched in front of the Marina like a crab waiting on its prey. Built at the height of 1960s brutalist architecture, the Marsh Centre for Enlightening the Youth was a cross between a prison block and a concrete slab. Two wings jutted out from its featureless façade; small wire-meshed windows, too high to open without a stick, squinted out to sea. At some point, the local Community Development Association had decided to make it more appealing by painting it bright green. The combination of sea air and funding cuts had left the building looking like it had leprosy.

A small spattering of cars dotted the parking lot, none of them quite in between the faded white lines.

A jeep twice the size of their own car had not even bothered with the pretense. Abandoned in front of the entrance, the driver's door was wide open, an insistent beeping expressing distaste at this development. At the rear, the open boot was a maw filled with odd lumps and bumps.

"I see she's here already," Sarah said.

Jim parked alongside the others and nodded.

"Truly it is a night for miracles," he said, hopping out of the car and scurrying around to the other side.

He hovered outside, jerking forward, hands outstretched as if she had fallen instead of just opened the door.

"I'm pregnant, not an invalid." She ignored his proffered hand and hauled herself out.

Jim raised his hands in defense. "Just trying to help."

Wrinkling her nose at either Jim's over-protective nature or the smell of the fish market (and she wasn't sure which), Sarah walked towards the door hidden behind the jeep.

It was lying wide open, a brick acting as a doorstop.

A short wide woman bustled outside. She smiled when she saw them.

"Health and safety, Danog style," she said.

"Hi Sylvia," Sarah said, "what horrors do you have planned for us tonight?"

Sylvia waddled over, wrapped her stout arms around Sarah and hauled her into a hug.

The smell of fish was replaced by the scent of coffee and just-baked bread. Sarah settled into the embrace, knowing from experience there was no sense in trying to fight it. Best to enjoy her aunt-in-law's all-engulfing arms than try to avoid them. Besides, Sylvia's hugs were rather nice.

Sylvia pushed Sarah back a step and looked her up and down. "Two weeks, isn't it?" she said, biting the underside of her lip.

Sarah nodded.

"I wouldn't be so sure," Sylvia said. Her bright gaze fell on Jim. She pointed a finger. "You, bring that box of fake babies in from the jeep." Her eyes danced as she looked at her nephew. "After the tide, we're practicing nappies."

He glanced at Sarah, concern flickering across his face for a moment. Sylvia cleared her throat.

"Righto," he said, lowering his head and scurrying to the back of the jeep. He lifted a clear plastic container from the boot. Small, empty-faced babies stared at Sarah as he passed.

Sylvia wrapped an arm around Sarah's shoulder.

"You've been drinking the tea?" she asked.

"Every day," Sarah said. The little, homemade bags had sat on the shelf for the last week. Sarah had ignored the gift until she had run out of raspberry leaf this morning. It had tasted vile, like sloes and twigs and god knows what else. The rest had found itself falling into the outside bin.

"Good girl." She patted Sarah's arm. "We'll get another cup into you when we get into the Centre."

Changing the subject, she nodded towards Jim.

"And have you named it yet?"

"No. I have a list, but Jim wants to wait until it's born

before deciding."

Sylvia nodded. "Probably for the best. You wouldn't want to get too attached." Her warm smile slipped and a flicker of something else took its place.

Sarah opened her mouth to ask what she meant when a knot twisted in her stomach. She shifted where she stood, trying to relieve the growing pain as it tightened. A small moan escaped her. She stumbled, her fingers grasping the door, and she squeezed until the blood drained from her fingers.

It faded as fast as it had arrived.

She stood for a second and rubbed her belly. The Passenger undulated below her palm, small fists poking through thin flesh.

"So, it's not wind, then." Patting the small hand, she straightened up and bit back the rush of fear that threatened to swallow her.

"Jim," she said. Her voice shook slightly. He looked over and raised an eyebrow. Sarah pointed at the bump and opened her arms. He shook his head. He didn't understand.

Sylvia, however, did. "Are you alright, love? Is it time?"

"Seems to be," Sarah said. "Although it's a bit early."

Sylvia looked at her watch. "Perfect timing, if you ask me."

She guided Sarah towards the jeep, helping her lean against the black paneling. Sylvia placed chubby hands on Sarah's tummy. Broad fingers probed the baby below.

"He's turned, and his head is down." She looked Sarah in the eyes. "He's on his way."

"Bugger," Sarah said. Jim appeared at her elbow.

"Get the car," she said. "We need to head to the hospital."

Another contraction grew, squeezing another moan from Sarah.

"How long's that since the last one?" he asked.

Sylvia *tsk*ed. "Not long. A minute or so."

Sarah gripped Sylvia's hand as the knot tightened, a burning pain running from her back to her belly button, crushing her in between.

"Right," said Sylvia, glancing at her watch again. "Time's moving on. Get her to the Birthing Pool."

The contraction faded. Sarah's muscles relaxed but the pain stayed, a dull reminder of what had happened — and worse, what was to come.

"Birthing pool?" Sarah waved them away and straightened, groaning at the effort. "I am going to a hospital with a doctor, nurses, and lots of lovely drugs."

She pointed at her belly. "You do what your mummy tells you and stay in there. Jim, get the car."

Sylvia grasped her arm, her chubby fingers squeezing. Sarah could feel the iron that lay below the soft folds of flesh.

"The baby is coming and you're going to the Pool." Sylvia turned to Jim. "Get the jeep started."

A slow stream of villagers trickled from the Community Centre. Concerned faces focused on Sarah and all she wanted to do was hide from their stares. Something about them seemed expectant, almost hungry.

Sylvia noticed them and began to throw out orders.

"Jennifer, get some blankets and boil some water. The

rest of you go spread the word that we're going to the Pool." She paused. "And somebody tell Simon we won't be needing his youngest tonight after all."

A meaty arm swung around Sarah's shoulder, holding her fast.

"Let me help you into the jeep," Sylvia said, a feral smile plastered on her face. "Small steps, dear."

Caught in Sylvia's grip, Sarah wasn't given much choice but to let herself be led towards the back seat. Jim held the door open, bouncing from one foot to the other.

"Almost time," he said, as Sylvia nudged her towards the seat.

Sarah pushed back, refusing to lift her legs. "Sylvia, I am not going to give birth anywhere but in a hospital."

The Doula stepped back and folded her arms. "The nearest hospital is over an hour away across the border. The Lisavaney is flooded with the spring rains so you'll have to take the long way round. That's another thirty minutes." She pointed a meaty finger at Sarah's belly. "That baby is at least ten-pound weight and your first one. Chances are something will go wrong, and you'll find yourself stuck at the side of the road giving birth and hoping you don't bleed to death. Or, you can go the Birthing Pool and let the cold saltwater help relieve the pain with a trained midwife and couple of nurses nearby to help. Your choice, dear." Sylvia stood like a rock. Around her, the rest of the villagers watched. Jim stood with them.

"Okay," Sarah nodded. "It's not that I don't appreciate your help. I just, I thought a hospital would be better."

"You would think that. But sometimes the old ways

are best." Sylvia flashed her grey, round teeth. "Shall we go?"

The contraction hit Sarah just as she lifted her leg to get into the jeep. She crumpled forward; her face pressed into the black leather. Her stomach hardened, her insides twisting as her muscles cramped. Dull, round pain grew in her back and swept around her midriff. She bit back a scream. A low growl worked its way free.

Behind and above the pain she could hear Sylvia's voice.

"The tea never fails," she said. "The third tide will be here soon, let's get her to the pool."

Hands gripped Sarah by the shoulders and she was half–lifted, half-dragged into the backseat.

"I don't want to give birth in a pool," Sarah said. "Please."

Sylvia stroked her forehead. "There's no need to worry. I've delivered hundreds of children over the years." She gestured at the procession of women behind her. "Nearly every child in this village was born in that pool."

She leaned in close, a faint odor of rotten fish on her breath cutting through Sylvia's usual homely scent.

"You let me do the work. All you have to do is get that baby out safe and sound."

Jim hopped into the front seat, the others rushing off to their own cars. Sylvia flopped into the space beside Sarah and patted the headrest of the seat in front of her.

"Off we go, Jim."

"Aye, Sylvia."

The jeep moved off, slow at first, Jim whispering

apologies at each bump he hit that drove a pained groan from Sarah.

A procession of cars followed them out of the car park and along the road. They beeped their horns and flashed their lights. Along the street, doors opened, and villagers appeared, shafts of yellow light falling onto the dark streets.

They cheered as the car passed, some running to their own cars and even more following on foot.

"Is the pool at your house, then, Sylvia?" Sarah asked, resigned that she was not going to have her preferred, pain-free birth in a nice comfortable hospital bed, partaking of various gases and drugs. Right now, she would have killed for a paracetamol, let alone an epidural.

Sylvia laughed. "You silly girl." She lifted Sarah's hand and began to count her heartbeats. The Doula's lips moved but no sound came out.

The car turned towards the beachfront, away from where Sylvia's big bungalow sat on the outskirts of the village.

"We're going the wrong way," Sarah said. "Jim, it's back that way."

"No, it's not." A wide grin crawled over his face as he turned to look at her.

"Don't you be worrying where we're going," Sylvia said. "Just lie yourself back and let me take a look to see how far along you are."

"No."

Sylvia's face hardened. "Do you want your baby to die? If that's what you want to happen, then keep arguing with me and I guarantee you'll be holding a cold dead thing in an hour."

"Damn it, Sarah, just do as you're told," Jim said, an ugly snarl replacing the grin.

Sarah sobbed and shuffled around, pressing her back against the door. The latch dug into her shoulder, another hurt to add to the growing list.

Sylvia hitched Sarah's dress up over her thighs and pulled down her knickers, tossing them into the foot well.

The woman hulked over Sarah, her head dropping down between her legs. Broad fingers poked and prodded.

Sarah winced. Sharp pain bloomed from inside her.

"Please Sylvia, stop."

She ignored her.

"No movement down there yet," Sylvia said, "but with the pace of the contractions, we can't be far off."

Sarah felt her abdomen tighten.

"Please, no," she said. "Jim, do something."

He kept his eyes on the road.

"Just do what Sylvia tells you - she's the expert in all this."

The contraction tore at Sarah. Pain gripped her back and squeezed.

Sylvia patted the bump.

"There's a good child."

Taken by the contraction, Sarah didn't notice the car stop, its wheels crunching to a halt on the shale. A blast of cold air broke through the fog of pain as the car door opened.

A hand gripped her forearm and dragged her from the backseat.

"Find your feet, dear," Sylvia said.

Waves crashed against rocks; the sound close enough that Sarah looked down to check she wasn't standing amid the rising tide.

Half a dozen figures stood around the jeep, draped in white robes, their faces hidden by the hoods they wore.

Two of them stepped forward, reaching out for Sarah.

She retreated, her back bumping against the jeep. She slapped away their hands.

"Get away from me." She turned to look for her husband. "Jim, do something."

Standing with the others, Jim finished pulling a robe over his head.

"Don't worry," he said. "This is just tradition whenever a baby is born in the pool."

Headlights washed over them, and more cars arrived. A stream of villagers followed behind on foot. Some were dressed in robes; others carried picnic baskets and drinks.

Jim waved away the hooded figures.

"Come on," he said, taking her by the hand and leading her through the acolytes and towards a large cluster of black rocks that sat hunched on top of the beach. "Let's get you into the pool."

The acolytes trailed after them, Sylvia at their head. The shale underfoot turned into slick rock that rose and fell in sharp runnels, puddles of stagnant seawater splashing under Sarah's feet. Thirty yards away, the sea lapped its way hungrily towards them, swallowing shale and stone an inch at a time.

They stopped at a rock pool that lay below the old

stone breakwater that had protected the village from the sea for decades. Sarah must have walked past it a dozen times in the last year alone. A wart of black rock, it crept its way above the surface of the beach, a jagged crown of some long dead king, its edges worn smooth by the sea and encrusted with jewels of seaweed and mollusks. Steps, worn into the rock by generations of villagers, led up to the lip of the pool, which then dropped into the water, its surface thick with rancid foam.

Sarah stopped, her husband bumping against her and trying to push her on.

"This is the Birthing Pool? I thought you meant one of those inflatable ones." Sarah said. "I am not getting in that."

"Come on, Sarah. It's fine." Jim tugged her arm, urging her on.

"What is this, Jim? This isn't normal."

He smiled; his eyes glassy. "You're in the country. We do things different here."

"I don't give a shite." Sarah turned and tried to push her way past the acolytes. They locked ranks. She would have had more chance of walking through a wall.

The whole village had gathered around them. Most sat on the breakwater above, chatting as they watched the drama below.

Strong hands wrapped around her.

"To the Pool," Sylvia said. She paused, looking up at a dozen men and women that stood in the viewing area above. The Council had installed it five years earlier to try and attract tourists. The robes they wore were the color of blood in the water. "With your permission, of course."

A few of them nodded.

"Thank you." Sylvia bustled up the steps and splashed into the rock pool, the water rising to just below her knees.

"Who are they? What the hell is going on here?" Sarah struggled against Jim.

"You know them," Sylvia said. "That's the Committee of the Danog Community Association."

Jim and an acolyte bracketed Sarah. She refused to walk but they hauled her forward.

She pushed back at the top of the steps, the black water below a void that could swarm with anything.

Jim rushed her in, one hand pinching the back of her neck. The ground was slick, remnants of generations of seaweed turning the rock into an ice rink. Her feet went out from under her. Sarah fell into the water, her bump dragging her down and into the pool. Brown silt washed over her face and shoulders. Burning cold saltwater covered Sarah, her head falling below the surface. She came up spluttering, spitting the taste of blood and salt from her mouth.

"Idiot boy," Sylvia said. "We need the child alive."

"Sorry, Sylvia."

Sylvia rolled her eyes.

"Men. Idiots, the lot of them. Still, you're down there now. You may as well stay where you are."

She gestured at one of the hooded figures. He splashed through the water towards Sarah. She curled into a ball, arms wrapped around her belly, protecting The Passenger.

Ignoring her curses, the acolyte rolled her onto her back.

His scarred hands pressed down on Sarah's shoulders. Stone scraped against her skin.

"Let's get a look at you, then." Sylvia rolled up the sleeves of her gown and kneeled in the water.

The Doula put her hand between Sarah's knees and forced her legs apart. Hunched over her like a toad, Sylvia pursed her lips.

"How long since her last one?"

"Since we left the jeep. Three or four minutes, maybe?"

Sylvia put her hand on Sarah's stomach. Squirming, Sarah tried to get away from her vicious fingers.

The Doula squatted over Sarah, her face a goblin's mask beneath the hood. Palms pressed down on Sarah's bare belly, squeezing into tender flesh and muscle.

"Her muscles have relaxed," she said.

"What does that mean?" Jim asked.

Sylvia ignored him. She stood, wiping her hands on her robes.

"Go fetch the green case from the Jeep." She waved a hand at one of her acolytes. The man scurried out of the pool.

Sarah tried to sit up. Jim pushed her back down, shushing her.

"Walter," Sylvia said.

Another man stepped forward, lowering his hood. The pub landlord bowed his head.

"Go tell the Committee that the vessel is in false labor. I'll need to perform a caesarean if they want the child out in time for the Third Tide."

"What?" Sarah struggled to rise. "You can't do this." The acolyte shoved her back down.

Sarah stared at Jim. "She'll kill me and the baby."

Jim simply smiled, his face devoid of fear. "Sylvia has delivered nearly every child in the village, me included. I'm sure she knows what she's doing."

"Please don't do this," Sarah said. Her voice broke as she reached out to Jim.

"There's a girl." He leaned down and stroked her hair. "After all this is over, we can have our own baby."

"This *is* our baby," Sarah said.

He laughed. "Don't be silly, love. The baby isn't ours and it never was. After it's given to the Heralds as a gift to the Bádh Rí, we'll be able to have our own child."

Sarah pushed him back. "Stay the hell away from me."

"I'm just trying to make you feel better." He scowled, the same face he would make when she refused to let him help her from the bath.

"What is wrong with you?" she asked. "They're going to cut me open and steal our child and you're going to let them?"

"It's not our child." His voice rose above the sound of the waves crashing down outside. It broke at the top, turning into a rasping screech.

Sylvia clapped her hands. Jim stopped, turning sheepishly to face his aunt.

"Jim, enough. I won't have you upsetting Sarah any more than she already is. It's not good for the baby, and it has to be alive for the sacrifice." She put her arm around him. "You were warned this could happen when you chose outside the village. They don't know our ways or what obligations we have."

"I know, it's just," he looked back at Sarah. "I love her, I want her to stay."

Sarah stared out to sea rather than look at his gormless doe-eyed face.

Someone coughed. The acolyte was back, a large green case in his hands, a winged serpent embossed on the front in white.

"Very good," Sylvia said. "Put it over there and go and fetch some boiling water, we'll need it to disinfect the scalpel and the sewing needle. Jennifer should have the big kettle from the Community Centre." The acolyte nodded and dashed off again.

She patted Jim on the arm. "Don't worry. I'll do my best to keep her alive, and after this is over, we can all sit down with a cup of tea and sort everything out."

"Fair enough." Jim nodded.

"Good lad. Now go sit with your wife. She's going to need you once the cutting starts."

"No cutting." Walter stomped up the steps.

"Pardon me?" Sylvia folded her arms.

"Sorry Sylvia. The Committee says to tell you that the tide is only a couple of minutes away. There's no time to get the sacrifice out."

"They're sure?"

Walter shrugged. "They took a vote. It's minuted and everything."

Sylvia looked at her watch. "Oh bugger," she said. "What do they suggest?"

“They said to leave the woman here and let the Heralds take both of them. The child will be still alive, so it should be alright.”

“Not a bad idea,” she said. She put the scalpel back in the green case and closed it with a snap.

“Go and fetch a rope to tie Sarah up and then get the others. Best they all go together.”

She stood, hefting the case, and turned to leave.

Jim stood in her way.

“This isn’t what we agreed.”

The pressure on Sarah’s shoulders eased as the acolyte behind her watched Sylvia and her nephew. Sarah stretched out her fingers, searching for something, anything that could give her an advantage.

Sylvia pressed her hand against Jim’s chest. “It’s not for you or me to decide. The wave is coming and there is no time to cut the child free.”

“But we were meant to have our own baby.”

“There are a dozen girls out there who are crying out for a man. You’ll have no problem finding a new wife.”

Jim lifted Sylvia’s hand from where it lay.

“I don’t want a new wife.”

Sylvia’s eyes narrowed.

“Then don’t get one. This is about more than you and your little outsider. This is about making sure we give the Bádh Rí gifts in return for the Village.” Her finger poked Jim in the chest. “This is not about you.”

She pointed at Sarah. Sarah stayed her fingers, a sliver of rock lying under her hand. “Or about *her*. The Bádh Rí demands a sacrifice and he is going to get it, one way or another.”

Jim nodded, admonished, and moved aside. Sylvia splashed through the shallow saltwater and out of the pool.

Sarah flinched as Jim knelt beside her.

He brushed a strand of her dark hair from her forehead.

"I tried." He shrugged. "I just want you to know I loved you and won't forget you."

"Oh, well, that's all right then," Sarah said.

"There's no need for sarcasm."

Sarah laughed, a long peeling cackle that echoed from the black stone of the Birthing Pool. Her voice cracked.

"What the hell is wrong with you people? You're going to kill us? For a wave?" She twisted in the acolyte's grasp.

"Not a wave, for the Bádh Rí, the sleeper himself. The Third Tide is his stirring from his slumber beneath the sea."

Jim looked off towards the ocean. The waves crashed against the shale and rock that passed for Danog's beach. On the horizon, where the dark storm clouds met the grey ocean, something roiled in the depths.

"Let me go, right now. Right. Now."

Wet lips pressed themselves against Sarah's forehead.

"Goodbye." Jim stood, moving aside for an acolyte carrying a length of thin blue rope.

"Jim, please, don't leave me here."

He didn't look back.

Sarah dropped the sliver of stone before the men levered her upwards. Walter wrapped the rough nylon weave around her wrists. Crossing it over her hands, he looped a length around her ankles. It burned against her cold skin. The other man tied a knot, wrenching the rope tight.

The pain ripped a gasp from Sarah.

A trio of children appeared at the lip of into the pool, Sylvia huffing up the steps behind them.

A little girl, no more than six, clasped her hand.

"A little bit of company for you on your way to see the Bádh Rí." Sylvia said, leading the girl to the rear of the pool. Water sloshed over Sarah as they passed.

"Jesus fucking Christ, what is wrong with you people?" Sarah struggled against the ropes, thrashing in the water. "Let me go, damn you!"

Sylvia ignored her.

"Here you go, dear." She wrestled her hand free from the child's grasp. "This is an honor for you all. Don't besmirch it like this one here."

She glared at Sarah. "You should have drunk the tea."

"I'm sorry," Sarah said, her teeth chattering, "but it tasted like ass."

"That'll be the Shan legs. Not a fan, myself, but it does hurry a labor up no end." Sylvia loomed over Sarah. Her habitual smile fell away, replaced by an angry scowl. "All you had to do was drink it. The child would have been born by now and there would have been no need for any of this. Our Jim could have been happy, and you as well."

"Happy?" Sarah struggled in the water, wrists burning where the wet rope cut into them as she forced herself upright. "You're delusional."

Sylvia shook her head like a disappointed parent.

"You were such a lovely girl." Turning away, she clapped her hands and addressed the children. The familiar, warm smile was back on her face.

"Now, in the next couple of minutes, the Third Tide will arrive, and you will all be taken by the Heralds to live forever with the Bádh Rí." She beamed. "Isn't that wonderful?"

"Yes!" A dark-haired boy, around nine, started to hop up and down on one spot, a wide grin splitting his face. The girl began to cry. The youngest, little more than a toddler, was oblivious, splashing in the water, his little yellow boots kicking up waves that washed over Sarah.

"Very good. Now I, and all your Mummies and Daddies, will be watching from the seawall, so be on your best behavior. And remember, what do we say when we first meet the Bádh Rí?"

As one, the children, even the youngest, began to chant.

Guttural, rotten words flowed from their young mouths. The sound sickened Sarah, twisting her stomach and driving a painful wedge into her forehead. Her skin burned, as each syllable crawled across her flesh. She shook her head, trying to get away from the words. A smell of corruption assaulted her nose. The world twisted, just a little, as they spoke. Sarah closed her eyes but the darkness that waited there had too many angles.

Each word they uttered sent foul unknown colors blooming in Sarah's mind, until everything she knew and felt was a chaos of light and sound, smell and touch.

"Goodbye, children. Sarah." With a last sad smile at Sarah, Sylvia left. The acolytes followed in her wake.

The children stopped chanting. The world became right again.

Sarah turned her head and vomited, stinging bile and this evening's dinner mixing in the brown silt of the pool.

She heaved in a breath and watched the woman who was the first to welcome her into Danog leave her to die in a rock pool. She faded into the night, the Doula waving people off the beach and up onto the roadside.

Sarah waited until the last of the villagers had gathered their blankets and sandwiches and flasks of tea, until the only sound was the crash of the waves and the quiet splashing of the children as they waited for their faith.

She raised her head and looked across the beach. It was empty, the sea only a dozen yards from where she sat. With a grunt of effort, she scrambled through the murky water for the stone knife, sweeping her vomit out of the way. Slow and steady, she searched the pool's floor. The sliver scraped her fingers.

Holding it in her right hand, Sarah bent her wrist, dragging the serrated edge across the rope.

Looking up, she saw the children watching her.

"I don't suppose one of you would like to help me?"

The boy shook his head and turned to face the wall.

Between sobs, the girl spoke.

"Sylvia said we were to ignore you, or our souls would be eaten for eons."

"Of course she did." Sarah sawed at the rope for another few seconds before tracing her fingers along the material. Frayed edges tickled the tips of her fingers.

The boy scuttled forward, standing at the edge of the

pool and looking out over the sea.

"The first wave is coming."

Ignoring him, Sarah tensed her arms, the rope growing taut and easier to cut.

More strands gave.

A wall of water smashed into the rocks that protected the pool. The wave smashed into the boy, spilling him across the floor. He slammed into the rock wall.

Sarah gagged on the smell. It was as if a trawler full of three-month-old squid had washed up with the tide. Things crawled in the pool now. Little more than a mass of tentacles and mouths, the tiny creatures propelled themselves towards the children and Sarah.

The boy struggled to his feet, the creatures squirming up his legs. He yelped, panicked arms sweeping them from his robes.

One, the size of Sarah's thumb, latched onto the meat of her leg. A needle stab of pain erupted from her thigh and she grabbed its slimy body. Its teeth ground into her as she tried to pull it from her leg, its tentacles latching tighter around her calf. She stabbed it with the stone knife. Pulsating grey flesh popped, brown ichor leaking from the creature. It drifted like a cloud in the seawater.

Turning back to the rope, Sarah hacked at it. It snapped. Shucking free, she heaved herself upright using the black stone wall of the pool as support.

"Sylvia said we had to stay here," the boy said, shivering in his wet clothes.

"Sylvia can go to hell," Sarah said. Large swells grew on the surface of the sea, the water turning as black as the storm clouds that hung above it.

The tide rushed in, careening against the rocks of the birthing pool. More of the creatures squirmed on the shale as the water retreated.

No one stood guarding the steps.

Turning, Sarah scooped up the toddler in one arm and grasped the girl's hand in her own.

The boy stepped in front of her.

"You can't go."

Another flood of water crashed down, the gathering wave on the horizon growing larger.

"We're leaving," Sarah said. "I will not let anyone harm my child, so either move or be moved."

He stepped out of the way.

"Come on, Barry," the girl said. "Auntie Sylvia said the Bádh Rí is our friend, and friends don't mind if you don't keep a promise sometimes."

Barry glared at Sarah, his fingers tugging at the dripping sleeve of his robe.

Another wave smashed into the rock face. Larger than before, it engulfed them, the force of the water driving Sarah to her knees.

Barry offered her a hand up.

"Good boy," Sarah said as she stood.

She passed Barry the toddler. "You carry this little one, and I'll take the girl."

"He's called Arthur and she's Callie," Barry said.

Arthur grinned when he heard his name. "Hello," he said, and waved.

"Hello Arthur," Sarah said. "Now, everyone out of the pool."

Barry and Callie led the way, clambering over the

crested stone bank, pausing at the bottom to offer Sarah a shoulder to lean on as she took the last two steps.

"Keep close to the wall," Sarah said, water reaching up to her knees.

Things squirmed in the foam thrown up by the rising tide. The baby in her belly weighing her down, Sarah moved slowly. The water did not.

Villagers lined the waterfront, staring down at her and the children.

"Should have stayed in the pool, love," Auld Pete said, having moved from his bar stool for the first time Sarah could remember. "The Heralds prefer a moving target." Beer sloshed from his glass and splattered Sarah's hair.

"Aye," the woman beside him said. "You could have got another couple of minutes if you'd stayed in the pool. Still," She said to Pete. "You can't be telling these young ones."

Ignoring them, Sarah sloshed on.

The stairs were a dozen yards ahead. Two acolytes stood a foot or two above the water level, watching them approach. Barry scampered ahead; Arthur held tight to his chest. He stopped at the foot of the stairs and glared up at them.

"Let us past," he said. "We don't want to go with the Heralds." He put a foot on the step.

One of them surged forward. He shoved Barry off the steps. Tumbling backwards, the two boys fell into the froth, the water rising above their heads. Sarah dropped Callie's hand and rushed forward. She grasped Arthur by the shoulders and hauled him to his feet, the little boy spluttering water from his mouth between sobs.

Barry pulled himself up, shivering but shoulders square.

"Let me deal with this." Sarah put her hand on his shoulder and passed Arthur to him.

Heralds swarmed around her feet as she moved. An acolyte raised his hand. "Don't bother, we'll just toss you back as well."

"You'd let a pregnant woman and three children die here?"

"It's for the good of all of us," he said, moving down a step.

"It'd be quicker for you to kill us yourselves," Sarah said, keeping her arms folded across the top of her belly. The water continued to rise. Callie was up to her chest as dark shadows circled them, seal-sized Heralds waiting on some unspoken signal to strike.

"Has to be the Heralds, otherwise the sacrifice doesn't count," the acolyte said.

"Really? Thanks for letting me know." Sarah unfolded her arms and revealed the serrated shard of stone.

She held it above her swollen belly.

"Don't," the man said. He pushed the Acolyte beside him. "Go get Sylvia, quick."

The other man bolted up the stairs, his robes catching under his feet as he ran.

"Too late," Sarah said. Standing two feet from him, she drove the stone blade down. He surged forward, reaching for her wrist. Sarah twisted to the side. The knife slashed through his robes as he overbalanced and fell into the waves.

"Up the stairs, go." Sarah ushered the children up the

steps.

The acolyte stood. He flicked the arms of his robes, splattering the wall with wet spots.

"That was stupid." He waded towards the stairs. A shoal of Heralds gathered around his feet.

Sarah pointed to the wall. Flecks of blood ran down the rough granite.

The acolyte looked at the long gash the knife had ripped in his robes, a faint glimmer of torn skin below. Blood beaded and dripped into the water for the growing swarm of Heralds at his feet.

"Shit." The acolyte surged towards the steps. His foot touched the stairwell. A Herald leapt from the water and slammed into him. It dragged him below the surface.

The water turned into a bloody froth. The acolyte struggled to his feet, screaming. Heralds covered his body, a seething mass of biting tentacles.

Sarah ignored his cries for help and climbed the stairs. The children waited at the top, Callie covering Arthur's eyes from the sight of the man below.

Cautious, Sarah peeked around the stone wall. Cars were parked along the harbor front, blocking most of her view. There was no one nearby. A small crowd was gathered around the entrance to the pub, halfway down the street from them. Cheery light spilled from the doorway and windows, and for a moment, Sarah wished she was with them. The acolyte was running towards them, waving his arms, and pointing back at her.

From the seawall, villagers turned to face them, glancing at the Committee, as if waiting for orders.

A warm wind blew in from the sea, pressing the damp

material of her dress against her back. Sarah shivered. The air was growing fetid, as if somewhere out to sea, some great rotting beast was making its way to shore.

Along the harbor, the fishing boats and private yachts rose on a swell, their bows crashing down into the saltwater. The noise rolled across Danog, a shattering end to the peace of the night. Throughout the village, heads turned to watch the sea and what stirred beneath the waves.

Villagers leaned across the sea wall, looking towards the surging waters, voices rising in alarm. The seawater raged in a violent froth, the Heralds searching for their sacrifice and finding nothing. A shout rose from the Committee. The group broke, swarming down the pavement towards the stairway.

"We have to go," Sarah said. She pointed towards the cover of the parked cars, scuttling forward as best she could with her large bump in the way. She put her back against a car and waved the children over to her.

"They're getting closer," Barry said, as the acolytes and villagers spread across the road, the Committee directing them to cut off the way out of the village.

"Over there," Sarah said. Parked at the far end of the street, wedged at a right angle to the other traffic, sat a familiar jeep. The door hung open and a silver glint of keys hung from the ignition, Sylvia, as always, immune to the normal worries of car owners.

They scrambled towards it, every pretense of stealth gone. The children reached it first. Barry heaved Arthur into the back seat and crawled in beside him. The boy helped Callie up beside him and he buckled her in.

Sarah waddled behind, moving as fast as The Passenger would let her.

"Sarah."

She turned her head, the response automatic after so many years spend listening to it. Jim pounded towards her, outpacing the other villagers.

Ignoring him, Sarah ran on, the children shouting at her to run.

Jim roared her name.

Heaving in a breath, Sarah levered herself into the driver's seat.

She slammed the door shut, hitting the central locking button just as his hands slammed into the window. Jim jerked at the handle, a thin line of drool hanging from his mouth.

"Open the door, open it." He pounded the glass with his fist. "You'll kill us all."

Sarah ignored him. She turned the key in the ignition and the engine erupted into life. Reaching for the gear stick, she looked up, ready to speed away from Danog.

A wave, twenty feet high at least, rushed in towards the wall. It struck the breakwater, washing over the street and sweeping villagers off their feet. The force of the impact slammed Jim into the car door, his face mashed against the glass. She had time to see the panic in his eyes before he was carried away.

Not looking, keeping her head down and away from the struggling froth around her, where her husband had been swept away, Sarah turned the key and started the jeep. She even indicated. A small, round woman stepped out in front of the jeep. Her lips pursed, Sylvia held up a hand, as if she could stop the moving vehicle. Or maybe slow it down, just enough.

"Get out of the way!" Sarah said. Sylvia didn't move.

Sarah slammed her foot on the brake. The jeep skidded in the water, kicking up a high spray.

Her eyes wide and desperate, Sylvia put both hands on the bonnet of the jeep as if she was going to try and push it out to sea.

"You have to go back," she yelled, "The third tide is almost here. You'll kill us all for the sake of four children."

The Passenger kicked Sarah's stomach as if to display its displeasure at Sylvia. Sarah patted her belly.

"Don't worry, I won't let her have you." She looked out the windscreen. "Can you hear yourself? You're insane, every single one of you."

Sylvia waved her hand as if chasing away a fly.

"For you it's easy. It's like drowning kittens," she said. "Best done quickly before you get attached. Have you thought about the little one's parents? What they've gone through to protect the village?" Sylvia shook her head, a froth of spit caught in the side of her mouth.

"You city people. Selfish, every one of you."

Sarah revved the engine. "Move."

Sylvia shook her head. "You'll have to run me over. Please," Sylvia said. "The village is all we have. Four children, that's all they need. Four lives to save three hundred. It's not that many." Sylvia lifted her hands, pleading with Sarah. "There's still time to cut your one out. You could have another."

Sarah could see the light of madness glinting in

Sylvia's eyes.

"Look at the village, Sarah. It's perfect. It's been here a hundred-and-fifty years, and with your help, it'll be here forever. Unchanged and pure."

Despite herself, Sarah looked out across the village. Heavy grey storm clouds heaved above the village, rain pounding across the roofs and pavements in sheets. Waves smashed into the marina, sending ships dancing.

Out to sea, beneath the water, something shifted. Colors flickered beneath the waves, flashes of something beyond the blue and green and red of the world. They pushed into her mind, sliding past her senses and down into something deeper within her, something that longed to be in the ocean once again. Thoughts of escape flowed from her. Why would she run? She was already home.

Behind her, the children urged her to drive, to move, to just help, please. But they were just burbles of sound, lost against the pulsing rush of the sea.

She felt the thing that lived in the harbor, which had gifted this place to the families in its deep wisdom, turn its gaze on her and it was beautiful.

What was the life of a child when faced with infinity?

Sarah turned and smiled at Sylvia. It would be better this way. The children would be happy under the sea, with all the others that had joined the Bádh Rí. She reached for the door handle. Sylvia dashed around and hauled on it, a beaming smile on her face.

Sarah's stomach twisted. A tiny palm pushed against her belly, warding itself from the sea outside and the thing that waited beyond. She hesitated.

Sylvia snarled and pulled on the handle. She thumped

the glass with her fist.

"I can't help you if you don't open the door," she said.

Sarah shook her head, trying to clear it. Sylvia was right, she needed help.

The Passenger twisted, small hands flexing inside her, butterfly kisses in her belly.

The world snapped back. Sound rushed in. The cries of the children, the roar of the waves as they swamped the beach.

In the water, something vast roiled and raged; colors that pulsed in hypnotic beats drew in the villagers as they rushed into the sea to join it.

Sarah pulled her hand back from the door and restarted the engine. Sylvia pounded on the window, her knuckles splitting against the glass and smearing it with blood. Cursing, she dashed in front of the jeep.

This time, Sarah didn't bother to ask her to move. She floored the accelerator. A jolt shook the Jeep. Sylvia bounced from the bonnet, the windscreen cracking where she thumped into it. The Doula tumbled into the seawall.

Gripping the wheel tight enough to turn her knuckles white, Sarah watched in the rear-view mirror.

Sylvia clambered to her feet, her left arm hanging limply, a trickle of blood leaking from a cut above her eye. She stared after the jeep for a moment, her eyes catching Sarah's just for a moment.

The Doula turned to face the sea, opening her arms wide as if to greet it. A fifty-foot wall of water slammed into the beach, breaking the stone wall. In an instant, Sylvia was gone. Black foam washed across the street, engulfing the village.

The wave rushed on. The temperature rose, and the stench of rotten air filled the car. Small things squirmed in the pools that had formed in the footwells.

The Jeep sped along the street, passing villagers clinging to the walls and fending off the Heralds that gamboled in the surf.

Following the coast road away from the harbor, the mass of parked cars petered out, the seawater receding.

Sarah allowed herself a small smile. Peeling one hand from the wheel, she laid it on her belly. A small knot of pain twisted in her lower back.

Faint screams rose from the harbor. Reaching the edge of the village, Sarah turned the car towards the border. She didn't look back.

Elegy

Sarah Johnson

The navy-blue dress swished over my calves as I twirled, taking in a panoramic view of the graveyard. I'd expected more headstones. Wailing angels, cherubs, and crosses. Dramatic stuff. I also thought the grass would be nicer, like a golf course. Most of the markers were small plaques set into scrubby turf freckled with dead leaves. I tried not to show my disappointment. Almost everything looks better in the movies.

"Ready?" Clem plucked the lens cap off her camera. "Just act natural."

I snorted. "Right, natural."

The nude branches of a weeping willow stretched down and around us like a cage of bones. At the base of the trunk I moved aside a wilted floral arrangement obscuring the inscription on a plaque. No name, and no dates. Just the words *Beloved Daughter* and a quote I recognized from Rilke's *Elegies*.

"Angels (they say) would often not know whether they moved among living or dead."

As a teenager I'd bonded with Rilke, wallowing with him in the fathomless pool of our shared existential depression. Even in happier times, his *Elegies* were something I returned to again and again. Comfort reading, in a weird way. Rilke's angels seemed more human than divine. Easily fooled. Easily hurt. Afraid to fly.

I brushed the dead grass from my legs, the skin smooth and unblemished by bruises, nicks, or other evidence of day-to-day collisions usually hidden behind high denier tights. Vain, perhaps, but I was glad to look put-together. I squinted at the sunset. "Are you allowed to do a shoot here? It's a graveyard."

"Cemetery, G. They're called cemeteries." Clem fiddled with some toggles and buttons. Then she glanced up, her brown eyes gold in the evening light. "Are you okay with this? When I called…I never considered that you might not want to come."

"Like I had something better to do?" I pulled the clip from my hair, letting it tumble down my back and wincing at the release of tension on my scalp. "How long has it been?"

"Over five years," she said. "I used to know it down to the day, but living like that, one sunset at a time—it's hard."

I nodded. Time didn't mean what it used to. I glanced down at the plaque again. "You picked the inscription?"

Clem took a whistling breath through her nose. "Your parents did."

"What?" An accusation as much as a question. "You let them—"

"You weren't there. I was a complete mess and they offered to take care of it. When they showed me the design and asked what I'd like to add...I was touched. Couldn't bring myself to change a thing."

I fidgeted, mollified but unwilling to concede. "How did you track me down, anyway?"

She peered through the viewer and snapped a couple shots. "Wasn't easy. I'll tell you that much."

Baby showers were the fucking worst. However, the new mom was on my team at work, and I felt obligated, despite my deep disinterest in her reproductive achievement. I dropped my expensively wrapped baby food cookbook in the heap of presents and headed into the kitchen, because a girl's gotta eat. I'd hoped to grab a snack in solitude, but instead found a cute blonde standing in front of the open fridge biting into a piece of fried chicken and washing it down with a swig of orange juice right from the carton.

Our eyes met. She lowered the carton and wiped her mouth with her sleeve. "Almost empty. No point dirtying a glass."

"You know there's a ton of food right here on the table." I peeled a paper plate off the stack and loaded it with a few veggies and a pile of cheese.

"This is my sister's place. She's used to me shredding through her leftovers. I'm Clem."

"Clem?" I asked, trying to match the awful name to the girl with butterscotch eyes, a soft pink mouth, and...Jesus, was that a dimple? Damn.

"Short for Clementine."

"Ah, hideous. Clem is much better." I shook her greasy hand. "George. Not short for anything."

The truth was, I'd always liked my name, and hadn't seen any reason to change it. As a kid I'd been obsessed with the Nancy Drew mysteries, but was too embarrassed to check them out of the school library, so I stole them, one-by-one, and hid them in my closet. I loved Nancy, with her titian hair and blue convertible. I saw myself as her best bud, a gamine tomboy conveniently named George. Plus, their fat little friend Bess sounded hot.

"So why aren't you out there with those Lululemon bitches?" Clem asked.

I noshed on a wedge of Gouda. Evasive maneuver. Stuff your face to avoid answering questions.

"The baby thing is so not my scene." Clem peeked out the kitchen door and studied the gaggle of ladies in the living room, passing around a sleeping infant. "Do you have any babies, George?" I shook my head as she approached me with a thoughtful expression. "We should be friends. You're stunning, by the way."

I gulped down a mini carrot dipped in hummus. "Eh?"

"Your face is perfectly symmetrical; did you know that? I want to measure it. Have you ever modeled?" Her nervous grin showed her molars. "God, that sounds sleazy, but I'm a photographer—which sounds even more sleazy—but I really am, and sometime, when you have time, I'd like to shoot you—with pictures—take pictures, of you, is what I mean."

I liked Clem. Her clumsy social skills, and her porcine grazing habits. I liked that she found me interesting. And what girl hates being told she's beautiful? I definitely wanted to know her.

"It'll cost you dinner," I said.

I took in Clem's ponytail, the frayed cuffs of her sweater, and the faded denim clinging to her hips. Thinner. Harder around the edges than I remembered. An acquired seriousness that suited her somehow. She still wore her wedding ring. I glanced down and saw a matching stripe of gold on my own finger, and a thin scar running over the back of my hand, up the outside of my forearm. Clem's eyes followed the pink thread all the way up to my elbow. I clasped my hands behind my back. We weren't there to talk about scars.

"You're all grown up," I joked.

She snapped pictures from different angles and heights while I strolled and twirled. "You look the same. Always a princess, even in your pj's. Navy is your color, perfect with your skin."

Turning my flawed arm from the camera, I gave her a dramatic, arched-back, hand-to-forehead glamor pose. "You picked this dress?"

"Figured you'd want something classic."

My laugh lodged between my collarbones, hardening like a clod of frozen earth.

Clem lowered the camera. "What is it?"

"The last time I saw you..."

"I was a whale."

"Pregnant. Crying all the time." I swallowed past the lump, thinking of how much I'd missed. "Now I get it, because you knew. Somehow, you knew."

"George..." Clem reached into her purse, pulling out her wallet. "I brought her picture with me."

I clutched my elbows and squeezed my eyes shut. "I'm sorry, I can't. I want to, but I can't."

Her arms surrounded me, and I inhaled the perfume of autumn and warm skin trapped in the weave of her sweater. "Let's not waste time being sad or sorry. We're here, now. Clem and G. Same as before."

"Except it's not." I skirted as close to the unspoken truth as I dared. "It's not the same at all. Why did you call me, Clem? Why did it take you so long?"

She held me tighter, whispering into my neck. "I was scared. I didn't know if you'd still be you. And right now, I just want to take your goddamned picture, okay? Can I do that?"

I straddled the ledge of the bathtub while Clem perched on the vanity reading the side of the box, her forehead knotted up. "Maybe it's too soon?"

"Okay," I said. "So wait another week."

She swiveled her head toward me so fast her hair flew out and slapped against the mirror behind her. "And sit around wondering? Forget it." She studied the box again. "Can you go downstairs and get me a mug?"

"A mug?"

"It says I can go right on the stick, but I'll end up peeing all over my hand."

I went downstairs and rummaged in the back of the cupboard for a mug. An *I ♥ NY* mug we hadn't used much before and I would certainly never use now.

"You're leaving?" she asked when I turned to leave the bathroom.

"We aren't pee-in-front-of-each-other people, Clem. No baby is going to change that."

Her face clouded. "A baby is going to change everything, and when it does, you're going to freak out because you actually have to take it seriously, and I'm going to have to take care of the baby *and* you."

"Cracking a joke doesn't equal desertion of duty. And we both know that of the two of us, I'm the serious one."

She had no idea. Being a mother was something I hadn't dared allow myself to want, for how unlikely it was. But now I had Clem, and I wanted our children more than anything. But I was terrified. More scared even than I'd been on our first date when all through the movie, I sweated through my capped-sleeve blouse reminding myself that it was better to be up front. Better to be rejected for who I was, than desired for who I wasn't. Afterward, we lounged on a Starbucks patio and I told her I wasn't a cis-fem. Her forehead wrinkled, and she blinked a few times. I told her it was okay to ask questions. I didn't want there to be uncertainty between us on that score. She asked if I had a penis. I asked if that was a problem, fearing she might be one of *those* dykes, savagely protecting her gold star status. She shrugged, slurping the dregs of her iced coffee. Then she grabbed my hand and took me back to her place.

Maybe it was stupid, and selfish, but that day, and every day since, I'd been the love of her life. Would the baby take her away from me? Things were tense with all the fertility stuff, and I'd already been shut out of one family. I didn't think I could survive losing another.

"Are you even listening?" she demanded. "Do you even care?"

My spine stiffened. "Just pee in the fucking mug."

"Don't yell at me!" Tears ran their twisting course down her cheeks. "I can't do this alone, G. I need to know you'll be there."

I bit my cheek but wasn't able to hold my tongue. "If you can't see that I'm in this as much as you are, then maybe you should get that thing scraped out before we make a huge mistake."

"Cunt," she snarled, and slammed the bathroom door in my face.

Leaves crunched under my ballet flats as I walked over to a large marker in the shape of an Egyptian obelisk. Eccentric, expensive, and cheeky in a phallic way. I wrapped my arms around it and laid my temple against the cold polished granite. Over my shoulder I heard Clem's camera click.

"Whoa, I think I've got it," she said. "Don't move, I'm going to take a couple more."

I hugged the obelisk tighter. "They show up on digital?"

"Well..." *Click, click, click.* "Purists would say you ought to use film, but the investigator I contacted said digital works just fine, better actually. Less artifact. And I don't want something that can be explained away as a blotch of unevenly exposed film. It's gotta be authentic—especially since I decided not to bring her."

I tried to keep my breathing invisible, and tried even harder to ignore the uneven expansion of my ribcage and the lopsided thump of my heart under navy blue georgette. Rilke said every angel was terrible. Clem couldn't have known what she'd be summoning. A ghoul, madness made flesh, a monster. I couldn't blame her for wanting to protect a child from that.

A hundred questions swarmed around my molars and I sealed my lips against their escape. Judging by the look on her face, Clem was itching to ask me the same questions.

Are you happy? I wasn't unhappy.

Is there someone else? Doubt it.

What have you been up to? Outcroppings of memory glimmered here and there but really, I couldn't say. Perhaps there were rules.

Do you still love me? From the moment we met, to the moment I left, to the moment I answered her call. I never stopped. That, I knew for certain. That, I could've said. Could have, but didn't.

I turned the key in the lock and shuffled into the foyer. Before I could kick off my pumps, Clem called out. "If I'd known you'd be late I wouldn't have cooked."

I sniffed the air cautiously. "You cooked?"

"Grilled cheese. Just something I'm trying," she said with a weary smile as she shifted her distorted body on the couch. I slid my hand over her belly, feeling a greeting kick beneath my palm.

We rested against each other in a rare absence of conflict. We were far from the picture of joyful expectation. I was banking overtime so I could take a month off. She was still working as well, weeping with exhaustion at the end of every day. Sex wasn't a thing that happened anymore. The first three months of her pregnancy she couldn't get enough, and I happily obliged, exploring her constantly changing body with equal parts awe and envy. Now I could barely touch her, and everything I said made her burst into tears or fly into a rage.

Over one persistent issue.

Clem insisted I was going to leave. I promised. I reasoned. I argued that I'd done nothing to indicate that I would bail on her. Over and over, but she would only shake her head, claiming she had a bad feeling.

"G?" she said, hesitantly. "It's getting close now. Don't you think we ought to tell your parents?"

"The parents who wouldn't even come to our wedding?"

"It's their grandchild. Babies have a way of softening people."

"As far as they're concerned, I died the day I wore a dress to Nana's funeral."

"You did?"

"Navy blue boat neck. Classy. I looked like Audrey Hepburn."

Clem smiled. "Still do."

I shrugged. "It was elegant, and Nana would've loved it, but Mom and Dad acted like I'd shown up in full fucking drag."

"Body glitter and platform stilettos. You could totally pull it off," Clem said, her swollen fingers toying with her wedding band, strung on a chain around her neck. "I just...I don't want you to regret anything, with your family."

"You're my family." I splayed my hand on her stomach. "You, and this little beast. Now, if you feel like being bad, I'll go out and get you an iced coffee."

"God, yes," she groaned. "I'll come with you."

"On those ankles?" I glanced at the puffy flesh spilling out of her socks.

"I've got your meatloaf squatting in my uterus and you complain about my ankles?"

I sighed. "Woman, did I not just offer to acquire contraband for you?"

"So you did."

"Your ankles are beautiful."

"Thank you."

"Prepare to be caffeinated." I kissed the tip of her nose, feeling safe and loved, knowing we'd always find each other. "I'll be right back."

A questioning look in Clem's eyes had me gazing down at

my legs, so smooth an hour ago, now a hash of scars. Trauma, gone silver with age. My vanity cried foul but my deeper self—the part that knew where I'd been, but couldn't talk about it—that part knew this body was a borrowed item. A summoned facsimile, fumbling towards entropy. And it could've been worse. Clem could have been in that car with me.

I twisted my wedding band on my finger, feeling the tug on my thin skin. "Clem...there's a lot we aren't saying."

She nodded.

"But there's something you need to say."

Another nod.

"Tell me."

"They invited us for Thanksgiving," Clem said. "Every year they invite us. Every year they send birthday and Christmas cards."

I scowled.

"They were devastated, G. And people change, doesn't the inscription on the plaque prove that?"

"*Too Little Too Late*, would've been more appropriate."

She snapped another photo. "Don't frown, it makes you look old."

I rubbed my arms, not surprised to feel the pattern of old wounds drawn to the surface. My whole life, my parents loved their fantasy son more. They chose a person who didn't exist over their actual kid. Now they wanted to be a part of their granddaughter's life. They wanted a chance to do better, but that was no guarantee they would.

Clem took my hands and kissed my knuckles. "You

don't need to forgive. That's not what I'm asking."

I pressed my thumb to her lips. The aperture of all her unspoken words. *Do you trust me to protect her?*

"Okay," I said. "Okay."

"Light's gone." Clem capped the camera lens and led me to the skeletal tree where we sat side-by-side in the thickening dusk. "I've always wanted to do it in a graveyard."

"They're called cemeteries, Clem. And why didn't you ever say so?"

"Probably, I would have, but we ran out of time."

She leaned in and I shivered, feeling her warm cheek against my bare shoulder, and the scrape of her teeth on my throat.

"Necrophile," I teased, and gave her a playful shove.

Clem grabbed my wrist, pulling me off balance. I fell on top of her and we laughed like a normal couple, goofing around on a morbid third date. She pushed my hair off my face, the only part left unscathed. "You still look like Audrey."

I kissed her then, really kissed her. The way I should have the last time. Her lips tasted like root beer. Still addicted to Lipsmackers. Still the adorable barbarian, raiding other people's fridges and drinking from their cartons. She'd held onto that part of herself, and I held onto her so long that it was nearly full dark when we clambered to our feet.

"I'm glad you called," I said. "We'll have to do this again."

A smile curved across her face like her own disfiguring scar. "Next time I'll bring little G."

"I'd love that."

"See you soon."

"Yeah."

We lied with all the love we had between us, and I saw myself reflected in the mirror of her eyes, not as a decaying revenant, but a princess. She slung the camera over her shoulder. I watched her walk down the path until her shadow slipped through the gate.

At least she got her photos. A few orbs to show a five-year-old girl with my name, my blood, and the love of my life watching over her. Maybe my parents would be a part of that. It wasn't up to me to correct or complete. Not anymore.

I wandered to the base of the tree, to a plaque with no names or dates. Just Rilke, his angels, and a *Beloved Daughter*.

Coyote

Jason A. Wyckoff

"We sat in the sun all day." My Great-Grandfather held up four leathery fingers protectively, his gnarled thumb across his palm, as though the late-day sun slinking through the plastic slats of the venetian blinds offended as much as the oppressive blaze of memory. Then he turned his hand and flipped the fingers towards him, as though beckoning. "The wind was constant; dusty wind that scraped the skin like sandpaper. But still we'd take off our costumes, because the wind was our relief from the sun. The first two days of shooting, one of the assistant directors yelled at us to keep our costumes on between takes, but he gave up. He was wearing himself out in the heat!" He chuckled; each "heh" marched out in rhythm. His voice was so hoarse that I couldn't help but swallow reflexively as I listened to him. He dropped his hand, gently pushing away the sixty-plus-year-old elements. "*He* didn't get to hide in a trailer like John Wayne did."

He was half-submerged in a faded faux camelhair

recliner. I leaned on a table, clutching a sweating bottle of La Croix, trying to keep still so the hardback chair I perched on wouldn't creak too much. At least twenty lobby cards were thumbtacked to the wall opposite the front door, photogelatin hand-tinted stills or Technicolor reproductions somehow yet vibrant. Three plastic tubs full of more cards and posters lined the base of one wall. I wondered if he rotated the display. I wondered how many comedy westerns Lee Marvin had appeared in. I could swear I smelled a lingering note of buttered popcorn above the stale musk of the old widower's quarters. The trailer wasn't old, but it wasn't the first he'd lived in set on the same lot. He spoke English. He could've spoken the Southern Paiute dialect of Colorado River Numic, but I wouldn't have understood him. Hell, I had to look up what language it was that I wouldn't have understood.

I'd never visited Joseph Gad Thompson at his home on the reservation. I'd met him only twice that I remembered, both times at family reunions at my Grandmother's house outside Albuquerque. But I started hearing his name mentioned much more often when, to their astonishment, I told my parents I intended to major in film studies at UCLA. I never knew we had another film buff in the family. My mother would say, "I've never heard of a trait skipping *two* generations!" Gad (as he preferred to be called; when I called him "Father Thompson", he told me he wasn't a Catholic priest) found out about my intentions and invited me to visit, but school—and disinterest, to be honest—kept me away. I didn't have the heart to tell him that the only reason I finally found time to make the trek was because I had dropped out of college after two years, and even then, might not have come if circumstances had been different. Scholarship money had helped with tuition, but I was flat broke besides. Perhaps it wouldn't have surprised my Great-Grandfather to find out the native scholarship hadn't helped *that* much; the first thing he did when he saw me was scowl and then lean in and say, "You got a whole lot of white in you, don't you, kid?" And he laughed. Of course, he knew my heritage; I'm three-eighths native. And the Shivwits are ruddy or dusky or whatever crap term you want to use, so even with all my white, I still get mistaken for Latino in L.A.

"We were the great Mongol horde of the Utah desert. And they put a Fu Manchu on 'The Duke,' did you know that?"

I knew it. *The Conqueror* was notoriously bad, from casting to execution. John Wayne as Genghis Khan didn't even look good on paper.

He read it on my face. "Of course you know. You're a college boy!" He beamed with familial pride, so I didn't take it as a jibe. Again, I didn't have the heart to dissuade him. "Of course, for years and years, Hollywood cast white actors to play Indians. So why did they cast Indians to play Mongols? Probably because we were the only ones willing to sit out in the sun and wind for two or three bucks a day. There were some Shoshone there, but it was mostly Shivwits. One of the Shoshone actually got a one-line speaking part as a soldier making a report to John Wayne. But they wanted him to do it in broken English! He pointed out it didn't make sense to have a Mongol speaking in broken English to another Mongol who spoke good English when they are both supposedly speaking Mongolian. So they fired him and put a white actor in redface and had him do it!" He let out another staccato chuckle. "I never did figure out why some people got paid two dollars a day and why some got three. I did some good trick riding, but I only got two. After the Shoshone man got fired, I didn't dare ask for more. I was excited to be in a film, no matter how terrible the conditions—or the film!"

Gad was much more loquacious than most of the Elders I'd met, so I was surprised when he abruptly fell silent. He looked at the lobby cards. I knew not to prompt him.

He said, "I was young enough to think it meant the start of something." He paused again before he said, "I took a different path." He looked at me and smiled. "But not before I took all of my earnings from the shoot and bought myself an eight-millimeter camera." He rose spryly from his concave seat and went towards the bedroom door. He reached up and grabbed a metal ring. Somehow, I hadn't noticed the projector screen mounted near the ceiling. He pulled it down; the seven-foot white square blocked half of the bedroom doorway. He turned the rod on the curtains to close them completely. "That same A.D. who told us to keep our shirts on had a Kodak Brownie. I bought it off him the last day of principal photography." He walked past me to the kitchen counter, bent, and brought forth a projector, already plugged into the receptacle above the sink. "He didn't realize he hadn't taken the film out." He set the projector on the counter and turned it on. It chittered. The screen bloomed. "You'll like this," he said.

The chair creaked as I leaned forward. A stream of short clips, most no more than five seconds long, was displayed in silent black-and-white. It was insignificant behind-the-scenes set photography, all surface greetings—Agnes Moorehead waved and smiled, John Wayne sauntered past, shooting a finger-gun—but I was enthralled. After all, how many people had seen this footage? It was the first time in a while I could remember being interested in anything, no matter how banal. A trainer fed apple slices to a horse. A panning shot captured the desolation of Snow Canyon. There was John Wayne again looking painfully bored. Someone handed him a lit cigarette.

"Watch close," Gad said.

I'm sure my jaw dropped open. I'd seen a still photograph of the scene before, but now I was watching it unfold. John Wayne was out of costume, sporting a broad-brimmed hat, leaning on one of his two shirtless sons to his left. On his other side, an unknown man adjusted the controls of the black box Wayne was holding in his right hand over a thatch of weeds on a large rock. Because there was no sound, we could not hear the reputedly violent crackling of the Geiger counter.

"Watch close," he repeated.

The son Wayne leaned on shimmered out of focus—only him; the rest of the picture remained sharp. Then a black spot burst like a sore on his face. I thought the film was burning, but then the sore closed again, before re-opening on his chest. It squiggled across his sternum and collapsed once more.

Wayne was all smiles. The other man appeared to be apologizing as he nervously continued to tweak the controls.

Wayne's other son, further away, shimmered out of focus for a second. The black crackle was a spastic snake coiling around his neck. Then it was gone again.

Wayne's face frayed into vertical lines and then came back together. His left eye yawned black. The spot opened wide across half his face. It writhed down his body, bubbling black scorches on his stomach.

The scene changed. Nameless crew bent over their lunches at a picnic table.

There were more clips. I failed to note them. Eventually, the film ran out and Gad switched off the projector.

"You know about *The Conqueror*," he said.

I breathed, "Wow."

I think he took it for 'yes,' but explained anyway. "They called it an 'RKO Radioactive Picture'," he said. "Ninety-one out of two-hundred-and-twenty people on the film got cancer. Half of them died from it. Wayne's sons each survived their battles, but The Duke didn't. Of course, he smoked like a fish, as the saying goes." He winked and grinned. "So who knows? For certain, though, is that St. George still struggles with leukemia rates five times the national average," he said, in reference to the nearby town.

I nodded. "The nuke tests."

"Surface tests in Nevada," he specified. "A hundred-fifty miles upwind. They gave 'em names, you know that?"

"What?" That was news to me.

"Each bomb got a name. Humboldt, Sally, whatever. Simon was fifty-one-kilotons." Once again seated in his recliner, he leaned towards me. "Simon was a *motherfucker*," he said, and then he laughed, open-mouthed, so that I could see his missing incisors.

"You think the radioactivity caused those errors in the film?"

"Errors," he scoffed. "Yes, I think that was the radioactivity, but not the way you mean. Bombs are eggs. Never forget: Death is a thing that is *in* the world." He leaned back and motioned towards the blank screen. "I think that was Simon."

I tried not to look at him like he was crazy, but I must have betrayed the thought.

He laughed again. "I have something for you," he said. He got up and brushed past the screen on his way into the bedroom. "You'll get all of this eventually," he said as he disappeared.

I think I protested (I was half-unsure I wanted anything of his, half-desperate to start cataloguing it all immediately); from out of sight, he countered, "Who else have I got to leave it to?" I heard him shuffling boxes. "I still have a few years kicking around before then, though. But there's one reel I won't ever watch again." I heard him grunt, lifting something. It finally occurred to me that I should get up to help. I had been stuck in place, thinking of the disappointment he might feel if he knew I wasn't sure film was going to be *my* future, either. The screen bulged out at an angle as he pushed the edge of a box against it. I pulled it to one side, and he came in.

"You can always go back," he said as he passed me.

"What?" I asked, incredulous that he had read my mind.

He set the box down on the kitchen counter. I saw that it contained another projector, slightly inferior to the one he had set up. He turned around. "That's what I always loved about film. Even the dumb little things I shot are memories I can revisit whenever I want. There's quite a few of your Great-Grandmother and me when we were young." He smiled his gappy smile. "Be kind when you inherit them." He patted the projector. "But, like I mentioned, the one in this box, I don't need." He looked at me and I saw his eyes had turned rheumy. He said, "I don't need it, but maybe you do."

Gad invited me to stay the night ("or as long as you like"). He said his neighbor had an air mattress he could borrow. I lied and said I was supposed to catch up with some friends in Las Vegas late that evening.

I drove in that direction on the I-15 highway. I had no intention of staying in Las Vegas, but I had no incentive to drive six hours or so across the desert at night to get back to L.A. I could've stayed in St. George, but my skin crept at the thought of the lingering radiation, even if one night sixty years after the fact wasn't likely to do me much harm.

I ended up at a lonely motel on the southwest side of Mesquite. The town reminded me of a clean, abandoned Albuquerque in miniature. With casinos.

I was away from the "strip" (more of a cluster). If anybody staying at the Pink Palms Motel had any connection to gambling, it was likely a damn sad story. Fortunately, my stopover for the night seemed nearly as uninhabited as the rest of the town. I counted four cars, including mine. Well, it was Tuesday.

A plump, balding man at the check-in desk seemed almost bemused anyone would choose the Pink Palms. Though he was affable and polite, once outside the office, I spied him shaking his head as he turned back to his sports magazine.

Number 16 looked like any other motel room, only more confused. The indeterminate wall color might charitably be described as "verde limón." It shared no tones whatsoever with the tiger pouncing from a void of black velvet on the wall or the powder blue checkered bedspread. I didn't care. The room seemed clean; that was enough for me. The air conditioning was functioning, and a scented plug-in emanated lavender or lilac, something that started with an "L"; I was never good with flowers.

I called Josh, my roommate. He sounded surprised.

"Just checking in," I assured him.

"Oh. I figured you'd just text."

I shrugged, which did him no good. He was still in school. We were drifting apart, just as I was with everyone I knew in L. A.

"Sylvie came by to get her stuff," he said.

I grunted. "Well, it was probably better I wasn't there, anyway."

He didn't say anything for several seconds, and then

asked, "So, you're heading back tomorrow?"

"Yeah. I'll be there early afternoon, probably."

"Cool. Alright, then. I'm, uh, I'm on my way out."

After we hung up, I reviewed our brief conversation. Josh's tone seemed unusually flat, almost furtive. It occurred to me that perhaps something had happened between them when Sylvie came by, maybe something that had been waiting to happen for a long time, and I felt a flash of anger. And then I doubled down, mad at myself for thinking such a thing was possible, and mad at the both of them that I wasn't convinced otherwise.

There was a carryout down the street. I bought a six-pack of Lone Star just before they closed for the night.

I had gone to see Gad for no other reason than I needed a destination to get away from my life. Maybe I was depressed, but I didn't like the word; depression was something other people suffered from—actually *suffered.* I thought my "blues" were inadequate to claim as a real struggle. I felt I had no right to my stagnation. I hated myself for my weakness.

Two beers later, expecting to engage my jealousy at an imagined tryst between two people I was once close to, I found myself instead unwilling to invest in the effort. As I opened my third, I said, "Fuck 'em both," but it was neither defiant nor desultory; it was rote. It was a bad line reading.

I took down the velvet tiger. The projector was a heavy, khaki brown thing, like a suitcase with a handle on top and one side cut away to accommodate the working bits. I set it on the small table (one leg wedged with a generic wrapped mini-soap from the bathroom) and threaded the film. I turned on the projector and shut off the lights.

My Great-Grandmother, Elizabeth, appeared on the wall in black and white. If I'd ever met her before she died, I was too young to remember. I'd seen pictures before, but she was different in motion. Her face didn't look plump; it was rounded from high cheekbones down, like a stone plucked from a river. Her upper lip was wonderfully pouty. She blinked with mock-Betty Boop flirtatiousness. She backed away from the camera and then turned towards a blanket spread in the clumpy shadow of an old pinyon tree. A basket sat on one corner. She paused, turned back, and scowled feistily at the camera. I guessed Gad teased her; maybe he said she was so short she needn't stoop below the low branches. She nimbly lowered herself to the blanket, and began removing objects from the basket, displaying them to the camera before setting them out: plates and silverware, a loaf of bread wrapped in a towel, an unlabeled jar, a small paper sack. She pulled out a wine bottle and winked coyly.

The film jumped clips. The shot was from a low angle at the base of the blanket. Gad scrambled into view and threw himself onto the ground. He reclined his head on Elizabeth's lap. She plucked a grape with her right hand from a bunch she dangled from her left and lowered the grape to his hungry-hatchling mouth. After two more grapes, he got up and leapt towards the camera. The film jumped but retained the shot. The actions were the same with the figures reversed. The bunch of grapes Gad plucked from to feed his wife was considerably reduced.

Another jump. A blur of motion as the camera raised—Gad stood and stepped from beneath the tree. He shot the landscape, down an incline. His left hand appeared, pointing. I didn't see anything but stratified rock mounds and sagebrush. Apparently, Elizabeth didn't see anything, either, as Gad's finger shook insistently.

Then something emerged from behind a jagged curve of stone. It was four-legged, with a canine gait. The subtle shades of the desert were lost in monochrome, making it difficult to judge how far away the blurry animal was. Once in the clear from obstacles, however, it moved directly towards the young couple. I thought it was likely lured by the scent of their food. But both I and the live witnesses were startled by its brazen approach. It ascended the dusty incline unhurriedly but steadily; it did not waver or crouch the way a skittish coyote would. For a second, I wondered if it might be a stray dog, as it did not have a bushy tail. But as it drew near, I could see the mottled grey of its boil-studded head and body, and a bald, stick tail. It was a coyote, sick with mange —and who knew what else.

Suddenly the black crackle I'd seen on the Wayne family crawled from the coyote's snout and slithered down its spine. The camera shook and then Gad's arm shot out in a pushing motion, urging the beast away. The coyote continued padding forward. The image blurred as the angle turned to the dirt. The camera shook and then rose up again. Gad had switched hands while he bent to grab a rock. He showed the rock and snapped his arm at the elbow to demonstrate his intent. The loathsome beast was undeterred. Elizabeth flashed halfway into frame, perhaps pleading with Gad, but he stepped to the side. The coyote was no more than ten feet away. Its mouth fell open, slavering. Black spilled out, trailed down its jaw, and bloomed into a hole on its chest before disappearing. Gad threw the rock. I couldn't see where it went. The coyote suddenly rushed forward. It leapt; in the blur just before the film ended, I saw blackness deep in its maw behind white, sharp teeth in perfect focus. I knew it couldn't be a still, but the power of the impression of that last image made it seem frozen in time.

The take-up reel flipped and flipped. Eventually, I reached over to switch off the projector.

I turned on the room light. I took the reel off and looked at the innocuous black film. The events it documented did not seem to me constrained to the past—"you can always go back"—but at least the vile creature was once again *contained* and made small in my hands.

What had happened after the film ended? Obviously, nothing too terrible, at least not for my Great-Grandparents. But then why had Gad wanted me to see it?

I considered calling him to ask him about it, but I noticed the time. It was after midnight, and according to what I'd told him earlier, I should have been with my friends in Vegas by then. It occurred to me that, not only was I not there, I wasn't really anywhere.

The logical thing to do was to cut across town and get

back on I-15 westbound. But a map search showed I was close to state route 170, which proceeded southwest for a short jag before turning north and eventually intersecting with the interstate. It would add only a few minutes to my travel time, and I thought I could do with a short spell of isolation on a "real" desert highway to start my day before settling into traffic on the split four-lane.

A couple of minutes later I passed Bunkerville and a few outlying houses, and then I was alone on a two-lane, gravel-bermed straightaway. The road passed through rocky swells; dashes of shadow marked stone shelves in the cutaways. The sides opened and I saw why the stretch was quaintly labeled "Riverside Road"; "Riverbed-side Road" would have been more apt. Tufty green stubble dotted the banks.

I slowed as the road curved northward. An idea flashed in my mind about something I'd seen in the film the night before (I'd watched it twice more), but it was immediately dispelled by the ring of my phone. I accepted my mother's call.

She asked how my visit with Gad had gone. I said, "Fine." I told her he'd given me an old projector, but I didn't mention the film reel. The road straightened again; on the bridge over the river I looked over the side to see a broad swath of mud with just enough of a shimmer to indicate shallow water rippling as it flowed. My mom asked me how I was and again I told her, "Fine." I didn't want to talk about me.

I asked something I didn't think to ask the day before, "Mom, did Gad ever have cancer?"

I was surprised at the pause before she answered. I asked, "Mom, are you still there?"

"Your Great-Grandfather has always had a vivid imagination," she replied.

"What does that mean?"

"He had throat cancer when he was younger, or so he said."

I didn't pick up on the caveat. I asked, "Is that why his voice is messed up?"

"My mother told me he says he had cancer *because* of the way he sounds, and that if he actually had had the cancer he *said* he had, he would be dead. I've never known him to be sick a day in his life."

I didn't know what to do with that information, so I said, "Okay."

"To hear him tell it, his 'treatment' was to go out into the desert every night and howl with the coyotes. Gad likes to tell stories."

I saw a shape to my right, moving quickly towards the road. I slammed on the brakes. The tires squealed, my phone flew and hit the floor, and I yelled, "Shit!"—too many sounds to be sure if there was another impact.

I checked my rearview mirror (angling it, as I was not straight in my lane when I came to a stop) to make sure there was no one approaching before I bent to retrieve my phone. My mother was yelping, "What happened? Are you alright?"

"Mom! *Mom!*" I had to interrupt her torrent of concern. "I'm okay. I think I might have hit an animal. But I'm alright, okay? I'll call you back."

It took another thirty seconds of assurance before she

would let me off. Finally, I hung up and got out of the car. I went around to the front, dreading to see some smashed furry thing stuck in the grill, mortally wounded but still alive. There was nothing there but a small dent adorned with an asterisk of red. I went around to the back and moaned. There was a streak of broken brushstrokes leading off the road into a ditch.

The ditch was six feet deep, terminating at the point of a "V" where a dirt road intersected with the state highway. I walked to the crumbling edge. There was a cluster of brush in the crook; the trail of blood seemed to lead there. I couldn't see or hear any animal, dead or alive. I moved to change my point of view. I took one step too far forward and the loose dirt gave way. I flung my arms in the air, but couldn't regain my balance or catch hold of the side before I tumbled to the bottom of the shallow gully.

Jagged rocks stabbed my hands and the skeleton of a shrub scratched my face. I cursed and sat up, and brushed my arms and knees. I looked to the end of the ditch but didn't see any creature crouching in the pit.

He wasn't there. He was pacing the rim.

I remembered what I had thought of right before my mom called: how the camera had jumped *before* Gad had bent to grab a rock—how it had jumped when he saw the black crackle on the coyote's face *as it happened*. The film was not damaged. It was recording.

I knew this because I saw it. The mangy coyote crooked its head at an odd angle as it regarded me. I thought my vision was streaked because the sun was behind it. But then, as it padded with only the slightest limp along the edge of the ditch, I watched the blackness erupt from one shoulder and smear along its emaciated ribcage like spreading talons. It turned and padded back, and the crackle flared and burnt out half of its head for a second before closing again. It stopped and faced me. Its eyes were charcoal to match the remaining fur on its cadaver-pink hide. Its black lips pulled back as it opened its mouth. And from between its sharp, white teeth, so different from the rest of its body, I heard a sound emerge.

It was the sound of a chuckle it might have learned from a human, where each "heh" marched out in rhythm.

I didn't take my eyes off it as my hand searched the ground in an arc. I felt a suitable rock and snatched it from the dirt as I straightened up. Like my great-grandfather, I brandished my missile threateningly, as though the beast would understand my intent. Perhaps it did at that, as it stopped "chuckling." It growled as it tensed its haunches to leap.

Suddenly it lurched sideways and whirled around, shrouded in a maelstrom of dark smoke. When the beast skidded to a halt at the brink of the drop-off, scattering dust and pebbles into the gulley, it was five times larger. The jagged black smears on its hide were now fixed stripes, though much of the rotting fur dangled in patches and tattered skeins. Splayed claws and exposed bones alike raked the dirt. One of the tiger's eyes was milky white; its fangs were yellowed, fractured stubs. Its roar was a horrid rasp, somehow distant; the howl of a lone, lost, bloodied animal.

Despair squeezed my heart. My hand trembled. The

threat was too large, too alien. I wanted to run, but where could I go? What hope did I have to fight it? What did I think I could do with one outsized pebble?

I thought of Gad, in the desert, under the moon, crying out with his coyote note for note. I opened my mouth to roar. My tongue was dry and no sound would come. I opened my mouth further. Dust went in; nothing came out. The tiger matched me. A tendon snapped and its lower jaw lolled sideways. Something like breath escaped; something cold and stinking of quagmire.

I closed my mouth and swallowed grit. And then I did not roar, but spoke instead.

"I can't just close my eyes and make you go away, can I?" I whispered hoarsely. "Maybe I could make you disappear, but it's never *that* simple."

The tiger leaned forward as though to hear. I saw something crawl in the orbit of its milky eye.

"Because if I deny your existence, you will kill me." A little louder, I said, "Better to keep you in sight—in *mind*."

I lowered my arm slowly. I slackened my fingers and dropped the rock to the dirt.

"Cancer isn't a sick dog you can throw a rock at or howl along with at night," I said, "any more than depression is a velvet tiger you can leave on the floor of an ugly motel room. Not really."

We stared at each other for a few seconds more, and then I turned away from it. I didn't look back as I walked towards the open end of the ditch where the sides were lower and less steep. I found a likely spot and scrambled to the top. When I turned to face it, the beast was once more Gad's coyote, standing where the tiger had been. I began walking towards him—no, towards my car. He was in my path; that was all.

"But perhaps the old man knows something important," I said. "He knows that we empower ourselves when we frame our perils."

When I got within a few feet of the wretched creature, it spun and ambled down the road towards the river. After several seconds, the black crackle spread from its belly down its legs, swallowing them. The coyote's body bounced in mid-air as the consuming darkness crept from its brittle tail to the tips of its cracked ears.

And then I was alone on the road once more.

Unto The Next

Amanda Helms

The rock sails up to the shutter, collides, and clatters to the ground. Cassie roots for another and pulls it back.

"Hey, did you see that?"

Cassie tries to follow Jerome's gaze up to the window, but all she sees against the faded orange-pink light of late sunset are the gray, weathered shutters, the piles of leaves in the gutters, the bare spots on the roof from missing shingles. "No." She winds up again.

Jerome yanks Cassie's arm down and cranes his neck at the window. "She's in there, I know it."

"If you'd let me throw the rock, we'd know for sure, wouldn't we?"

Jerome sucks in his lower lip to chew on. Cassie feels herself staring and tears her gaze away, thankful for her dark skin; it helps hide her blush.

Spitting out the *(biteable)* lip, Jerome says, "I don't know if we should be here."

She grins. "This is, like, a rite of passage. Every kid has to throw rocks at the creepy old house."

Jerome glances back up at the window. "What do you think she is?"

Withholding a sigh- —it'd been going so well— Cassie says, "Most people say she's a ghost."

As Jerome turns toward her, Cassie experiences an epiphany regarding all those clichés about falling into someone's eyes. "Yeah, but what do *you* think?"

Shock-desire-fear rattles up Cassie's spine, suffuses her cheeks, her chest, her heart. She backs away.

Hates herself for doing it.

"Does it mat--"

The knocker bangs, without a hand to touch it. When Jerome's fingers fit themselves against hers, she forgets to blush.

"Maybe we should go," he says. "Come back tomorrow?"

They're three houses away from Jerome's and eight away from Cassie's when she finds something to say. "I think we should spend tomorrow night there."

"You're crazy." Jerome's hand remains in hers. Cassie's grip tightens a little, breaking the spell; Jerome drops her hand to smooth back hair that wasn't out of place to begin with. "We can go back, sure, but I was thinking, like, during daylight. When she's, you know, *quiet*."

Cassie tosses her head, though her curls are so tight it has little of the dramatic effect she'd envisioned. "People disagree on what she looks like. 'Short- —no, tall. Blond hair— no, black.' But everyone says she stays in the attic. We'll be fine. You're not afraid, are you?"

Jerome scowls. The smile that crept at her lips

disappears, and she ducks her head.

They've reached Jerome's now. Cassie tries unsuccessfully not to think about what it must be like: kitchen done in warm, neutral colors, walls dark beige, furniture a deep mahogany. Pictures on the walls of Jerome and his older brother and their parents, all of them beaming because they genuinely like one another and are genuinely happy.

Some families fake it, but she's been around Jerome long enough to hear the fond exasperation when he talks about his brother and parents. Sometimes you define things by knowing their opposites, and that's how Cassie knows Jerome's house is full of love.

Feeling stupid, she toes the ground, feels stupider for toeing the ground, and stops. But Cassie can't let the house go. "C'mon, Jerome, it'll be fun. Promise. We can go to Lucky's after school, buy a whole bunch of candy and chips and junk. You bring your tablet, and I'll hack us into the McCaffertys' Wi-Fi. Stream a movie or something."

"While the ghost's in the attic."

"We'll have an awesome story to tell everyone on Monday."

He rolls his eyes. "Are we supposed to do the dumb thing about telling our parents we're spending the night at someone else's house?" What goes unspoken is that Jerome says "someone else" to mean not-Cassie because she's a girl, and on her end, it means not-Jerome because he's a boy, and they're barely fourteen, and what would their parents think?

Not that her father cares enough to need a story, but

still. "Yeah, I'll tell Dad I'm staying at Laura's."

Another eye-roll, but there's still light enough for Cassie to catch the split-second sparkle. She has him. "Chris might cover for me. You really think it'll work?"

"'Course." She points to the phone in his back pocket. "You'll only be a phone call away the whole night." Good. She doesn't sound at all bitter about not having her own.

Jerome grins so wide it's like he wants to split his head open, and Cassie trembles, because she'd crawl inside him if she could.

"Okay. Lucky's tomorrow at six. Then the house." He laughs. "It's stupid, right? But also . . ."

"Kinda cool."

But what sings in her head is *It's perfect, perfect, perfect.*

A note about Cassie's family, before her mother disappeared, before the lake was dredged and found empty, before the forest was searched and found bodiless, before the authorities heard the words *chronic depression* and concluded she was dead somewhere else, or a runaway from her own life:

Before all that, they were happy. Or so Cassie's father said.

If he found Moira sitting in front of the mirror, tilting her face this way and that, and he asked her what she was doing, she would say, "Trying to see if I feel anything," and he would wrap his arms around her and say *Of course you do. You love us; you're happy.*

Six-year-old Cassie twined her arms around her mother's knees and held them tight. Her father said it. It must be true.

Is it ever a kindness, to lie to a child?

Is it less a lie, when you also lie to yourself?

It is night, and Cassie and Jerome are in the maybe-haunted house. They climbed in through a side window, landing in the living room.

Ever since hitting Lucky's for sugar-filled supplies, they've been snickering at private jokes. Mr. Durban's new hair plugs. Nellie Gleason presenting her unicorn collection for the public speaking assignment. They're keeping it light.

While smacking his flashlight to make it turn on, Jerome stumbles into a weather-warped pedestal end table, knocking it over.

Cassie's pulse thuds in her ears. Jerome rights the table and flashes her a sheepish grin. Even with the poor illumination of her flashlight, it's enough to make her stomach twist.

She wasted her ten dollars at Lucky's, because she's not going to be able to eat a single thing she bought.

"Sorry," Jerome says when it's clear Cassie is smiling back.

He could set fire to the house and she wouldn't be mad.

"You think she heard us?"

"Doesn't matter if she did. She never comes out of the

attic." Cassie sets her flashlight down long enough to shrug off her backpack. The left strap is coming loose. She tried to fix it with duct tape, but she's not sure how long it'll hold. Jerome's gaze landed on it when he saw her at Lucky's, but he didn't say anything other than to ask her if she wanted Jujubes or Starbursts. If she hadn't loved him already, that would've clinched it.

Bag deposited in the middle of the floor, she retrieves the flashlight. "C'mon. Let's see what's here."

The far wall bears a large, empty fireplace. Though plastic covers most of the furniture, the whole place smells of dust and the danker, loamier scent of nesting rodents. Cassie and Jerome start to uncover the couch, but it makes the smell worse.

A brief debate ensues about whether they should arrange their sleeping bags on the couch and its perpendicular loveseat, on top of the plastic, or if it's preferable to just lay them on the ground. Jerome is concerned what his mom will say if she sees the grime on his bag. "She'd never believe Chris's house is this dirty, and if she did, she'd threaten to have Child Protective Services called in."

Cassie doesn't have to worry about what her father would think if her old, holey sleeping bag with the fill poking out comes back unsalvageable. But while Jerome knows enough not to comment on the state of her backpack or sleeping bag, the thing he won't get is that there's a much larger difference between his family and Cassie's than money, even forgetting that his mother is still around. Cassie's mother didn't take the sadness with her when she left.

For the time being, they table the discussion.

There's not much in the living room besides the couch, loveseat, and fireplace, so they head down the hall to the kitchen. The spot where the oven should be is empty, and there's no room for a dishwasher. Rust lines the sink, and when Cassie tries the tap, nothing comes out.

"Who owns this place, anyway?"

Cassie freezes; Jerome comes up right next to her. While their previous handholding was based on nerves, now his closeness is extravagant. There's plenty of room for him to be a step or six away. He doesn't have to stand so near. He's *choosing* to.

She turns. While she doesn't close any of the remaining distance, she's careful not to let it grow.

"I mean, someone's got to own it. They would've torn it down, otherwise."

Cassie starts to cross her arms, forces herself instead to grip the counter. "Some family in Florida. They try to sell the place every so often--last time was about three years before you guys moved to the neighborhood. But no one wants it."

"You'd think they'd raze it. At least sell the lot."

"Yeah."

"How did she get here?"

Their proximity is too much. Her emotions are a boa constrictor choking her in its coils. "How the hell should I know?"

In the glow of her flashlight, Cassie sees Jerome's face close off, how *his* emotions are anger, disgust, disappointment. "It was only a question."

The house should collapse upon her. Only her, not

Jerome. She doesn't know how to apologize —or she does, on a theoretical level; she should say *I'm sorry*.

But with Jerome, she lost her footing long ago —his first day in school, she thinks, when he complimented the felted superhero patches on her knees, and when, even after the other kids told him that she wasn't making a statement, that she was poor, he kept talking to her. She can do nothing to regain her steadiness.

Cassie tries, though. She can't help but try. "I mean, there's no real stories about her. Other than she's a she, and she stays in the attic, and it's an old, old house, so she has to be a ghost. But there's nothing about a murder, or an accidental death, or anything that explains her. She's just always been here, in this house, for as long as I can remember. Sometimes blond, people say, sometimes brunette, but always here."

It says something else about Cassie's family that she has no memory of when she first learned about the attic woman, that it is now entwined with what makes Cassie Cassie.

She shivers.

"Cold?"

She's not, but what she said is apology enough, for Jerome looks soft, somehow. Cassie nods and rubs her goosebumpless arms for good measure.

"I have an extra sweatshirt in my backpack. Let's go back to the living room."

"Sure. And if you brought your tablet, I'll hack into the McCaffertys' Wi-Fi."

They settle on the plastic-covered couch. Cassie almost can't concentrate well enough to do her hacking (which isn't real hacking; Mrs. McCafferty took pity on her and gave her the password when she visited one day, knowing her father couldn't afford Internet service). But she manages, despite wrapping Jerome's smell around her. Wearing his sweatshirt is the closest she'll get to her earlier wish to crawl inside him, so she keeps finding reasons to subtly inhale against her shoulder, enjoying the sensation of having Jerome both wrapped around and beside her. His fingers flash over his tablet, bring up Netflix, and pick a horror b-movie.

A zombie cheerleader has just torn off the arm of a zombie football player when Jerome turns to her, so close she can count his eyelashes, and smiles, a tiny uptick at the corners of his mouth that makes Cassie grin in Pavlovian response. The tablet falls to the small crevice between their laps, and Cassie tries not to let her breath catch in her throat, and Jerome leans in, and she can feel the warmth of his breath on her lips—

—Which then say, "We should go up to the attic."

Amid the glow from the tablet —now a zombie football player is gnawing on a thighbone— Cassie sees Jerome's chin tighten, just his chin, and she's amazed for a moment that he has such control over this one part of his face, and then she realizes what she said and what she ruined, and she wants to cry.

But like someone who's stepped on a nail and thinks they might as well drive it through to the top of the foot, she must carry on.

"Let's find out if she's really there."

"Cassie." He says it like he's scolding a dog, and it makes Cassie cringe like she is one.

Which means she wants to stomp her second foot onto the nail, as well.

"So you *are* scared?"

Jerome picks up the tablet again. The picture had rotated, and he turns it until it goes horizontal again. "I came here because. . ."

She wants to ask *Yes, Jerome, why did you come?* But while she may be a masochist, she's not suicidal: she won't stab her heart on the nail.

"Because I like you, and I thought it'd be fun, hanging out here. But Cassie, this place is *gross*. And this is only the living room. Who knows what crap's up in the attic?"

"That's why we should go see." It's a small miracle that Cassie said so much, when she is silently thrilled. Jerome *likes* her. Well enough to come to an old abandoned house with a maybe-ghost hiding in the attic.

She grips his wrist, feels his pulse thudding under her fingers. "Don't worry. If you're scared, I'll protect you from the scary attic woman." She strokes his pulse point once, twice, three times. "She'll have to go through me to get you."

She leads the way to the stairs, flashlight shining a thin, frail beam in the darkness.

A note about Cassie's mother:

Moira liked to walk, because it made it easier not to think. It made it okay not to think, not to worry whether feeling nothing was normal. She also liked dark, quiet places, which she found conducive to not-thinking.

She felt little compunction about trespassing—which wasn't what she called it— when she went inside the abandoned house; boarded-up is not the same as locked. No, she did not trespass; she wandered.

When Moira couldn't avoid not-thinking, she pressed her hands to her face and ran her fingers over forehead, noting a creased brow, over nose, noting flared nostrils, over lips, noting rapid breath. She tried to think what emotion they indicated, because in naming it, she could perhaps let it go and return to not-thinking. It often didn't work.

Wandering worked. The dark quiet of the abandoned house worked.

As for the ghost the neighborhood children prattled about, well, they were only children. Moira felt nothing about that, either.

Once on the second floor, Cassie and Jerome follow the hallway to its end, and shine their lights up at the ceiling, where they see the attic hatch. An old wooden chair from the next room provides Cassie a boost.

The hatch creaks as she pushes it up and shoves it to the side. A cord dangles; she tugs it and squeaks as a folding staircase snaps out, top rung broken.

"You ok—"

Cassie shushes Jerome, pauses, and shakes herself. Then she climbs the stairs, stopping before she reaches the broken rung, and pokes her head into the attic.

"Do you see anything?"

Another time —or even if they were still downstairs —Cassie would've teased Jerome for his cracking voice. "Not yet, quiet." She heaves her torso onto the attic floor, then wrests her legs up, stands to dust herself off.

The glow of her flashlight falls on a figure seated by the window.

She freezes. Maybe it's a dressmaker's dummy. She's seen those in movies—

The figure holds something up to block the light. A fan, with the face of a blond woman painted on it. A small rip bisects the woman's forehead.

Cassie can't breathe, can't speak Jerome's name to warn him off.

Grunting, he pulls himself up into the attic and stands beside her. He places a hand on her shoulder. "Do you see any—"

Then he notices the woman.

The woman lowers her fan. Her skin is dark. Thin scars spiderweb across her face. Staring straight into Cassie's eyes, she pinches the ball of her jaw and starts to pull, peeling off her face. It trails strings of red like stretchy bands of mucus. The *slorp* sound reminds Cassie of a gelatin dessert sliding out of its upended mold. She is aware of her own breath inflating and deflating her lungs, of Jerome's hand gripping her shoulder hard enough to bruise, of him whispering "whatthehelldamndamn" in a litany.

The flashlight trembles in Cassie's hand. Her stomach churns; she places a hand on it, urging it to settle, trying to keep her mind from focusing too much on the fact that the woman is flaying her own face.

It's halfway off; she can't watch anymore, but neither can she shut her eyes. Jerome tugs at her, gesturing back downstairs, and her brain wants to leave, oh, it wants to, except her legs are petrified blocks of wood that refuse to obey.

But she can force her hands to turn the flashlight away from the woman, so she does that. It lands on rows and rows of shelves, full of jars, and things float in the jars, dark blobs with holes in the middle—

With eyeholes, with noses, with mouths open in silent screams. Her stomach churns again. She sweeps the flashlight along the wall, counting five jars, ten, rows and rows more. There must be hundreds.

This whole time, Jerome hasn't released her shoulder. His hand spasms and she grimaces. She starts to swing the flashlight back toward the woman; the slopping noises have stopped. But Jerome catches her arm.

"We should leave."

Her light rests on the jarred face farthest from her, the one at the bottom right, closest to the woman. Its skin is a warm brown, like her own, and though the faces should all just be flaps of skin floating in liquid, this face has a shape to it, a high brow, a proud nose that flares at the nostrils, full lips that, even now, look tense, as if they've been swallowing their own words for a long, long time.

Cassie's blood leaves her head and lands in her stomach. Her light roves across the other faces. As the faces progress beyond the woman, they shift to scowls, then open-mouthed rage, then the tight-lipped sadness of the first face.

Then, jar after jar of emotionless void.

She turns the light back toward the woman. "Mom?"

"Cassie!" Jerome grabs her other shoulder, but she breaks free.

The woman holds the face she's just tore off, angling it just like this and just like that, as if she doesn't recognize and is trying to name it. The place where her face used to be is nothing but red meat with bits of bone showing through. Except it roils. As Cassie watches, it gains something that might be dusky skin, at the very top of the brow, just below the hairline.

Cassie tries to focus on the face in the woman's hand. She can't quite see it, but it might be her. Adding on six years, it might be her. She takes another step. "Mom?"

The woman goes still, then retrieves the fan she'd set down. With an expert flick of her wrist, she expands it again and holds it in front of her head, in front of the place where even now, her skin is re-growing. When she rises from her chair, her joints groan like warped boards pried up.

Cassie hesitates, then takes another step, and then she's running. Jerome calls her name, but she ignores him, skids to a stop in front of her mother, whose face is blocked by the fan, held so that the blond woman's face is a perfect fit over her mother's.

The blue eyes are too sharp, the mouth curled in a cruel moue. Cassie prefers her mother's face, whatever she looks like now. She tries to push the fan away.

Her mother's hand locks on her arm. It doesn't hurt, but it's a shackle.

Jerome shouts behind her, runs to them, tries to yank

Cassie away. "Let go of her!"

"It's okay, she won't hurt me—"

"Like hell she won't, who says all the faces in the jars are hers?"

When the woman —*Cassie's mom*— won't let go, Jerome takes a fortifying breath, squirrels around them, and draws back his fist.

A note about Cassie's father, in the form of a rhyme he taught her after her mother disappeared:

Once at night a woman went walking
Stopped at a house and did some knocking
"Invite me in, I can take no more
Of my family's needling, wheedling, wanting more."

In she went, and up the stairs
Never minding her family's prayers
"At last I'm free, and I can see
How'd they never, ever let me be."

Cassie used to beg for another verse, but none ever came.

Cassie watches Jerome's fist fly toward her mother, rising over the edge of her fan as if he's trying to hit her through a wall of water.

Moira releases Cassie and catches Jerome's fist, tightens her grip around it. Jerome screams, and so does Cassie. Moira stiffens, starts to relax her grip—

Her attention catches on his face. Tears run across the expanse of reddened cheeks and his lips are peeled away from his teeth.

She pulls him closer.

Sweat beads at Cassie's temples. "Mom, what are you doing? Let him go!"

Her mother ignores her. Setting the open fan in her lap—its eyes blink at Cassie— she pinches the point where Jerome's jawbones meet.

Jerome screams. Head tilted, Moira stops.

For a moment, Cassie thinks maybe everything will be okay.

Jerome's hand finds Moira's left breast and twists. Her face forms a snarl.

She yanks him and settles her grip on the flap of skin she'd already tugged free, pulls a little more. Jerome's scream heightens.

"No! Stop it, you're hurting him!"

Cassie throws herself at them. Moira glances up, releases Jerome's cheek to shove back Cassie, bowling her over. The flashlight skitters back toward the hatch.

Jerome's gone quiet. The only sound is the wet squelching as his skin comes free, as Moira peels it back.

Red tinges Cassie's vision. Her ears buzz with phantom noise. She doesn't register sprinting back to her mother. She's aware of herself in pieces: the hand that slaps her mother's arms, the feet that kick at her legs, the throat and mouth that sob.

The hand that reaches for Jerome pulls so that half his face comes free.

Cassie whines and lets go. "Mom, stop, please—"

She hadn't realized she'd retrieved the flashlight until Moira plucks it from her. Jerome remains quiet; in shock, Cassie thinks, and oh, she must be in shock, too.

Her mother is staring at her.

Moira sets the flashlight in her lap, next to the blinking fan. Hand free, she strokes Cassie's face, tracing the bone beneath her eye socket, her cheek, finishing with her chin. The spiderwebbed scars stretch as Moira works her mouth. "Love."

Wetness trickles down Cassie's cheeks. "Please, he didn't do anything. Let him go. "

Moira does. Jerome drops to the floor.

Cassie's chest is tight; she's been holding back her sobs. "Yes, oh Mom, thank you—"

Moira grabs Cassie's wrist in one hand, and in the other, catches her neck. Snakes her hand toward the hinges of the jawbone. Pinches.

A note about the woman in the fan:

It's simple, really. She used not to be in it, but she *was* in the attic, and she *was* stuck there.

And she wanted out.

The only way out was to bring another in.

Her misfortune, that it didn't work as intended.

Cassie gasps at the first feeling of her skin peeling back from her face.

Her mother's fan on her lap rolls its eyes toward Cassie and blinks. Then it smiles a smile with teeth as red as her mother's peeled skin.

Cassie forces herself forward. Her mother's grip is relentless, and Cassie's own momentum strips a long hank of flesh off, all the way to her cheek. Fiery-hot pain flares, even sending shocks down her spine, but Cassie keeps going ...

... Reaches the fan.

Her fingers find the small gash at the top. The fan's mouth opens in a rictus, and screams echo in the room; all her mother's faces, screaming loud enough that Cassie wants to clap her hands over her ears, to tear out her own eardrums so that she cannot hear.

Instead, she rips the fan.

Air implodes around Cassie, blowing her back from her mother. Her face throbs.

The glass jars shatter. The screaming intensifies, turns to a howling gale as the faces, beginning with those closest to the hatch —farthest from her mother— rocket through the air and throw themselves onto Moira. Absurdly, Cassie thinks the *thwapping* noises they make sound like the blades of an oscillating fan hitting paper.

A hand wraps around hers. She turns to Jerome. He has the flashlight. She traces the new scar that lines his scalp. It ducks behind his ear before curling down to his jaw. He touches her cheek. They must have a matching set.

The last face flies through the air and slaps on her mother's head, shrouds it like wet papier-mâché.

The fan lies on the floor, torn in half to its handle, its two sides a blank white.

Cassie bends to pick it up.

"No!"

Her mother smacks aside her hands, seizes the fan and holds it close to her chest. Jerome puts Cassie behind her, and she has a moment of happiness before the irritation sets in, and she scoots around him. After all, Moira's *her* mother—

"Mom? Are you—"

"Cassie," her mother says, like the syllables are foreign. "I made a mistake." Her mother's hand, the one that doesn't hold the fan, clenches her arm. Cassie can't remember when her mother took it.

"I shouldn't have left, but I couldn't— I tried to love you. I *did* love you. I couldn't feel it, is all." Her fingers tighten on Cassie. "But you feel it, don't you? Maybe that will save you."

"What?"

"I'm sorry," her mother says again. She holds the fan before her, placed just so.

The rent in the fan heals. The grip on Cassie's arm is inexorable.

Her mother's eyes appear on the fan first. The nose follows, and when the lips appear on the paper, the eyes shift to somewhere over Cassie's left shoulder. "Run," she says.

Jerome doesn't, not until Cassie says she loves him,

and repeats her mother's command.

A note about Cassie:

She sits in the attic beside the shuttered window, her face in a jar beside her. Every so often, she flicks a fan to stir the air. A woman's face, spiderwebbed with scars, stares back at her.

"Love," Cassie says, to her jarred face and the fan both. It's important.

She wishes she remembered why.

At Least the Chickens Are All Right

Trisha J. Wooldridge

Chickens are way cooler than most people think. First of all, they're the closest thing we have to actual dinosaurs—which I always think more people know than actually do. But chickens are also smarter than most people think. You can train them to do tricks...and like pretty much any animal, they train their humans to care for them.

While there are diseases and mites that affect chickens, there's a lot of stuff they're immune to. So besides laying eggs and generally being cute, chickens are good for barns because they eat insects and bugs that carry infections to other animals, including humans.

Chickens are also omnivores. They will kill and eat small animals, like rodents, birds, or snakes that threaten their eggs or their coop. It was the dead things that stayed dead that clued me in to the relationship between chickens and surviving an apocalypse.

The dead things *not* staying dead started up a couple

of weeks ago. Day-Day, the barn cat, brought a chipmunk into the office. A chipmunk that shoulda been dead but, after ten minutes and having its back half eaten, started running around, trailing its intestines and dropping squirming worms. It traumatized Lenore, one of the stable owners and the mom of our riding instructor and horse trainer, Macy (aka Stable Mom's Mom, aka Stable Gramma). No one else was around, and no one started talking about it until after Chuck, Macy's Dad, (aka Stable Grumpy Grandpa) set another dead-but-not-dead chipmunk on fire.

'Course we were already under quarantine for lessons because someone reported a rabid skunk in the neighborhood. I got around the quarantine and could volunteer because I'd gotten a rabies shot when a bat got into my family's house last fall. Macy's family and the horse's actual owners (we boarded six horses at the stable) were also allowed access.

When Day-Day ended up dead-but-not-dead, though, I started wondering if it was really rabies that the skunk had.

I hate to use the term "undead," because I've seen plenty of monster movies, and the animals weren't like zombies or vampires. They basically acted like they *did* have rabies—only, if you looked at their bodies, they were definitely dead. At least Day-Day was, for sure. I saw her before... well... I couldn't watch when Chuck took out the heavy shovel and kerosene, but I heard.

I heard about the chipmunks from Gail, who was horse-mommy to Candy, a gorgeous paint who boarded here. She was there when Day-Day came in on three legs, blood smeared over half her side, looking like she'd gotten hit by a car. Wriggling strings—like maggot earthworms—hung from her hip and wounds. She'd been carrying something. I didn't get close enough to see if her prey was also dead-but-not-dead. She'd dropped it and started meowing her proud, "Look what I caught" call—like she always did when she brought us gifts. Chuck, who'd been cleaning stalls, cussed (which he tried not to do around us younger kids) and grabbed the heavy shovel. That's when Gail grabbed me and pulled me into Candy's stall. I didn't fight her; I'd just frozen in the middle of the hall.

Gail pulled me close to Candy and wrapped us in a hug that muffled the sounds. I won't ever forget the hissing yowls and the *clang-crunch* of the shovel. Then the *scrape-scrape*. I was still plastered against Candy, Gail's arm around me, when the smell of kerosene, burning meat, and hair overpowered the pleasant smell of warm horse, citronella, and sweet grain.

I didn't say anything to my mom when she picked me up. She mouthed an "I'm sorry" as she tapped her bluetooth headset and gave a series of "uh-huh...yes...yes...no, we need to adjust that procedure for the client" responses. That was fine; I didn't *want* to talk about what had happened. A quiz on Friday was my excuse for being quiet and not hungry at dinner. Both my parents asked if they could help. I told them it was American history, knowing that was both of their worst topics, and promised them I was getting help. I sometimes wonder if "good parent" guilt is a thing like survivor's guilt; all my friends complain about their parents. Mine? Let's just say they've put up with a lot between me and my sister and they *still* take time off from work when the school does something stupid, like puts the wrong gender and my deadname on formal paperwork.

I worked at the barn Monday through Thursday unless I had a doctor or psych appointment. Or was sick or had massive homework piles. When I got out of school the next day, I did debate which bus to get on: the one that'd take me home to study, or the one to the barn.

I chose the barn. As sick as I felt climbing the stairs, I really wanted to know what was going on.

When I got to the barn, Macy said they were burying Day-Day's ashes that afternoon. I joined the circle of her family and a few boarders for the beginning, then just had to go. I felt bad, but the few who noticed me leaving gave me understanding looks.

I went to clean the chicken coop. It's a gross job, but it's hard to let your mind wander between the cleaning and watching whatever weird antics the chickens are up to. Normally, if I get done early, I pull out my sketch pad and draw them like the little dinosaurs they are.

The coop is a converted stall that has plenty of space for them to roam inside or outside but lets us easily lock them inside at night. You can look from the stall-turned-coop into the stable's main hall. Across the way is Candy's stall.

Candy was stomping around and letting out little squeals. "It's okay, Candy," I called to her without looking, because the first challenge of coop cleaning is getting *into* the coop without the chickens escaping. I felt bad; horses, like all animals, know when their humans are upset. And Candy had been so good yesterday, letting Gail and me snuggle her rather than freaking out herself when something scary was happening.

But I didn't want to think about yesterday.

I slipped into the coop with the wheelbarrow and pitchfork and shut the door behind me without any escapees. Then froze again as I wheeled into the outdoor part.

Miss Kate, Pepperoni, and Murica were squawking, taking turns pecking at a half-gone mouse body. I swallowed hard and edged closer. I didn't want to—but *wanted* to—see if it was dead-but-not-dead.

Dead dead. I let out an exhale that hurt my chest. There wasn't much but skin and a few bones to the carcass. And definitely no movement outside the chickens' efforts.

Then Gail screamed for Macy. I hadn't even heard her come in.

I wanted to go help Gail—especially after yesterday—but I froze once again. I hated myself for being a coward.

The little rooster, Chickaletto, pecked at my ankles and made me jump. Which made him puff his chest and lunge. With a frown, I squatted and managed a soothing voice as I said, "Hey, buddy, it's me. It's Drew. We're cool, remember?" I put down the pitchfork and showed him my open hand, appreciating the distraction from the voices and stomping outside the coop.

Though my fingers shook, the rooster didn't seem to care as he hunkered down in his "You may pet me" stance—wings relaxed, half-squatting, beak up, and eyes half-closed. I rubbed one finger against his comb and over his eyes. After a few minutes, he informed me we were done with a shake of his wings and a dart of his head.

The din outside had quieted. Gail was talking softly to Candy, though I couldn't make out the words. I decided to check the nest boxes, which were closer to the hall, and listen in.

"Everything's going to be all right, Candy. You're gonna be okay..."

I peeked through the slats to see. All the stalls had bars, which kept the horses from being able to stick their heads out (and kept annoying unsupervised children from easily sticking their hands in). Gail was a few steps back from the stall, and I could see why.

Candy was circling and stomping. A froth of black, red, and white foam made a beard around her mouth, which was disturbing enough, but hardly the worst. Along her snout, cheeks, and neck, the skin was cracked and peeling—like when you forget gloves during winter chores, only it was a really hot May. No blood was flowing, but the tears were red and angry. I couldn't see very well because she was throwing her head around, snorting and squealing like she was in pain, which she probably was.

Her eyes, though... They were dark and shriveled in their sockets, with yellow and black pus oozing from them. Dead eyes.

Every so often, she'd get close to the bars, bang her head and squeal, stumbling.

The other stalls were empty. Macy must've had everyone move the other horses. Good idea.

Gail was shaking even more than I was. Sometimes

she'd edge close to the bars, but a quick turn and squeal from Candy would make her flinch back. "I'm so sorry, baby! The vet's on his way. He'll make this better..."

If it were my horse, if I had a horse, I'd probably be lying to it, too. Because I honestly didn't think Dr. Mac could make Candy better. My stomach turned and I felt like I'd puke out the chocolate milk and two slices of pepperoni pizza I'd gotten for lunch at school.

I focused really hard on collecting eggs and piling them on a hay bale outside to be brought in later. I checked the dead mouse every time I passed it. It stayed dead.

I wondered how long it took for the dead things to change. It'd been two weeks since Day-Day had brought in that first chipmunk, and it hadn't been till yesterday evening that anyone'd noticed something wrong with her and had to...kill her. Kill her *again*? Candy had been fine yesterday.

I wondered if I should set the mouse body on fire... but, to be honest, I'm a pretty boring kid. My parents didn't smoke, and I never actually played with matches. I basically sit alone and draw things. I figured I'd do that forever because I hated interacting with people. Then my older sister dragged me out to the barn because she had to "babysit" me one Saturday when both our parents had to work, and I loved it. That was two summers ago. Now she was in college and couldn't come with me as often. But Macy gets me. She always calls me by the right pronouns. Sometimes I'll watch / hang out with her youngest son, Rayce, who's five, while she teaches a lesson. Rayce and I both love dinosaurs, animals, and being covered in dirt, so it's cool. I wondered how he was doing—he'd been at the burial—as I berated myself for being a loser who didn't know how to start a fire, even if it meant preventing the infected-dead-rodent-and-barn-animal apocalypse.

I'd cleaned out most of the coop when I heard the diesel pick-up truck rumble and stop in our dirt parking lot. The door opened, heavy boots hit the dirt, the door slammed, and Dr. Mac and Chuck started talking in voices they were struggling to keep quiet. I checked my phone. It'd only been a half an hour. Record time for the vet to show up.

They weren't close enough for me to make out words, but their tone squeezed my lungs so that just breathing hurt.

Macy came down the barn hall. "Dr. Mac needs you to sign some paperwork..."

"I didn't bring c-c-cash or a ch-checkbook with me today..." Gail blubbered.

"It's all right, sweetie, we know you. We'll work something out."

They headed back toward the barn office.

I didn't know what was left of Candy behind her dead eyes, but she didn't seem to like Gail leaving. She squealed, groaned, and started beating at the stall door. Cowardly loser me froze again, holding a pitchfork full of hay and chicken shit over the wheelbarrow.

The chickens looked mildly curious about the ruckus.

Chickaletto let out a low crow that reminded me of the velociraptor noises in the *Jurassic Park* films. Even though I'd heard the sound a hundred times or so, it sent goosebumps over my arms.

The office door shut, and the voices of Chuck and Dr. Mac approached. Twisting my sore arms, I flipped the shit into the wheelbarrow and stepped closer to listen.

"...Yeah. Like the others," Dr. Mac said.

"You think it spread to the other horses?"

"Hard to say. We think the flies might be carrying it. We'll know for sure when..." He trailed off.

I couldn't see them, but I felt a tenseness in the pit of my stomach in those few seconds of silence, in the soft shift of a canvas and leather and jeans.

"Hmm. Sorry, Candy," Chuck said with a crack in his voice I hadn't heard before. "Do what you need to, Mac."

Bang.

The gunshot sound punched me in the gut. I staggered backwards, tripping over my boot ties and falling ass-first into the pile of chicken shit and hay I'd raked up.

Th-thud. THUD. The sound of something big stumbling. Falling to the ground.

The pitchfork handle fell into my lap as I slapped one hand over my mouth and the other to my chest because I thought my heart had literally stopped.

The stall door rolled open. Not the one to the coop. Candy's. Did they know I was here? The chickens clucked and crowed and flapped up a storm. Maybe their noise covered my fall.

"Yeah..." came Dr. Mac's voice. It was soft but sounded perfectly clear over the quieting chickens. "It is."

"Shit," said Chuck. "What do we do?" Pause. "Fire in here'll send up the whole barn."

"Mmn." Dr. Mac sighed audibly. "Let's check the other animals first. Text Macy. Tell her not to let anyone in the stall."

"Shit," was all Chuck said back.

Candy's stall door rolled closed. Its metal slide-lock *thunked* louder than I'd ever heard it before. Their footsteps headed toward the other end of the stables.

I picked myself up and did my best to clean off my ass. The clearest thought in my head was how pissed Mom would be if I got chicken shit in her car. Maybe I could borrow a towel to sit on.

Making myself think normal things, I stared at the coop's wooden slats as if I could see through them, across the hall, and into Candy's stall. Up until yesterday, I hadn't seen anything die before, seen it killed.

Dr. Mac shot Candy.

Also in my head, I knew, *I knew*, that she hadn't really been alive. Or if she was, she was in a lot of pain. That she couldn't've been fixed.

Dr. Mac shot Candy.

I'd heard gunshots before, in the distance. The stables were near woods where people hunted. I'd never touched a gun—boring kid, remember? Couldn't even think of a time I'd seen one up close. Not even at Walmart. I didn't frequent the sporting goods section.

Dr. Mac shot candy.

I looked over at the mouse. Still dead. Mostly skin and bones. The chickens kept pecking at it.

Not knowing what else to do, and not wanting to leave the chicken coop—my sanctuary—I finished shoveling crap into the wheelbarrow. It didn't take but a minute. I was staring at the wheelbarrow, not ready to push it out to Poop Mountain across the street, when I heard the office door slam and feet come jogging up the hall.

"H-hey, Candy..."

It was Gail. I crept back inside. Candy's stall door rolled open, freezing me in place (a trend in my life right now). I'd unfrozen and taken two more steps before I was shocked still again.

"Fucking God! Fuck! Fu—" Violent puking cut off Gail's last swear.

It was all I could do to not throw up, too.

"I'm sorry..." Gail apologized. "I didn't mean to... but *God*! How do you have all those maggots in your face already? How fucking strong was that gun? There's like nothing but—those *worms*..."

Worms? Like the things on Day-Day? And the chipmunk?

"Ow!" A hard slap rang from the stall. "Stupid fucking fly. Killed you, you bast—*the fuck?* Ew! My God, ew!" Gail ran from the stall, each stride punctuated with another "Ew!"

Holding the pitchfork in one hand, I chased the chickens away from the inside door. I slowly opened it so it didn't squeak, closed it behind me so the chickens wouldn't get out, and crept over to where Candy's stall was still open.

The horse lay on her side, a stained blanket over her neck and face. The opposite wall was splattered with black and red...*bits*. As well as tags of skin and tufts of hair. And long pink-white worms. Longer than maggots, but smaller than earthworms. Some were half-splattered with their intact body squirming, stuck, on the wall. Others curled and crawled between the wall's boards.

Keeping my distance, I reached with the pitchfork to lift the blanket off Candy's face. I only saw motion, squirming, before—

Bang!

From the office.

What! The! Fuck?!

I dropped the blanket and ran back to the coop, barely closing the door without a sound while keeping the chickens inside.

What even...? As I fought the pain of just breathing, Chickaletto ran up to me and started pecking at my boots.

"Hey! Hey!" I breathed, backing away and dropping the pitchfork.

Another peck yanked one of those worms from my boot.

"Fuck! Fuckfuckfuckfuckfuck!" I scraped backwards several steps and then checked my boots. No more worms. But Blueberry, Machete, Murica, half the flock went at the pitchfork, fighting for the couple of worms that had clung to it. I checked every inch of my feet, ankles, legs, clothes, *everything*. When I felt I was safe, I grabbed the now-clean pitchfork and wheeled the barrow out of the coop and across the street to dump it.

Would the chickens get infected now? If the chickens got infected, that would be my fault.

What did Dr. Mac shoot in the office?

Macy's kids had been here for Day-Day's service. They usually hung out in the office. Had they been in there?

And seen...what?

Another barn cat? One of the office rabbits?

I shouldn't have looked in Candy's stall.

Not Gail. I thought of her screaming, running to the office. No way he'd shoot an actual person... No way!

I probably shouldn't have still been in the barn. I don't know where I'd've gone... I still had to wait for one of my parents to pick me up. On autopilot, I put away the wheelbarrow and the pitchfork.

Who—*what*—did Dr. Mac shoot in the office?

Everyone was still in the office when Mom pulled up, so I hopped in the car without saying goodbye. I didn't want answers to the awful questions in my head.

"Hey, sweetie," she said, ruffling my hair, which I normally hated because I was almost fourteen and too old for that. This time, though, her silly touch felt comforting and I found it just a little easier to breathe. "What's wrong? You look bothered."

Shit, what was I going to tell her? I sucked at lying. "The cat died and one of the horses was sick... so it was a tough day." Not a complete lie.

With a frown and creased brow, Mom asked, "Rabies? Did anything bite you?"

"No. Not rabies." That wasn't a lie. "It was just... hard. Y'know?"

"I'm sorry, kiddo." She one-arm hugged me before putting the car into reverse. "Still, anything I should know about? Are you going to come straight home tomorrow?"

"I dunno. Macy'll probably call if it's something important." Like creepy-ass worms or the barn being burnt down to stop them...

She scrunched her face. "Well, throw all your clothes right in the washer when we get home and take a hot shower...okay?"

Normally, I was annoyed at being told to wash my clothes and take a shower, but this time I couldn't agree more.

I spent the next day in a gray haze where I didn't remember anything and managed to be even quieter than usual. Enough that Mrs. Lambert, my science teacher, stopped me on the way out of class and asked me if I was all right or if something was happening in my life. I don't remember what I said, but it was enough to appease her.

I hesitated after the dismissal bell, debating once again which bus to take. Home or the barn?

I didn't remember deciding; I didn't even know what I chose until I recognized the suburbs thinning into the hilly farmland on the way to the stables.

We were about ten minutes from the stop closest to the barn when everyone-on-the-bus's cell phones—maybe eight altogether—screamed that emergency broadcast tone.

"What the fuck?" said one kid; I think his name was Brian.

I didn't say anything. I just stared at the screen.

> *This is an urgent message from the U.S. Department of Health and Human Services (HHS). The U.S. Centers*

for Disease Control and Prevention (CDC) has confirmed that individuals in Central and Western Massachusetts have been diagnosed with an unknown parasite transmitted via bug bite.

Public health officials are working together to identify those who might have been bitten by the insect carrying the parasite. They are also working to identify all those who have been in contact with the individuals who have been infected. Authorities will continue to assess the best course of action as they learn more.

At this time, it is unknown how many people have been exposed to the parasite. The first symptoms are asymmetrical welts with raised lines; intense itching and pain; open, bleeding sores with colored discharge; or the appearance of a worm-like parasite on the skin or within an open wound. Based on the information available now, public health authorities have determined that the best course of action is for everyone in the area experiencing these symptoms to report to one of the specialty clinics in the following cities...

My heart hammered. The rest of the information was where the "specialty clinics" were and contact info and an all-caps note about NOT reporting to hospitals. I closed the message and clicked over to my messenger app. My foggy brain hadn't thought to check it before the buses, and I'd had to keep it disabled while in class. A message from Macy said not to come to the barn. *Shit.* I was almost there; what was I supposed to do?

Not coming up with any other ideas, I got off at my usual stop and trudged my usual route. The air felt cold, but it was still May and there were birds singing in the trees. A horsefly buzzed by me and I spazzed out, slapping and hitting and spinning and running till I was sure it was gone and had not bitten me.

"Hey, Drew, what are you doing here?" Macy asked, coming out of the office with a look of concern on her face. "Didn't you get my message?"

"I just got it." I held up my phone. "Didn't see it till I was on the bus."

"I left a message with your mom, too." She frowned, folding her arms. Her eyes were red like she'd been crying, or trying not to.

"What's going on?" I asked. Playing dumb helped way more often than most people realized.

Macy sighed. "A shit-storm. Did you get that emergency message thing on your phone?"

"Yeah, but it was confusing. Bugs?" I swallowed. "Is that what got Day-Day?"

"We don't know. Probably, maybe... Dr. Mac's looking into it..." Her voice trailed off.

With or without a gun? I thought but didn't say.

"Hey, did you get bitten by any bugs lately?" She wore her full-on Worried Mom face now.

I shook my head and pulled out the giant spray can of Deep Woods Off that I always kept in my bag. "I pretty much bathe in this daily."

"Good! Keep bathing in it. Bugs are nasty things. Put another coat on now while we figure out what to do with you..."

I did so, then asked, "Can I go see the chickens?"

"Yeah, go ahead, but stay outside the coop." She pulled out her phone and began texting. Probably looking for someone to drive me home.

I walked along the coop's edge, chatting with the chickens, sticking my fingers through the wire to pet the ones who wanted to be petted. As I walked, I kicked up what, at first, looked like a dead leaf, but stiffer and heavier. I squatted to take a closer look, then recoiled.

It was a chipmunk carcass, but this one looked at least a week or two old. Holey skin and some bones, it was definitely still dead. A flattened, pecked husk. Pursing my lips, I checked the rest of the wire's perimeter and the corners I hadn't done quite as good a job of cleaning yesterday. I found one more very dead mouse carcass and a dead barn sparrow. No worms. I studied each of the chickens. They all looked bright-eyed and not-rabid.

My phone rang, making me jump.

"Drew, where are you?" It was Dad.

"At the barn."

"Okay...can you stay late? Or can someone drive you home?"

"Why?" I asked, not liking the panic in Dad's voice.

"Nothing to worry about, really," he said in a voice that meant otherwise. "It's just, your mom got bit by a bug of some sort yesterday or the day before and it's swelling. The hospital sent her to this special clinic and I have to drive her... It's probably nothing, but we just want to be safe. Especially after that weird broadcast message, you know? But, like I said, it's probably nothing. In case we're late, there's leftovers in the fridge... Are you there, Drew?"

"Yeah... Here..." I choked out.

"You all right?"

"Fine. I'll ask Macy for a ride home." I don't know how I managed not to stammer.

"Good, good. I'll keep you posted on things. Love you, kiddo."

"Love you too, Dad. And...and tell Mom I love her."

"Will do. See you later."

I stared at my phone, not hanging up my end even though the screen said Dad had hung up his. My stomach churned icy numbness.

"Was that your parents?" Macy strode toward me and stopped. "What's wrong, Drew?"

I turned slowly to face her. "Mom. Got bit by a bug. And was sent to...one of those..." What had Dad and the message called them?

Macy's face got really pale. We stared at each other for a few moments until a low growl interrupted us.

"Drew, get behind me!" Macy ordered.

I did, looking in the direction of the sound.

Pibly was the black-and-white-and-brown, wire-haired, third-generation mutt that belonged to the closest neighbor a mile down the road. He'd gone missing over this past weekend. Now he stood, growling at us. Half his head was bashed in and his whole side was torn open, revealing his ribs.

Both injuries were teeming with worms.

"Motherfucker," Macy cursed, assuming an alpha posture but backing away, herding me with her. "Chuck's heavy shovel is just inside the doors," she said to me softly. "If we keep backing up, how quick you think you can get it for me?"

"I-I don't know," I said honestly, picturing myself tripping over my feet and falling as the infected dog leapt at Macy and mauled her.

The chickens were all clucking and crowing again, flapping and hopping around. They weren't running away, though. That seemed odd, against a bigger predator. Macy narrowed her eyes at them, too. She'd raised chickens since she was a kid; I didn't know anyone who knew chickens better than her.

"We're by the coop's gate..." I suggested.

"I'm not letting that thing near my chickens!"

A thought was clawing my brain like a hungry raptor. "Trust me?" squeaked all the way up from my stomach.

Macy screwed her mouth up, looked at me, looked at the wormy dog, then looked at the chickens fluttering and squawking at the gate. "Fuck." She dodged to the side long enough to unhitch the coop door. It swung open. Chickaletto and the hens surged out and onto the dog.

"That is *not* normal chicken behavior!" Grabbing my arm, she darted toward the open barn doors and Chuck's shovel. Next to the shovel was the kerosene tub.

The dog broke through the chicken mob and Macy swung the shovel, hitting it right in the head. It fell and the chickens swarmed the body.

"Did you get any of those worm things on you?" she demanded, checking the bottoms of her feet and pant legs.

I did the same. "No."

Backing away, Macy took the kerosene I'd thought to grab and glared at the birds. "Y'know, guys, I can't burn it with you all on it!"

The chickens were undeterred and continued to feast.

"Chickens are still dinosaurs," I muttered.

"Not gonna argue." She put down the kerosene. As she bent, her shirt rode up her back and I saw an asymmetrical welt just over her jeans' waistband. A thin line of black and red liquid and yellow-white pus dripped from it. Just above her belt, I swore I saw a wriggle—like a worm under her skin.

"M-Macy ...?" I started to ask.

"Mommy! Mommy!"

Eyes wide, Macy turned to face the two children running up the hill from the farmhouse she lived in. "What are you two doing here?! I told you to stay home with Gramma!"

"Dreeeewwwwwww!!" Rayce came running right at me, arms wide. Outside of his mom, I was the only one he chose to hug. He threw his little arms around me before I even registered what he was doing.

"I asked you two a question!" Macy demanded in mom tones.

"We came up because Gramma won't wake up and Keelie's kittens got worms!" Jaylin, Macy's nine-year-old daughter said.

"Worms?" Macy choked on the word.

"Yeah! Worms!" Rayce pulled away from me and held up a handful of wriggling white and pink. He frowned with an "Ow!" and I saw the lines of movement crawling up his chubby little forearm, under his skin.

I backed away, patting my hands under my shirt, and yelped as I felt slimy movement on my back, crawling under my binder. I slapped at the things, trying to brush them off, but I *felt* them still there, going in with pricking bites.

"Fuck, fuck, fuck..." I whispered.

Tears were pouring down Macy's face as she dropped to one knee. "C'mere, kiddo," she croaked.

"What's wrong, Mommy?" Rayce asked, hesitating.

Jaylin hadn't moved. She was looking at her arms. Panic darkened my vision, so I could only imagine what she was seeing.

I heard a growling crow behind me, like one of the velociraptors from the *Jurassic Park* movies, and turned around. Chickaletto fixed me with a sharp, predatory look.

"H-hey, b-buddy," I stammered to him.

He hopped away from the feasting flock, darting his head between Macy and me. Miss Kate, Murica, and Machete followed him, their eyes bright and hungry.

Groomed

Liam Hogan

"Happiest day of your life," Ma muttered through a mouthful of pins. "Happiest day."

She was adjusting the dress; the dress she'd worn the day she was married. The same dress my grandmother had worn and, if the tale were to be believed, my grandmother's mother and grandmother's *grand*mother before her.

The dress I would wear tomorrow.

Though I did not yet know who I would be marrying.

Trembling in the chill evening air, trying not to move, I was glad the slender ivory silk and lace dress was such a good fit. I'd been stuck once already, sparking a sharp yelp from me and a "hush, child" from Ma as she dabbed the tiny red bloom from my pale leg.

Despite her declining years, Ma was still taller than me. At the end of every harvest she had me stand barefoot on the cold kitchen floor, slowly circling and doing her best to straighten the stoop in her back.

"Not quite," she'd said, two years earlier.

"Almost," she'd said, this time a year ago.

"You'll do," she said one wet and windy evening a week gone, her eyes a fraction higher than mine. "And it can't wait much longer. Girl, it's time you were married."

I stood on the chair while Ma adjusted the delicate hem of my wedding dress. For perhaps the first time I could look down on her from above. Her hair was thinning, gray and wispy, failing to hide the ugly, thick bubbling of skin at her crown. Some ancient injury, badly healed. So that was the reason she always wore her hat, a peaked one that left the word '*witch*' muttered in her wake.

Ma always said she was 'eighty, going on eight hundred'. The rest of the kids my age had mothers in their early and mid-thirties, with one 'darling miracle' in her forties. Ma claimed to be older than the fossilized spinster who taught us to read and write, who never dared raise her cane to me and who, despite her advanced years, reacted with obvious fright every time Ma made an unexpected appearance in her classroom.

She needn't worry anymore. Ma had pulled me from the village's two-room school when I turned seven. "Old enough to help out, young enough not to have learnt too many daft things," she'd said.

I'd hoped that would be the start of my true education. People were always coming to ask Ma questions. Not just from the village; from up to three days' walk. No matter where they came from they were always respectful, as Ma sat solemnly in the solid wooden chair some previous petitioner had gifted her, the chair I was stood on now. Even when she told them things they didn't want to hear, even if they grumbled as they left, they followed her advice or regretted it later.

But Ma didn't answer any of *my* questions. "You'll find out, soon enough," she would say, as I labored away, scrubbing and sweeping, sewing and cooking.

Sometimes I wondered if Ma was really my grandma, or great-grandma. Perhaps my real mother had died in childbirth and this already elderly relative had begrudgingly taken over my upbringing. It always seemed impolite to ask, and being impolite was one of Ma's bugbears. Politeness was taught with the liberal use of a hazel-wood switch.

Still, I stumbled out the question, once. Ma squinted narrowly at me.

"Who's been talkin'?" she asked, her voice cold iron.

I shook my head in fear. "No-one, Ma! I just... I just wondered, is all."

"Well, don't," Ma *tsk*ed. "It might have needed magic, but you're my flesh and blood, girl, and don't ever forget it!"

I didn't dare ask who my father was.

Even so, I'd have risked asking the name of my intended if Ma hadn't kept me so busy. When I wasn't out collecting herbs and roots, I was slicing, mashing, and boiling them into noxious brews I'd have thought inedible. Ma retreated to her small bedroom, insisting on solitude as she meditated. Half the bowls I passed through the narrow gap of the door she returned untouched, with precise instructions for their replacement. The others were scraped clean. For both, she warned me repeatedly not to lick the discolored spoons.

Ma removed the pinned wedding dress, gently folding it over her withered arms, and made to vanish back into her room. I stuck my foot into the closing gap of the door, even as she pulled against it.

"Ma," I pleaded, peering into her glinting eyes. "Please; who am I to marry tomorrow?"

She laughed, until it cracked into a crow's cough, and smushed her foot against mine, pushing it clear. "Patience, child. They are well-known to you," is all she said as the door shut firmly in my face.

It wasn't yet dawn when her crabbed hand prodded me from my fitful slumber beneath the kitchen table. I brushed the straw from my nightdress and scurried to light the stove, but Ma shook her head.

"No breakfast. For either of us," she ordered.

A village tradition, I thought; the first meal of the day to be taken as a married couple, the wedding breakfast. I wasn't hungry anyway, my stomach fluttering as though full of small beasts, a tumult of excitement and fright.

"Strip," she commanded.

I stood on the bare stone floor, the water icy as she wiped me down with a wet cloth, itself the color of the just-lightening sky. She lowered the ivory dress over my head, gently, gently, the silk smooth and cooling against my freshly scrubbed skin. Her fingers worked the narrow laces, face twisted in concentration, birds beginning their morning lament.

With the last lace tied, Ma took a step back and tilted her head to one side, scrutinizing me. I began to turn slowly for her, and for myself; towards the aged and blemished mirror propped up against the equally distressed dresser. Her expression became a scowl. "Stay put!" she barked.

From a locked cherry-wood box, Ma pulled out a web of twisted metal: a headdress, of sorts. One that fit snugly, like a cap, the dull, silvery wires covering all but the crown of my head. Ma fiddled behind me and I felt a tug at my upper back as she tilted my neck, realizing then that the crown was secured to the stays of my dress.

It was an odd thing, that crown. Crooked limbs splayed out like roots, like the thorned branches of a dead or dying tree. It was awkward, tortured, and strangely disturbing, despite being the only piece of jewelry I had ever worn.

When I turned away from the mirror, Ma stood wearing the diadem's exact copy, a weird and terrible look on her face.

I trembled. For a moment, I had the feeling I was still staring into the mirror, that despite the gray smock she wore, despite the deep lines on her aged face, I was seeing myself.

"Come," she said, turning briskly to the door. "The chapel awaits."

She took my arm on the short walk through the still sleepy village. The dawn mist wrapped its cold wet shroud around us as I stepped carefully, lifting the hem of my dress away from the mud —and worse.

It was only when I saw a gravestone underfoot, lichen

smothering the etched letters, that I realized we had arrived.

I raised my head, expectant. The wooden doors of the chapel were flung open, a glimmer of candlelight came from within. But it was silent, deserted.

"There's no-one here!" I exclaimed in surprise.

The hold Ma had on my arm, the arm that had supported her across the uneven footing of the graveyard, tightened painfully, and she lurched forward with me in tow. Eyes glancing from side-to-side in the flickering light, wincing at the grip, I wondered who had lit the candles and where they had gone.

Wondered where my husband-to-be was.

Ma dragged me towards the altar. I expected at least to see the priest, a thin, sallow man who was no less afraid of Ma than the schoolmistress; than anyone else in the village. But the chapel echoed in a way that told me it was truly empty. Just Ma and me.

There was a large chalk circle sketched out on the ancient flagstones. Five candles in pewter holders rimmed the circumference. Something acrid stung my eyes, some burnt incense or herb, making me feel faint and dizzy.

"Kneel," Ma said, after pulling me deep into the circle. I looked around for something to rest on, to keep the wedding dress clean. Impatient, Ma yanked my arm until I was at her level, facing her, our knees a half-yard apart. Bowing her head as though in solemn prayer, her eyes flicked up, skewering me through gray eyebrows.

"Lean forward," she said.

I tentatively obeyed, careful not to clash, but Ma

reached out and pulled with a strength I did not know she had. The metal crowns touched, interlaced, locked. When I tried to tug my head away, her hand snapped out and slapped my wrist.

"Be still!" she commanded, spittle flecking my face.

Imprisoned by her fierce stare a scant hand's breadth away, my gaze escaped into that twin nest of wires. I saw the skin of her old wound flex and heave. I thought it a trick of the wavering candlelight, but there it came again, pulsing, moving. Acid burnt at my throat and painfully I swallowed it down. Her hands, old, withered, liver-spotted, settled on my shoulders, seizing me tightly. She began to mutter in some foreign tongue, the sound a mixture of hisses and clicks.

The tangled crowns held my head firm and the motion at the upper edge of my vision kept drawing my eyes back to the emerging horror.

When the bulbous, pus-yellow body burst forth, I sobbed, helpless, my limbs weak and trembling. "Ma!" I cried, my shaking body rattling our conjoined heads. Her voice had fallen silent and, though her bony arms still gripped me just as tightly as before, her eyes were fixed blindly in front of her.

The fat grub, its segmented body the size of a full-grown toad, slimed its way up through the metal nest. The sickly, swollen, pale-colored mass was broken only by a pair of black, curved and serrated pincers that clicked and waved in the air, feeling their way.

"Ma!" I shouted again and again, over and over, trying to wake her from her stupor. I twisted an arm up between hers to wrench the crown from my head, but the fastenings were too tight. I felt the pull of the laces and stays at my back and knew I would not be able to remove it without help.

As I struggled, the bloated maggot squirmed ever forward, questing, questing, disappearing from view as it crossed into the fronds of my crown. Not being able to see it made it worse. I became aware of a sound, a sucking, wet gurgle. I wrapped my hand around Ma's fingers, trying to pry her off.

They were stuck like iron, like gnarled tree roots growing through masonry. I gripped her index finger, levering it angrily away from me. It gave with a sickening crack and I dry retched as I stared in horror at the bent-backwards digit.

I could remove her hands. If I was prepared to break every finger.

I blinked away tears and peered into Ma's blank eyes. Did she not know what I had just done? There had been no scream, no cry, not even a whimper. Was she dead?

The wet, soft lump dropped onto the top of my head and I cringed and twisted in disgust. But the funnel-web of metal held the grub snugly in its grip. There was a stab of pain, washed away by a numb, warm feeling that spread like honey through my limbs.

Somewhere, far off, I heard rasping, a rusty wood-saw in a distant forest. Something warm trickled down the side of my face.

Agony! Searing pain like nothing I had ever felt before. Pain that burst from behind my eyes, flared the dim candlelight into white hot lances. Oh god... the pain and—

I looked down at my hands in wonder. So smooth, so young! The crippling ache of two decades of arthritis gone; even the memory of time's cruel torment was beginning to ebb away. I reached up, expertly unsnagging the transfer harness, and lowered Ma's inert body to the stone floor. The joy was so overwhelming I could almost dance and sing. The happiest day of my life!

With the renewed strength of my youthful body came knowledge. So much knowledge. I knew the names of all the planets in the solar system, even those invisible to the naked eye. I knew what to say to the terrified priest to stop him doing something stupid. I knew all the petty little intrigues from the village, and beyond. I knew that the coming winter would be a hard one and how much grain should be set aside.

There was much to be done. Things I had let slide as my body had aged.

That, fortunately, was no longer an obstacle.

True, it was replaced by others. A testing period during which people would doubt, unable to reconcile my youth and my wisdom. I would struggle to be believed, trusted, respected.

That too would pass. I would prove myself once again. Had I not been through this many times before?

My head was full of alternative names for the herbs I had picked since I was a child. Names and uses. Instead of knit-bone, *symphytum asperum*. Instead of nightshade, *atropa belladonna*. I knew which remedies I would need to treat the entry flap high on the crown of my skull. I knew which balms would ease the passage of the mindless husk I had once been.

And I knew how to bring about the birth of my replacement—my exact, genetic copy— without any need of a father. *Parthenogenesis*, the process was called.

But, as the one lying insensate on the cold chapel floor had done, I knew that I would seek other ways, other means. Like her, I'd leave the process as late as possible, worried that it was cruel, even inhuman.

But necessary. Not just for me, but for this remote settlement, for the good that my multiple lifetimes' experience and knowledge could and would do.

And so I knew that one far-off day, I too would dress my replacement in this gown and marry my ancient mind to her young one.

"Happiest day of your life," I muttered, the sun filtering through the chapel's stained glass as I blew out the candles.

"Happiest day."

Beneath Her Skin

KT Wagner

Beneath the bathroom's flickering light, Tamsin attempted to tell Mother about the bird lady at her bedroom window. About how the wind whipped the lady's silver hair as she wept tears of moonlight. About the angry words the lady whispered through the rain and the mullioned glass. About how the fury slithered past Tamsin's ears, slipped under her skin and down her spine.

"It's the middle of the night. You were dreaming." Mother motioned for her to stand on the rickety beige stool she'd pulled out from under the sink. "Besides, birds don't fly at night, only bats."

"Owls do. She had grey feathers, but she wasn't an owl."

Mother snorted; the corners of her mouth turned down as usual. "Be quiet, child."

Tamsin scrunched her toes and tried to ignore the curls of paint scratching the soles of her feet. She wished she were taller.

Just two weeks earlier, Auntie had held a super-secret birthday party for her and her cousin Kaya. Their birthdays were only one day apart, and they'd both turned seven. For the first time, Tamsin had lied to Mother about where she was going after school. Lying hurt her tummy, but Auntie said it was okay. She'd told Tamsin what to say and claimed it was just a little white lie to protect Tamsin's mother. The little girl hadn't really understood, but she'd nodded along.

A bunch of kids from the apartment building were there and they could all reach high enough to whack the piñata. Auntie brought out a stool for Tamsin—a nice smooth plastic one—but she didn't need it because a bigger boy broke the piñata before she or Kaya got a turn.

Mother wouldn't talk about Auntie. Auntie shook her head and cried when Tamsin asked her why. Auntie explained about being fraternal twins. They were alike, but different, and Mother didn't like some parts of Auntie. If Tamsin didn't think about it too hard, it made sense. She didn't like some parts of Mother, either.

She wished she and Kaya were sisters, not just cousins. Kaya said she felt the same way.

"I like being older than you," Kaya said, then giggled. "Even if I'm only one day older. We're best friends forever."

Each night before Tamsin fell asleep, she would wish to grow tall enough to decide for herself where she lived. She hated the dark, narrow townhouse. Kaya and Auntie lived in a sunny apartment high up in the sky.

Mother refused to consider a move but complained about the gloomy townhouse all the time—the narrow rooms, the sketchy neighbors, the crappy location.

Tamsin wanted all four of them to live together. A three-bedroom apartment would be big enough. Mother and Auntie could each have their own room. Tamsin liked having her own room, even if she wasn't allowed to have anyone over to play, but she'd love to share a room with Kaya. They'd have matching superhero duvet covers and share their favorite books, and read by flashlight under the covers each night while eating giant bowls of strawberry ice cream with chocolate sauce.

Mother rapped her knuckles on the bathroom counter and interrupted Tamsin's thoughts. "Hold up your hair and hunch over. I need to see." She didn't touch her daughter. She only touched her when angry. "It's a bite! Damned house. Now spiders are invading through the hole in the bathroom ceiling and attacking us while we sleep."

"A spider didn't bite me. The grey bird lady did." Storm winds whistled in the distance. The windowpanes in her room rattled. The little girl clenched her fists and told herself it didn't matter what Mother thought, but it did.

Mother pinched her arm. "What have I told you about making up stories?"

Tamsin expelled a breath. Crying or complaining would invite Mother to do worse. Instead, Tamsin stopped listening and studied the pale-blue porcelain sink. The color of a robin's egg, except for the brown stains no amount of scrubbing had removed. Glistening black sludge coated the inside of the drain. How far down could she see? She leaned closer. All the way to the basement?

The basement had never held much interest, but now she wanted to explore it.

The hole pulsed. A whiff of rot. She jerked back and grabbed the rubber stopper. Its chain wound around the corroded faucet.

"Tamsin Louise! Stop messing around."

"But—" It was no use arguing. With trembling fingers, Tamsin freed the chain and plunged the stopper into the drain.

Mother used the handle of Tamsin's pink toothbrush to poke at the spot on her back just below her neck. Something under her skin scurried out of the way. She tried to reach back and feel it herself.

Mother smacked her hand. "You'll infect the bite with your dirty hands."

Tamsin held her hands out and examined them. She'd scrubbed them before bedtime, and Mother had laundered the sheets from both their beds on the weekend.

Mother squinted at her from the middle of the tarnished spot on the mirror. On either side of her eyes and mouth, deep brackets scored her face. Her short spiky hair lay flat and misshapen, and her turquoise-framed glasses were nowhere in sight.

Tamsin loved those glasses, especially the rhinestones on the arms. She'd begged for a pair of her own, but Mother had laughed at her. "Be thankful you have perfect vision."

Tamsin hadn't laughed. She didn't have perfect vision, or she wouldn't be seeing creepy things out of the corners of her eyes. Mother claimed glasses helped people see better. She'd hoped wearing glasses would help her, but she'd tried her mother's on when Mother was sleeping and they hadn't helped. They must only work for adults, she'd decided.

The mark on her upper back burned. Her own reflection appeared to have a slight double image, like the television on a stormy day.

A word fought to escape Tamsin's mouth. She bit down hard and tasted feathers. The word escaped anyway. "Bitch."

"Tamsin!" Mother's eyes widened, then narrowed.

Tamsin cringed. She'd never say that word out loud and on purpose, especially not in front of Mother. In the mirror, sweat beaded on her forehead.

Her tummy cramped. "Sorry. It hurt when you poked."

She studied her bare feet and wished she hadn't cried out when the grey lady had burrowed into her back. She hadn't meant to wake her mother. If only she were stronger and bigger and more able to control what she said.

A rancid taste coated her mouth. She reached for her toothbrush, then decided to wait; Mother would accuse her of stalling a return to bed.

Mother yawned. "You'd better mind your tongue at school. I don't need any more trouble."

"There really was a lady at the window." Tamsin's words echoed in the tiny bathroom. She held her breath. Maybe Mother would believe her for once?

"Give it up, child. You're on the third floor."

"Can I go back to bed now?"

Mother nodded. Tamsin scampered back to bed and pulled the covers to her nose.

Mother tapped the bedroom window. "No one is getting in this way. It's painted closed, but you know that." She pulled the tattered brocade drapes. They dampened the sounds of the wind, but didn't block all the light from the streetlamps.

One hand on the door, Mother paused, silhouetted by the hall light, while behind her a smoky shape loomed. Tamsin half waved. The shape rippled.

The lock on the door clicked, and long shadows shrouded the room.

The stairs creaked. Tamsin counted the thumps and thuds of descending footsteps. Thirteen stairs down to Mother's second floor bedroom. Tamsin counted sixteen footsteps.

While her eyes adjusted to the dark, she continued to count, all the way up to five hundred. The new skill surprised her; she hadn't been studying or practicing her numbers lately. She stared up at the ceiling and scanned it for spiders and faces hiding in the popcorn stucco.

She pictured living somewhere else, like an apartment in the green-glass high rise where Kaya and Auntie lived. Their ceilings were a smooth, soft white. A month earlier, before the school year began, Tamsin had carefully cut out a newspaper ad for a two-bedroom apartment in the same building and taped it to the fridge.

When Mother noticed the ad, she'd turned ghost pale. "My

sister's no good, Tamsin. You make sure you tell me if she shows up at the school again, and we're certainly not moving anywhere near that woman." She'd ripped the paper down and tore it into tiny pieces that fluttered onto the kitchen floor like confetti.

The memory made Tamsin restless. She retrieved the flashlight from the drawer of her bedside table.

Wrinkling her nose against the faint mildew smell, she pulled back the drapes. Far below, rain churned the surface of black puddles. The windows of the townhomes across the road reflected the rippling dark. Often, if she stood still for long enough, the wispy shapes of children would float into the empty street, but their presence never tugged at her the way she felt drawn to the bird lady, who wailed without sound and always appeared to be searching.

Tamsin waited at the window. Her feet grew cold. The children arrived, but not the bird lady. The hole in her back throbbed. Why had the lady hurt her?

Unaffected by the wind, the pale children milled, their faces twisted with expressions of longing and regret.

Tamsin replayed Mother's words in her head. Maybe Mother was right, and she'd dreamed everything. She needed to know.

She dragged the chair from her desk into the bathroom. Mother had rescued the chair from an old dining room set a neighbor had placed out on garbage day. It only had one broken spindle, and, unlike the other chairs, the crossbars were intact. The feet scraped against the wood floor with a low moan.

The spider hole lurked in the ceiling behind the bathroom door and next to the shower cubicle. Tamsin pushed the chair into the corner and climbed onto the seat, but couldn't quite reach. She stacked the stool on top, clutched the plastic shower curtain for support, and clambered up.

The spider hole wasn't big, and the perimeter appeared moldy and soft.

Wings rustled.

"Look," the bird lady whispered. The stench of rot worsened.

Tamsin glanced around, but didn't see her. She hooked her fingers over the edge and peeled away chunks of spongy plaster. The beam of her flashlight illuminated a web. At its center loomed a black spider with thick, hairy legs.

Her hand darted up, and she closed a fist around the creature. Careful not to crush it, she shook her hand a bit. The panic of the creature radiated into her flesh, but it didn't defend itself.

The spiders in her room didn't bite. Mother had lied.

She grasped the spider by one leg and lifted its writhing body. A soft voice wondered how it would feel against her tongue.

"Gross!" Tamsin squeaked, and tossed it into the sink.

It tried to scramble up the porcelain walls. She reached past it, unplugged the drain, and turned on the faucet before running back to bed.

At breakfast, Mother growled, "Good morning." Bony elbows on the kitchen table, eyes stained by yesterday's mascara, she slurped from a chipped mug.

She'd been like this for the two weeks since Tamsin's birthday, which she'd ignored. It was the same the year before. Tamsin couldn't remember it ever having been different.

A sour, burnt odor filled the room. Blackened toast lay in the sink.

Tamsin warmed a packaged pastry in the toaster and munched on it while packing her food for school. "Is it okay if I take the last yoghurt? It's expired."

Mother didn't respond. She didn't ask about the spider bite.

Tamsin rubbed at the numbness at the base of her neck. She'd ask Kaya to look at it when she got to school.

Words not her own tumbled, musty and hard-edged, out of her mouth. "I've always wanted a sister."

The chipped mug smashed against the tile floor. Dark liquid spread around the shards.

Tamsin backed against the stove.

Mother lunged and shook her by the shoulders, hard. "What game are you playing?"

"I'm going to live with Kaya and Auntie." She hadn't planned to say anything until Auntie had spoken to Mother. She wanted to add, "and you, too" but Mother's expression had darkened and twisted.

Tamsin ducked under Mother's arm and ran all the way to school.

Tamsin's teacher stopped her at the door to the classroom. He held out a hand. "Homework."

She'd forgotten. Behind him, Kaya bounced on the balls of her feet, and motioned for her cousin to hurry up. Tamsin hunched her shoulders and moved to pass her teacher.

"Not so fast, Missy. Your homework?" He shook the stack of papers in his other hand.

A voice in her head whispered. Tamsin's heart sped up. A dank scent crowded her nostrils. She tried clamping her teeth together, but the words had already flown out of her mouth. "Bugger off. I didn't do it, but I did see you kick a homeless guy Saturday night, and there are dirty magazines behind your hot water heater."

Her teacher stepped back, eyes wide. "What the—?" His expression hardened.

She felt the blood drain from her face. Maybe if she explained her mother said she'd been bitten by a spider? No, no-one ever believed what she said. She turned to run but found herself yanked back by the collar.

"If I catch you snooping…" he ground out.

She trembled and shook her head.

"Principal's office. Now."

Tamsin swung her dangling legs and wondered why the chairs outside the principal's office weren't kid sized. Never had she seen an adult sitting on one of the hard, wooden seats.

The bird lady was teaching her many things, like the ability to spot a lie and how to walk softly, but she was most pleased to be able to count to five hundred. Sitting on the chair, she'd already counted to five-hundred four times, but mostly in her head because the school secretary had shushed her the first time.

She hadn't paid much attention to the principal's words. Instead she studied the severe lines of her hairstyle and her ruby-red glasses. She wondered what powers the glasses held, and whether the principal was lucky enough to live in a new apartment building with no basement.

"Tamsin, I'm very disappointed to have to call your mother. You're normally a better-behaved young lady."

She'd heard that part.

The round, black-and-white clock over the school secretary's desk clicked past each second. One hour, twenty minutes, and thirty-seven seconds. Her mother would come when she could, the secretary had told her.

The recess bell rang.

Kaya stood outside the office on the other side of the glass wall. Her hand low, next to her knees so only Kaya could see, Tamsin waved.

The secretary gathered up a pile of papers and went into the principal's office.

Kaya slipped through the office door and stood at the counter. "Mom wants you to move in with us, but she's scared of your mother."

Tamsin's chest hurt. Everything was messed up and it was her fault. She kept saying things she shouldn't. She stared at her feet and blinked against the prickling behind her eyes.

"I'm tired of being all by myself." Kaya's voice cracked.

"Me too." Tamsin reached out and grabbed Kaya's hand. "We'll share a room. We'll make good sisters."

Kaya smiled. "Best friends forever."

"Promise?"

"Promise."

The secretary bustled out of the principal's office. When Tamsin turned back, Kaya was gone.

A light, windless rain fell. Mother turned the key in the lock of the faded-black front door. "Go to your room and stay there. I have three more cleans before I can call it a day."

Tamsin slipped past her mother, ran up the stairs and slammed the bedroom door behind her. Mother wouldn't be back for hours.

Maybe she could go over to Auntie's. Tamsin dialed the wall phone in the hallway, but there was no answer.

She prowled around her room, restless and unhappy, until her stomach began to growl, and she tip-toed downstairs in search of food.

In the kitchen, a towel lay across the mess from breakfast. The stains formed odd shapes that were not quite recognizable. She stood at the other side of the table eating stale crackers from the box. Her back itched.

Thump. Thud. Thump. Thud.

Soft footfalls on the basement stairs.

She stopped chewing and listened. The sound ceased and after a minute she decided she'd been mistaken.

Mother didn't like the basement. She kept the door locked and the key hidden, but Tamsin knew where to find it, and her curiosity had been growing since the night before.

In the narrow living room, she climbed onto the back of the threadbare chair next to the fake fireplace. She teetered there, and the frame of the chair creaked and popped. She carefully moved aside the large red vase and several guttered candles, then worked one hand behind the heavy, garage-sale mirror. It crushed her knuckles. She ran her other hand along the back of the frame until she felt the taped key.

Moving the red vase back, its smooth surface warmed to her touch. Sadness wormed its way up her arm. She hugged the vase, felt silly and stopped. Maybe Mother kept something interesting inside it? Setting the vase back on the circle it had left in the dust, she slipped a hand inside. A jolt like electricity burned through her, and she yanked her hand out with a shout.

A whisper that sounded like her name drifted up through the floorboards. Like a magnet it drew her down, below ground.

The cold and damp basement wasn't interesting at all. One large room, about the size of the first floor, dusty and empty, except for two items—an unplugged freezer with the lid propped open and nothing inside, and an open-slat wooden crate bristling with rusting tools. A couple looked like the ones the school caretaker used on the flower beds. Odd. Their tiny back patio consisted of a cracked concrete slab and a few half-dead dandelions.

Three walls were cinder block, the far wall rough concrete. She looked around for spiders. One high, filthy window interrupted the concrete monotony. Tamsin headed for the stairs, then paused to scratch the base of her neck. The crate might be more interesting than it looked. She pulled it away from the far wall.

The concrete behind it crumbled slightly. She ran a finger over the surface. Dust billowed and formed two wispy shapes: the grey bird lady and a much smaller person. For a second Tamsin thought it was her shadow, but when she moved, it didn't.

The wall whispered, the murmurs soft and welcoming, begging her to explore and discover. She pulled a long-handled weeder from the crate, fell to her knees, and wielded it like a chisel.

Dust surrounded her, settled on her, and crept into her ears, eyes, and mouth.

"Dig," the bird lady whispered, and even though it felt like something she might get in trouble for, Tamsin dug with the talons of metal. A hint of sulphur wafted past.

The coarse tone of the scraping weeder changed. A bright note rang out.

She sat back on her heels and wiped at her eyes. Visible at the back of the hole, a patch of familiar red.

She chipped around it; hands guided by the grey lady. The stench of rotten eggs worsened.

She'd been wondering, so she asked, "Who are you?"

The response formed within a series of sighs and chirps, "I punish."

Tamsin frowned. The answer didn't tell her much. She thought about asking another question, but before she could put one together, a palm-sized shard of warm red pottery dropped into her hand. She recognized it as part of a jar; its twin was sitting on the fireplace mantel in the living room.

Her stomach lurched and for a moment, nausea swept through her. She straightened, cradling the shard with cupped hands. "I'm not doing this anymore," she said to the empty room, knowing the bird lady could hear her.

Tamsin climbed the stairs.

Back in the kitchen, she cleaned the piece of pottery with a tissue. She cut a lone piece of butcher's twine from the roll in the utility drawer and wrapped it around the shard, creating a necklace. Against her chest, it pulsed warmth.

Tamsin sat at the kitchen table, rested her palms on the Formica, set icepacks on her knuckles, and waited for her mother to return.

The kitchen light snapped on.

"What have you done this time?" Mother filled the kitchen doorway and glared at Tamsin. "You're filthy."

"I found something in the basement." Tamsin's voice emerged small and insignificant. She pictured herself as a bird unfurling her wings. She lifted her chin.

Mother's face turned chalk white; her gaze fixed on Tamsin's chest.

"Tell me the one on the mantel fell."

"I dug it out of the basement wall." Tamsin placed her hand over the shard. It pulsed, warm and slippery.

"Give me that." Mother grabbed at the cord.

Tamsin dodged her and raced up the stairs.

Boom, boom, boom. She tried to count, but the pounding footsteps behind her were too fast. She couldn't make it to her room. She hid in the second-floor linen closet.

Mother was on the landing. "Have you been talking to my sister?" her voice cracked. "You have, haven't you? She kept calling, wanting to see you. Then she stopped…I should have known."

"They're our family," Tamsin whispered. She wasn't sure Mother could hear.

"I hoped you'd never find out."

Tamsin blinked. Mother wasn't making any sense. Carefully she pushed open the closet door. Mother stood there, her face blotchy, the turquoise glasses pushed to the top of her head. She didn't look angry. She looked sad.

Tamsin crept onto the landing. She felt the bird lady stir and tense, like this was important. "Mother?" she asked.

"You're only seven. I hoped you would at least be older, if it had to come out at all." She stared at the necklace. "We'll go see my sister, but stay close to me."

Tamsin felt the grey lady's beak curve into a smile. It wasn't a very nice smile.

Mother held Tamsin's hand on the city bus. She also made her wear a sweater and buttoned it up to her chin, despite the warm sunny day. Sweating, Tamsin stared out the window and hoped Mother would consider moving once she'd talked to Auntie.

Sunlight glinted off the green glass apartment building. Beautiful. Tamsin gazed up and wondered if Kaya would notice her get off the bus. She'd kept her promise and hadn't tattled about having been here before. She hoped neither her aunt nor her cousin would think she had.

Auntie answered the apartment door. At first Tamsin thought Kaya wasn't home, but then she saw her standing in the doorway to the kitchen. She didn't appear happy to see Tamsin.

Kaya smiled a sad smile and waved.

"You brought her." Auntie reached for Tamsin. "Thank you."

Mother yanked Tamsin behind her, her grip a vise. "She found a piece of the red vase in the basement. I can't...won't protect you anymore. From her. From anyone. I'm telling Tamsin the truth. You may have been the one who birthed her, but I've looked after her all these years. You need to move far away. I don't want to know where."

"No," Tamsin struggled to get away from her mother. "I want us to be with them."

"Them?" Tamsin wasn't sure which grown-up sister said it. The bite on her back pulsed.

Kaya cried out and ran to Auntie. "Mom!"

A black rage crashed through Tamsin as the grey lady took control. She squeezed Mother's hand, hard, curling her fingers and pinching the skin.

Mother yelped and let go.

Kaya stared at Tamsin, her eyes dark and haunted. She shook her head. "I don't want to move away."

Neither Mother nor Auntie looked at Kaya. It was like they didn't see her.

Auntie reached for Tamsin. "She's mine."

"She's only alive because I knew something was wrong. God, if only I'd arrived a few minutes earlier. I'll never forgive myself."

Tamsin stared up at her mother. The grey bird lady quieted, like she was waiting for something.

"I made a mistake," Auntie wailed, and held her arms out toward Mother.

The bird lady unfurled her wings. Tamsin darted into the apartment, straight into the kitchen. The bird lady directed her to where the knives were kept.

Auntie followed close behind. Kaya pulled at her blouse and

yelled, “No, Mom, no!”

Auntie grabbed for Tamsin, but the bird lady materialized between them, her wings a blur of black fury. The back of Tamsin’s neck throbbed. She whimpered and clutched at it with one hand. The other hand closed around a knife.

Auntie’s eyes rounded, her mouth worked, and her throat opened up, red and smiling. She crumpled to the ground. A dark stain spread across the floor.

Mother screamed.

“Kaya?” Tamsin looked for her cousin.

Wind whipped through the apartment. Kaya stood trembling in the doorway.

Eyes flashing silver, the bird lady folded a dark wing around Kaya. Together, they dissolved into a wispy mist, blew into the corner of Tamsin’s eye, and disappeared.

Tamsin tasted feathers and dust.

Mother picked up the phone and turned to Tamsin. “Did she hurt you?”

From deep within Tamsin, the bird lady snarled and tried to push words into her throat.

Kaya stirred and warm strength flowed through Tamsin.

Kaya spoke to the bird lady, “No. We are together now, and we don’t need you anymore.”

Tamsin swallowed hard and spoke to Mother. “We’d like to go home, Mom.”

Brother Mine

Rohit Sawant

When I saw a sparrow poke its head out of my brother's hair, I should've felt a lot of things—startled, bemused, horrified—but I just burst into a giggle. It was so comical. It reminded me of the time a boy at school accidentally stepped into the girls' bathroom, froze, reddened, and disappeared.

The absurdity of what had happened didn't strike me until later.

Tarsem sat jackknifed on the floor, the tip of his nose almost kissing the page of his coloring book, when it happened.

His hair wasn't what you'd call "shaggy." It could hardly have trapped one of his smaller fidget spinners, let alone a freaking bird, even a dead one.

I slid off the couch, dropping the remote, over which we'd had a fresh battle only minutes earlier, and ruffled his hair. No sparrow.

My examination elicited a protracted whine-growl.

"Archana!" came my mom's voice from somewhere in

the house.

Because obviously I was choking him. Okay, I can't blame her entirely, since I did give him his share of sibling hell.

Expecting the sparrow to make a reappearance, I remained vigilant throughout the day.

Every glance at his head sparked a frisson of anticipation. It was as if the universe had flashed me, showing me its secret place.

During dinner, Mom periodically flicked a puzzled glance my way when she caught me staring at the crown of Tarsem's head. He, however, didn't notice. He was too busy stuffing himself with the kind of gusto that made my dad, a lifelong foodie, beam at him, proclaiming for the thousandth time how Tarsem had inherited the defining trait of the Kapurs, which invariably triggered an eye-roll from mom.

When I was brushing my hair later, I gingerly tapped my scalp for any feathered intruders. Of course, there was nothing. But can you blame me? My definition of impossible had been turned on its head.

I never broached the subject with Tarsem, afraid it'd shatter the new status quo.

Part of me expected *him* to bring it up. He had to have known *something* was up, right? Finding him absently scratching his head, as if trying to ferret out an itch rather than douse one, certainly seemed to suggest so.

I told Patricia about it one day. We told each other everything. She stared at me for a second then snort-laughed. A feeling of having shrunk a few sizes seized me, affirming I should've heeded the flutter of hesitation

I'd felt before I blurted it out.

So, I laughed along. Not doing so would've made things weird. Strange, isn't it? That brand of weirdness left me scrambling for normality while I was perfectly okay with the weirdness surrounding my brother.

I wonder if everything that occurred later could have been avoided if I hadn't fallen into the YouTube rabbit hole one evening.

It started with a movie trailer and ended with me making an origami bunny; or *trying* to make one. Even on my third attempt, what I ended up with looked malformed as opposed to crisp and clean-angled.

I balled it up in frustration. Since Tarsem sat close by, I couldn't help throwing the scrunched up craft paper at him.

It bounced off his shoulder and he shot me a sidelong glance, too wrapped up in the cartoon he was watching to lash out.

I proceeded to fold a paper plane into existence; the only thing I could make with finesse.

Taking aim, I unleashed it at Tarsem. The plane looped through the room, the tip of it bound to strike his cheekbone, judging by its trajectory.

The doorbell rang, and when Tarsem briefly turned at the sound, the paper plane swooped into the back of his head, vanishing into his black curls as if it had arced out a window and into the night.

My breath hitched. I jolted in my seat, my hand

knocking the stainless-steel ruler to the floor, where it clinked with the delicate ring of a fencing sword.

"The fuck?" I whispered with an adult unconsciousness. Usually I was mindful of using the f-word, delighting in letting that single forbidden syllable roll off my tongue.

The idea of something inexplicably manifesting itself in my brother's hair was less shocking than something disappearing *into* it. The former could've been a quirky set on *Magician's Got Talent*, stripped of all the prestidigitation. The latter was downright freaky in its casualness.

Tarsem didn't seem to register a thing. He carried on with his stupid cartoon, as if something that could potentially land him in a secret government facility hadn't occurred.

I kept to myself for the rest of the day and steered clear of him.

As night approached, the shock wore off and my fright shaped itself into fascination again.

A pen, a broken hair clip (mom's), a paperweight no one cared about, a half-eaten slice of pizza, a rolled-up newspaper; these were just some of the things I "dropped" into my brother's head after he was asleep.

I say *dropped*, but I hovered the objects close without touching and felt this magnetic tug before they were sucked in.

This development made me itch to spill to Patricia again, to behold that look of wonder on her face. Because what good is the best of magic tricks if no one could watch you perform?

It was on the tip of my tongue when we were at Bryson's Burgers. We'd fallen into a tradition of dropping by weekends for a snack-grab and alternating picking up the bill. Since it was my turn, I was glad Bun Lady wasn't taking our orders and it was Mr. Monroe instead. He was pleasant to talk to, made Dad jokes, and didn't expressly slide the check to Patricia like the bun lady always did, even as I was fishing out bills from my purse. In a way, what she did was worse than Conrad Warner calling me "dothead" in class, because at least I could flip him the bird in response. But what can you do when someone simply doesn't acknowledge you?

My heartbeat quickened as I dipped fries in my milkshake, close to telling Patricia again, but I stopped myself, recalling how it'd gone the last time.

I needed a way to disclose it in sips. If I called her over and just flung a soda can into Tarsem's head, she'd faint. Might want nothing to do with me. I'd be the freak by proxy. Perhaps it's a disservice to her to think she'd be quick to shun me, but I didn't want to risk finding out.

I started recording a series of videos on my cell, a my-eyes-only vlog.

I'd be lying if I said I wasn't having fun. I pretended I was in a movie, maybe a starship captain keeping logs.

Now I find the self-absorbedness cringeworthy, but back then, a frenzy clutched me. While my brother might be a conduit for the uncanny, I was convinced all of it unfolded for me to witness. I mean, think about it. Mom could've noticed it, Dad as well, or any number of people. But it was me. It was a glorious, heady feeling, like I was "chosen." That sounds trite in movies, but if it happens to you in real life, it's anything but.

The videos didn't turn out too hot. They seemed tacky, shot in the night lamp's bubble of light. Had I uploaded it online, a hundred YouTubers would've made reaction videos, "debunking" it.

I needed something that couldn't be argued with, something jaw-dropping, inexorable. Final.

And oh, did it fill me with a sickening mix of nausea and excitement when it came to me.

I waited till Tarsem was drenched in sleep, then turned all the lights on.

After a brief commentary about what I was about to do, I moved the camera around Tarsem in a "nothing up my sleeves" maneuver, making it clear there was no funny business.

I fed random crap into the back of his head, and for the finale, I pulled out my dad's gun.

A sheen slid along the black metal as I showcased the Smith & Wesson Governor to my propped-up cell to prove it was real.

It seemed to weigh twice what it had done when I'd plucked it out of the safe.

I fished the .45 round out of my pocket, expecting my hand to shake dramatically as I loaded it in the chamber, but it didn't. My heart, making up for the lack of tremor in my hand, thumped madly. I could barely hear the whisper of my own voice over the pulse in my ears.

"Okay now," I said. "Unless your brother has, like, a

black hole for a head, don't do this."

I chuckled at my lame joke, then fell silent as the cylinder clicked into place.

The moment I held the gun a few inches from the back of his head, *execution style*, as they say in cop shows, I felt that familiar magnetic tug on the snub-nose's tip but knew the black hole wouldn't suck it out of my grasp. The pull, while insistent, wasn't powerful, akin to me yanking Mom's index finger as a kid while she remained rooted, chatting with some acquaintance at the supermarket.

Not wanting to dwell—I knew I'd chicken out if I did—I pulled the trigger. A clipped scream broke the silence a beat after the loud boom.

Sound and pain dominated my senses. In my haste, I hadn't braced myself for the recoil.

My gaze sought Tarsem in the red fog of pain, and regret and relief washed over me in a mingled tide when I found him looking across his shoulder at me, his face still on.

I wanted to sweep him up in a hug.

"Hey," was all I managed.

He flinched when I spoke.

I'd seen him cry countless times; I had been responsible for the waterworks on at least half those occasions, but they were always petulant, enraged sobs, mostly accompanied with the flinging of a mildly heavy object in my direction, but presently my heart folded in on itself watching tears leak soundlessly down his cheeks.

"I ... It's—"

"Put the gun down!" My dad.

"Tarsem!" My mom.

I shouldn't have been surprised to find them standing in the doorway. As loud as the revolver had been, finding half the neighborhood crowding the entrance wouldn't have surprised me.

Dad took a step back when I involuntarily lifted my hand and looked at the gun, a little dazed.

"Archana, put it on the floor. Jeet, wait--"

I think my mother would've shoved a bear out of the way if one had blocked her path.

Before I set the gun down she had Tarsem in an embrace and cooed to him, examining him, as if any injury he'd have incurred in a worst-case scenario would've been akin to a bump on the head.

She threw a venomous glance at me, and I think that was the precise moment when she truly began to hate me. Even before the way things ended.

Had her arms not been too busy fussing about Tarsem I'm sure she would've smacked me in the face.

Soon as I stepped away, Dad rushed forward. As he swept the gun up, I read the look in his eyes: *I'll deal with you in a minute.*

He gazed about the room with a clouded brow, no doubt searching for a smoking hole in the wall. The windblown drapes caught his attention and, hurrying over, he peeked out past them. The tightness in his shoulders softened after a few moments.

Turning the lights off, he joined Mom, a hand on her back.

It was time for a family meeting.

I was expecting to be hung upside down and skinned or something, but I didn't get half the hell I was dreading.

Even Mom, who sat on the couch with Tarsem's head in her lap, didn't fire daggers at me. She reserved that look for Dad whenever their eyes met.

Dad delivered the talk I expected, about the revolver not being a toy, how Tarsem could've gotten hurt, or I could have, that my job as a big sister was to shield him from harm, not put him in its path, which was what I'd done. When Mom put in the occasional word about irresponsibility, she only made eye contact with the carpet.

I sat silently, nodding through it all, summoning tears. I was grateful when they came.

Later, Mom carried Tarsem back to their room and I went back to bed. It was almost four in the morning.

I lay awake, knowing that if sleep did come, it'd only be a wink. I pawed the dresser for my cell phone and realized it must still be in my brother's room.

I'd forgotten about it entirely. I lunged from my bed and found it face down. It had stopped recording.

I played the clip. Despite the improvement in lighting, it still looked no different than a hacky student film. I forwarded it to where I'd pulled the trigger. I shuddered at the sight of my brother stirring and the bright muzzle flash a split second later. He'd been soundly asleep until that moment. It was the gun's report that scared him into wakefulness with a scream. This might sound awful, but it was kind of funny the way he started awake, like something from a slapstick comedy, but any comical notion I was nursing faded when I saw myself stagger back and Tarsem turning to pin me with his shock-stricken face. And the tears, though they weren't visible in the vid. Moments later my parents appeared in the foreground, my dad's hip bumping against the desk, which tipped the camera over, causing the video to go dark.

Thank God for small favors, huh? Imagine how much worse the situation might've gotten if it had fallen screen up. If they had noticed the camera and watched the video I'd just recorded, anything coming out of my mouth would only have served to dig myself in deeper.

But you know what? Even if they had seen it and interrogated me, they still wouldn't have believed me. They'd have accused me of sleight of hand or some video editing magic, momentarily forgetting how ridiculous it sounded. And here's the kicker: if either of them *had* humored me, all poking him in the back of the head would've accomplished is poking him in the back of the head. I know this with the surety of plugging in a USB the wrong side in no matter what.

I deleted the video, sick at the lingering smell of burnt powder in the room, my desire for any show and tell smothered for good.

I came out of the brief doze I'd drifted into. The sound of my parents having a screaming match did it.

I only got bits through the closed door:

I told you I've never liked that thing under my roof.

Listen, I'll change the pass code.

She's a twelve-year-old girl, not a dog. I'm sure she could figure it out again if she wanted to.

That made me smirk. Sure, I was tenacious, but she was giving me too much credit. After my unsuccessful attempts at cracking the code, I'd considered dropping the idea, which honestly would've been dandy for everyone involved, and thwapped the small safe in frustration. And the door swung open.

My father didn't get rid of the gun. He did get a new safe, though, one *not* from Walmart.

Out of curiosity, I entertained a notion about having a go at cracking (or smacking) it, just to see if it'd yield, but figured if my parents caught me anywhere near it, they wouldn't hold back on the ass-whooping this time.

That's not to say I didn't face any repercussions for what I did. I called Patricia to tell her I wouldn't be able to hang out for a while, or even join her for our scheduled snack.

"Didn't you hear?" she asked.

"What do you mean?"

"I thought that's what you were talking about."

She told me about the yellow police tape blocking the entrance to Bryson's Burgers.

Mr. Monroe was dead.

Patricia had overheard her mom (no one in town could fart without her mom knowing) talking about it on the phone. She called it their homegrown locked room mystery.

Apparently, Mr. Monroe had stepped into the

bathroom a little after opening up and someone had shot him.

"Right through the neck." Patricia repeated her mom's words. The closet-sized bathroom was locked from within, and the only other way in or out was an unbroken square of frosted glass.

I pictured the window she mentioned, patterned with curled leaves. I could barely have crawled in, let alone a grown-up.

"But that's impossible," I said.

"I know! Forget *how*, though. I'd like to know *who*. He must've pissed someone off real bad for them to do it while he was on the crapper. I'm thinking what if an assassin stopped by for a snack or someth —Archie?"

"Yeah, I—I'm listening."

My thoughts had snagged on the word "impossible." A drain uncorked in my center, and everything warm cycloned down it, leaving me numb.

All the stuff I was putting into my brother's head. I'd never paused to think where it might come out. Was there random junk from our house scattered across town? Across the country? The world? *Another* world?

I shivered.

The thought that I was somehow (*you literally pulled the trigger*) responsible for Mr. Monroe's death, Mr. Monroe of whom I always thought as someone "on my side," was too much.

I told Patricia I agreed with her (stupid) assassin theory. Anything but the possibility of the cops matching the bullet that killed him to the gun sitting in my dad's new safe.

For days my only exchanges with Tarsem were of the "pass the salt" variety.

The frenzied fascination that had gripped me had melted away. I regretted having seen the stupid fucking sparrow that started it all.

My mom occasionally pinned me with an almost sympathetic gaze, taking my distant demeanor for guilt-ridden silence. And she wasn't wrong.

She didn't extend any comfort, though. I almost wished she *had* slapped my face that night she burst into the room. It would've served to vent the bundle of disappointment and rage that had so visibly calcified within her. She kept a watchful eye on me as if any moment I might go berserk and stab Tarsem twenty-seven times.

Dad was just awkward. I'm sure he must've been normal with Mom the way he was with me when it was just the two of us. When we were all in the same room, it was a different matter. His forced good cheer accomplished the opposite.

Tarsem, however, bounced back sooner than any of us. By the following week, *he* was the one bugging *me*. I was stretched on the shag carpet watching TV when he took his coloring book and planted himself right in front of me, blocking my view.

I could see him trying to resist the urge to peek over his shoulder.

The sofa cushion I flung at him struck the small of his back. He briskly twisted around, an impish smile on his face, and hurled it back at me.

It escalated to a full-blown cushion fight. My mom rushed in at the sounds we were making, and her alarmed expression morphed into one of bafflement.

I don't remember which one of us threw a cushion at her but she instantly adopted her "Oh, it's *on*" face and joined us.

Cushions spun across the room, giant puffy ninja stars.

It was the last time I saw that unblemished look of joy on my mom's face. She leapt and ducked and yelped and laughed; she was beautiful. Immortal. In that moment, we all were.

I wish I could stop writing here. Tell you we lived happily ever after. But of course, that didn't happen.

Our post-cushion-fight buzz carried over into the next day, then plummeted when Tarsem got sick.

He was in an exceptionally charitable mood after dinner and was helping me carry the dishes when he stopped midway to the kitchen and threw up onto the plate he was clutching, so that vomit fanned all around him.

I screamed for Mom and just stared, amazed that his seven-year-old frame could house so much gunky fluid. As if something had moved into his body and was making room for itself.

He spouted his insides like a burst hydrant for almost ten seconds. That's a long time in vomit o'clock. He fainted into my mother's arms when it was over.

Tarsem spent the next few days in bed, recuperating. The doctor said it was food poisoning.

There were spots under his eyes and he had lost a few pounds, but he gradually regained his health and his appetite. While the former was only temporary, his appetite not only returned but redoubled. No matter how much he ate, however, he kept losing weight.

Tarsem had never been chubby but he wasn't skinny either, so being able to count the knobs of his spine was rather jarring.

During his brief stay at the hospital they couldn't find anything conclusive. How could they? They were operating on incomplete information. I'm not sure what difference it would've made had they known about the black hole in his head, but there was no way I could tell my parents. I knew that would seem like I was making it up, seeking attention.

I had thought it would just go away if I ignored it. Now I couldn't shake off the feeling that my involvement had unwittingly caused it to alter, the way continually picking at a snag in a sweater would widen it enough for an entire finger to poke through it.

I brushed the flop of hair aside from Tarsem's brow one night and playfully asked him if he wanted a trim.

One corner of his mouth meekly tipped up as he said, unblinking, "You could try..."

Before bed, I made my brother a hot chocolate, which he

accepted with a frown, baffled by my sudden generosity. But he probably guessed I was being nice because he was unwell and sipped the drink containing two of my mom's sleeping pills. As I'd crushed them in a folded tissue, I hoped to God they would be strong enough to keep him under but wouldn't drag him into a coma or cause irreparable brain damage.

I raked a comb along the bottom of his head, stopping well short of the crown, and snipped a tangled tuft. I was clueless about what my actions would accomplish, if they would accomplish anything, other than a hair day from hell, but I was functioning on instinct. Also, it wouldn't hurt to try, I reasoned.

Clumps of hair pooled on the pillow. As I drew the comb across part of the hair carpeting the hole beneath, my grip tightened over it in response to that magnetic tug.

Gnawing on my bottom lip, I gingerly dipped one end of the comb into his head, not knowing I'd planned to until I saw it disappear. Encouraged that it hadn't slipped out of my fingers, I lowered it. The pull intensified. It was like dipping a stick of wood in a fast-flowing stream.

This prodding also stoked up the embers of the feverous fascination I'd been in the grasp of. Not smothered altogether, after all.

I waded the comb around as if stirring a bowl of soup. Something about the sight made my gorge rise, but I was helpless to stop. The urge to explore the shape of this darkly magical interior blotted all else. In an effort to reach deeper, I pushed it in until my fingertips brushed his hair. A surge in the pull plucked the now vibrating comb out of my grip and eased my fingers inside.

A wave of goose bumps exploded across my skin. What struck me wasn't panic, but astonishment as an intense chill slapped my senses. I experimentally wriggled my fingers, which felt like I'd dipped them into ice-water.

I sank my hand further in, moving it much like Mom pawing for something in her purse. The coldness encasing it, amber-like, seemed to pulse. Tarsem's scalp thrummed in sync. His hair stood on end, live with a static charge I felt dancing in my teeth. Alarm ballooned in the pit of my stomach.

I yelped as a vicious tug yanked me forward, forearm deep, knocking me off-balance. The scissors, dangling from the hooked fingers of my free hand, clattered to the floor. Of all the things, what flashed through my mind was a scene from *Roman Holiday* where Gregory Peck slips his hand inside the Mouth of Truth and fake shrieks, sending poor Audrey Hepburn into a wild panic as she scrambles to extricate it from the dark maw in the unnerving stone face.

I struggled against whatever had its solid grip on me. Grabbing my trapped arm around the elbow, I pulled, my bones crackling. I was dimly aware of pain that was more like an afterthought, numbed in that icy interior.

With my stance widened for support, I jolted my shoulder back, wrenching myself free, and bumped into a chair as I fell on my ass.

A bright spangle of pain snuffed the momentary flutter of relief when my harried gaze locked onto the ruin of my left hand. I trembled taking in my ring finger, bent unnaturally sideways, lacerated and oozing blood like its brethren.

Just then my ears popped, as if at a shift in a plane's cabin pressure, and what initially appeared to be a giant braid with a knotted end rose from Tarsem's head. Every inch extruding into the air tented the fabric of my sanity. Emerging like some chthonic periscope, it stopped shy of the ceiling.

It dallied a moment, seeming to harbor a predatory awareness that the sight of it was the optical equivalent of curare, wanting me to drink it in.

I ducked as the horror towering overhead whipped at me across the room. While it resembled a scorpion's tail, the fluidity of its movement was tentacle-like. Each chitinous segment bore respiring gashes which I only placed as mouths when I saw the begrimed, yellow barracuda teeth. Instead of a bulbous barb, the tail ended in a cancerous mass, a slab of it hooding a piss-yellow serpent eye the size of a golf ball.

An undulating buzz filled my head, a song of cicadas pouring from the mouths along the tail's length, the sounds out of sync and faraway, the sort that leak from headphones.

When it descended again, it bit down on the nexus of bone and gristle in my left elbow.

The only clear thought besides the underlying *fuckfuckfuck* was *who even bites an elbow*? As if I expected the thing to conform to some kind of fighting etiquette. But it was foolish to think this was a fight. It was more like someone crunching a bug underfoot.

The drive to survive is a funny thing, elemental and obdurate, and impels even a bug, pathetically outmatched, to scamper away, seek refuge, or die trying.

My feet drummed in protest as it dragged me closer. I scanned for anything that could've served as an anchor, but nothing stood out. Suddenly, a gleam on the floor jumped up at me.

I lunged for the scissors; my fingers, wriggling like spider legs, almost kissed the steel. I managed another stuttering step away at the cost of a fresh pang in my arm. The fledgling hope I allowed myself to feel guttered when I accidentally kicked the scissors. I watched in dismay as they skidded across the floor.

While my body continued to resist, my mind simply unplugged itself. In the same split-second, it was back online when the scissors glanced off the nearby chair leg and bounced in my direction.

I won't be able to grab it.

But my fingers closed on a plastic loop just as I was heaved to the bedside.

I swiped the scissors blindly at the thing as it began its descent, my heart knocking against my ribs like an insane inmate. The surface the blades struck was akin to a tightly woven mesh of steel. This should have disheartened me, but I was too rabid with panic and, surprisingly, rage, to stop. This enabled me to land a blow, more by chance than design, slashing a snaking tongue.

The resulting mewl had an emboldening effect and elbowed room in my mind for inspiration. I swung, aiming to jam the blades into the writhing mouth stacked below the one latched onto my arm, and voiced a mewl of my own as they dug into Tarsem's head instead.

I abruptly found myself flat on my back before this fresh horror had entirely settled in. Stars formed before my eyes, sparked by my skull thudding against the floor. I wasn't shoved, but rather tugged like a marionette.

My body continued to quake, and it took me a moment to register that the grinding on my elbow had stopped. Curling up, I braced myself for the tail/tentacle to wrap around me in an anaconda grip, its many mouths feasting on my flesh.

The mad cicada song had stopped. I tipped my head up to a room empty save for Tarsem and me.

Tarsem.

For a second, I was reluctant to move, believing it would pop the bubble of tranquility and the thing would return.

It didn't, though, as I got on my knees and scrambled closer to him, my good arm still clutching the scissors in a death grip.

My stomach plummeted. A red gash gleamed wetly above the nape of his neck like a mouth, as if grimacing at the injury I'd dealt in my frenzy.

Had it not been for the fire in my gored arm, I would've questioned my sanity, whether any of it had actually happened.

Hardly a minute had elapsed since I was cutting Tarsem's hair, but it felt like an hour or more. And seeing the sky drained of darkness, I wasn't sure if it was just a fear-induced time warp.

I ran my fingers through his hair with trepidation. A

squeal teetering on a cackle escaped me when my fingertips just pressed down on soft tissue.

As if startled by my laugh, Tarsem's arm twitched.

"Call 911," I said to my parents as I woke them up. "I did something to Tarsem."

My dad is the only one who drops in to visit me at the Juvenile Detention Centre.

He invariably gets choked during our conversation and says things such as "This is my fault" or "I've failed as a parent." I just purse my lips. After the first few times, I gave up trying to console him. It isn't because I agree. He gets to go home after our little talk while I return to my cell. If anyone could use comforting, it's me.

They don't like that word here. Cell. What they call it is "living station." You're escorted in through two locked doors, handcuffed, which I was spared because of my arm cast, and there are barbed wires around the property. It's a freaking cell.

During his recent visit, Dad told me Tarsem will finally be released from the hospital; that his overall health has improved. *Overall health* being code for the stab wound and the illness eating away at him.

"He misses you," Dad said.

I wanted to say I missed him, too, but I only smiled.

Boy, did I wind up giving him one hell of a trim, huh?

I've had a lot of time to dwell. I don't mean dwell on what I did —given how Tarsem is on the mend I'd do it again— but on the result it achieved.

I was staying over at an aunt's once, years ago. She was moving the plants on the deck indoors for winter one afternoon, and I wanted to pitch in. After one or two successful relocations, I tired of the bending and lifting and just grabbed a plant by the stem and dragged it. Aunt Heena's squawk froze me in place, with the plant half-uprooted in my grip. Although we replanted it after the lecture she gave, it didn't survive. I believe something similar happened when the scissor blades gouged into my brother's head; it severed whatever link that doorway branched into his being.

Dad never brings up what happened that night except in the oblique self-flagellating manner I mentioned. Minutes after I'd woken them up, mom finally delivered that lip-splitting slap I'd longed for. He had to restrain her as she screamed in my face. Up until then I'd held off crying, more out of shock than conscious restraint, but seeing her snarl pushed me over. In my mind, the sting in my cheek hurt just as bad as my arm, lit anew with pain.

Unless you'd been there, you couldn't have placed my wounds for what they were. There were no neat little arcs suggesting bite marks, and it looked more like it'd been stabbed at repeatedly.

Everyone thinks my injury was self-inflicted, and I don't confirm or deny it. Dr. Wei, the center's in-house shrink, brought up the subject during our sessions, asking how long I'd been self-harming, but I just kept mum. If I told her the real reason, she'd ship me off to the nuthouse.

Earlier, when Dad asked how my arm was, I just shrugged my other shoulder. I kept the cast hidden below the table where he wouldn't see the mess of ink, blotting out the slur scrawled on by an older girl.

I was grateful when she first offered to tag it, already casting her in my imagination as a second Patricia, until I saw her handiwork. My eyes sprung tears, not because of what she wrote, but the initial casualness of the whole situation had made me ache for the world outside, and the instant betrayal broke me.

She really singled me out for persecution after I tattled on her to a supervisor. During the outdoor activities, I had spotted her and a boy trying to cram a kitten up a downspout.

The kitten was all right. Me, not so much.

All of it stopped the day she followed me into the bathroom with two more girls in tow. Soon as I saw them in the mirror, my heart began to thud. A moment later, their grins wilted as their eyes left mine; I traced their line of sight in the mirror to a point above me. I gasped seeing the dandelion-like wispy halo surrounding my face, my hair raised in static shock. The wind went out of me and I leaned on the counter for support, squeezing my eyes shut, a metallic taste blooming in my mouth.

I don't know what they saw but their screams were deafening. One of the girls had a seizure.

I knew it wasn't the scorpion tail thing.

There was no sound of cicadas singing. Besides, it would've killed me.

It's beyond me to speculate on the *hows* of the incident; whether it resulted from the bite, some cosmic strain coursing through my system, or whether it had all the rhyme and reason of a slip in the shower. But it didn't frighten me.

She was different. She spoke to me later in my dreams, sang me stories.

Whenever I thought about Tarsem, my mind would ping a nebulous sensation, equivalent to a dog pricking its ears.

I was surprised at the reflexive stab of jealousy at this Other Mother's avid interest in my brother.

But I have to do something, for both his sake and mine. And I have an idea what that would be. I have it written down. She can't poke around for stuff in my mind if I write it out of me. Amnesia by written word is a blessing.

I don't think she means to kill me; just use me, ride along till I'm in the same room with Tarsem again.

How infinitely crummy for something so infinite?

All I'm waiting for is the right opportunity. I just need one other thing. I've already filched a Zippo lighter from one of the supervisors.

I'm not going to play cabbie for some starworn bitch.

Mirror, Mirror

P.D. Cacek

"Come back to bed."

He'd said it softly, whispering in the same hushed voice he'd used since they'd brought the baby, their son...*Benjy* home from the hospital because that was one of the things you did when you became a "New Dad," you whispered. He'd been given a list of what New Dads were supposed to do.

The list—provided by family, friends with children, and the stack of books they'd bought since Laney's OB/GYN had confirmed her suspicions—had grown throughout her pregnancy, which was unremarkable and undramatic. There'd been a few points of conflict, naturally, but there was one thing everyone agreed on: you kept your voice low so you wouldn't scare the baby.

So he kept his voice low, even though Benjy was beyond hearing it.

He whispered for her now, only for her.

"It's late and you need your sleep."

She looked up at him then and the breath caught in

his throat. His wife was only twenty-eight, two years, six months, and four days younger than he was, but the last ten days had aged her almost beyond recognition. There were still bits and pieces of the beautiful, vivacious woman he'd married. Her eyes were still the same green-gray, her pixie face still heart-shaped and framed by autumn-brown hair; it was still her, but not. Those eyes had gone dull and the hair he'd once loved to run his fingers through was matted and oily. The face that looked at him now had withered, with lines etched deep across the once smooth skin.

They'd known about their son, about Benjy, for ten days, but for the last two, his wife hadn't eaten more than a mouthful or slept longer than a few minutes at a stretch, and then she only slept in the chair next to the crib, her hand resting against the baby's back, and each time she woke, it was always in a panic.

Until she assured herself that he was still breathing.

It was like she knew it was almost over and wouldn't allow herself to miss it.

Ryan held out his hand and watched her eyes follow the movement.

"Sleep." Concentrating hard, he forced himself to smile and felt the muscles quiver from lack of use. "Come on."

Her eyes shifted away from him and back to the crib. "No, it's okay, I'm fine. You get some rest."

"I have," he said, only realizing the depth of his transgression when she turned to glare up at him. "I mean, I just laid down for a minute and—"

She dismissed him with a tired nod and turned back

to the crib. "Whatever. Go back to *sleep*, Benjy and I are fine."

Ryan wondered if it would have hurt less if she'd just slapped him across the face. He took a deep breath so he could say, could whisper, everything he needed to without stopping.

"No, you aren't, and you won't do Benjy any good by wearing yourself down. Now come on."

Forgetting, he reached out and brushed her shoulder with his fingertips. She jerked away as if scalded. She didn't like to be touched now, couldn't stand anyone touching her, especially him, and hadn't since the NICU doctor had told them what was wrong with their beautiful baby boy.

Ryan still cringed when he thought about it; not about the diagnosis, which was beyond reason, but that he'd almost laughed out loud upon hearing the name. It wasn't funny, but the name of the rare genetic fluke that would kill their son, *DiGeorge Syndrome*, sounded like a brand of frozen pizza.

He'd had to inhale to stop himself and heard Lanie do the same, but knew it wasn't for the same reason. While the doctor explained the condition that caused Benjy to be a faint bluish-lavender color *(cyanotic)* instead of pink, and why he had such difficulty nursing *(velopharyngeal insufficiency)*, and what exactly was meant by the term "failure to thrive," Lanie had gripped Ryan's hand so hard his fingers had gone numb.

Then, very quietly and gently, whispering the way a New Dad was supposed to talk to his baby, the doctor told them there wasn't anything else they—the doctors, the specialists, the machines—could do, and told them to take Benjy home and love him, sing to him, take pictures for the family album and then, in a few weeks, maybe a month if they were very, very lucky, let him go.

That would have been enough, more than enough, but then the doctor told them, reminded them again, how extremely rare *Di George Syndrome* was and how it might not affect any other children they might have...but that they should consider getting tested beforehand. Just to be on the safe side.

They were safer still, for the last ten days Lanie hadn't let Ryan touch her.

"I'm sorry," he said, and pulled his hand away.

She turned back to the crib, a mother bear protecting her dying cub.

"I'm fine."

"No," he said, "you're not."

"Go away, Ryan. Please, just leave us alone."

I wish I could. "Look, Lanie, you need to rest...for both of you. I'll sit with him."

She looked up at him again.

"You can't help him if you get sick." Ryan tried to smile again but gave up after the second try. "Go on. I made the bed, fresh sheets and everything. You don't have to sleep. Just rest, just for a few minutes, okay?"

There was a question in her eyes as she turned back to the crib, and Ryan knew she was wondering if a few minutes, if just a few minutes, would be too long. They were on borrowed time already, but then she stood up and he had to back up quickly to give her room.

"Okay," she said, and walked to the door leaving

behind the scent of unwashed hair and a faint musk that reminded Ryan of stale winter loam. The long, soaking baths she'd once indulged in had been traded for quick showers that barely dampened her skin, but even those had stopped. Ryan followed her across the room, making sure he stayed far enough back so they wouldn't accidently touch.

The plan, when they were still just expectant parents, was to keep the baby in their room, with the crib next to her side of the bed so she wouldn't have far to stumble, even though Ryan had graciously offered his side of the bed.

Parents, friends, and the books all agreed that having the baby in the parents' room, for at least the first few weeks, was a good idea. It helped the new parents learn their baby's sleep pattern, vocal signals and breathing sounds.

The only problem was that it only worked for new parents not dealing with anything other than standard-issue babies. Newborns were supposed to cry when they were hungry or wet, but Benjy never did; he never had the strength. He slept straight through the night from the day he was born and probably would have slept his life away if Lanie didn't rouse him every two hours to feed him. But even then, he never fully woke up.

Lanie hadn't even noticed that Ryan had moved the crib into the nursey. She'd just put Benjy into it and took her place in the chair, keeping watch.

Lanie stopped at the door of the master bedroom and looked back at him. "Just a few minutes, you promise?"

Ryan nodded. "I promise."

His wife nodded back then walked into their bedroom like a prisoner entering a gas chamber. Ryan waited, and started counting by one-thousands. On those other rare occasions when he'd been able to drag her away from her self-imposed vigil, he'd only make it to twenty-one-thousand before she'd reappear in the hall to tell him she couldn't sleep, wasn't tired, it was okay, she was fine.

When he got to fifty-one thousand, he stopped counting, but didn't move away from the door for another minute. When he finally convinced himself she wasn't coming back, he walked back into the nursery and sat down in the chair next to the crib.

His son was a small, still lump in the center of the mattress decorated with dancing bears, covered by the blue-and-white blanket his mother had crocheted for him. He was on his tummy, turned away from him, but Ryan could see his son's face in the crib mirror someone had given them as a baby shower gift. Set into a padded red fabric frame shaped like a flower, the mirror was supposed to be tied onto the crib bars by two Velcro straps so the baby could see himself and *"develop a sense of self and help develop a better self-image."*

But that's not how Lanie used it. It was the first item she put into the crib after Benjy, placing it flat against the mattress next to his face so she could see he was still breathing.

The room was getting darker; autumn had arrived the day he was born, but thanks to a teddy bear shaped light on the crib-side table, Ryan was able to see the ghosts of his son's breaths dance and fade, dance and fade across the glass.

"Daddy's here," he whispered to the partial refection—only a nose and part of a cheek, lavender-blue in the growing shadows—and folded his hands in his lap so they wouldn't be tempted. There was nothing Ryan could offer or give his son that would help. There was nothing he could do but sit there and watch and wait for the end to come. "It's okay. Mommy's resting, but I'm here. Daddy's here, it's okay."

The tiny body under the blanket didn't move at the sound of his voice, but he never moved. He was such a good baby in some ways, never complaining.

"If you need me, I'll be right here."

For as long as it takes.

Ryan continued to watch his son's breaths come and go across the mirror and began to understand how his wife could sit there hour after hour, day after day, night after night. There was something peaceful about it, something safe and serene and almost hypnotic.

When he woke up, the room was dark and there were no more ghosts dancing on the glass.

Ryan felt every muscle in his body tense. He wanted to scream and knock over the chair as he leapt to his feet. He wanted to grab his son and hold him and yell his name over and over until he woke up.

He wanted to, but he didn't.

Instead he moved slowly, the way his list and the books said a *New Dad* was supposed to so he wouldn't scare the baby, and held onto the crib railing as he leaned down, farther and farther.

"Benjy?" His breath —and only his— fogged the mirror. "Benjy."

Then he held his breath, but no other ghosts appeared.

He looks like a doll. Slowly, carefully, Ryan reached out to run the back of his fingers across one tiny cheek. The flesh beneath his was already cold and felt like the soft, malleable plastic rubber they use for baby dolls.

Ryan stood up.

That's what he looked like, a sleeping baby doll; a toy, not real, and as long as he kept that thought with him, it was easier to leave the room and walk down the hall; easier to sit down on the edge of their bed and take her hand.

"Lanie?'

She muttered once, then her hand tightened and her nails gouged the back of his hand as she pulled herself up.

"What? What's wrong? Oh God, why is it dark? I told you only a few minutes. Benjy! It's okay, momma's coming. I'm coming, baby!" She tried to push him away, to get off the bed, but he grabbed her and held her. "Stop it! What's wrong with you? Let me go! Benjy? Momma's coming. Ryan, let me go!"

"He's gone."

She stopped moving. It was dark in their room; there was no night light, so Ryan couldn't see her face as he let her go.

He couldn't see her at all, and that made it easier, too.

The first slap caught him high, just below the temple, and set off a starburst of red and yellow behind his eyes. The second ignited more fireworks and toppled him to the floor.

She kicked at him, probably accidentally, as she was scrambling off the bed, but he wasn't sure. Accident or not, it still hurt, and that pain gave him something to concentrate on besides the screams that ricocheted back to him from the nursery.

The rest of that night and the week that followed were a blur.

Because Benjy had been under a doctor's care and his condition known, they were able to forgo an autopsy, which meant there were no sutured incisions that needed to be hidden beneath the blue-and-white sailor's outfit with red trim and matching cap that Lanie's mother had picked out to contrast with the powder-blue satin lining and the crocheted blanket his mother had made.

The funeral director had tucked the blanket around Benjy and the small yellow teddy bear someone had given them as a baby shower gift.

The morning of the funeral was warm, the service respectably short, and the tiny white casket all but lost among the floral offerings that surrounded it. Blue Mylar balloons had been handed out to their friends and family to be released into the sky as the coffin was lowered.

Ryan thought it in bad taste when the funeral director had suggested it, but finally agreed because he thought it would redirect everyone's attention—and it had, except for Laney. Her eyes never left the grave.

Their friends left them at the cemetery; their family came to the house and stayed only long enough to make sure that he and Lanie ate something while they finished packing away the nursery.

He'd agreed to that, too.

"It was better this way," his mother had told him when they came home from making the funeral arrangements to find her and his father and Lanie's mother packing away the toys that would never be played with and the clothes that would never be worn. "We'll just put them in the closet and close the door until you need them again."

Ryan just nodded and Lanie seemed okay with it until they started to move the chair that had been next to the crib—the chair she'd sat in to keep watch every day and night of their son's short life, the chair he'd fallen asleep in on the last day of that life.

Ryan would have been just as happy to see it burn, but she demanded it stay where it was, next to the crib's ghostly outline on the rug in the otherwise empty room.

That's where he found her after their parents left the day of the funeral, sitting in the chair holding the only other thing she wouldn't let them put away, the crib mirror. The light coming in through the sheer curtains behind her was fading into twilight.

He stood in the doorway, hoping she'd look up and see him, but when she didn't, he reached over and turned on the ceiling light. Without its cream-colored man-in-the-moon cover, the light from the bare bulb made his eyes water.

"Turn it off."

Ryan's finger touched the dimmer switch. "I can turn it lower if you like."

"Turn it off."

He flipped the switch down and put his hands in his pockets.

"Are you hungry? You haven't eaten anything, and the folks left a ton of food."

She was sitting slightly forward in the chair, looking down into the mirror cradled in her hands.

"I'm not hungry."

"You have to eat, Lanie."

"Did you do it on purpose?"

A chill ran down his spine. "What?"

"I won't be angry, just tell me." She looked up, her face blank. "Did you not wake me up so you could...so he'd die?"

The cold settled in his stomach. "Do you think I...I killed him?"

"I won't be angry."

"How can you think... No! I didn't do anything." *But fall asleep.* "I'm sorry, I'm so sorry, but how could you think that? He was my son, too."

She shrugged and looked back into the glass. "I just wondered. Benjy was alive when I sat with him and then you made me go to sleep and he died. If you woke me up like you promised, he might still be alive."

"No." He kept it voice low, soft, the way a new father is supposed to, but it still seemed to echo off the bare walls as he stepped into the room. "No, he wouldn't be, Lanie. You know it was just a matter of time. The doctors said it was a miracle he lasted as long as he did. You know that."

When she didn't answer, Ryan took a step closer. "You *know* that, don't you?"

"I should have been with him."

She looked so broken all he wanted to do was wrap his

arms around her and lie and tell her everything was going to be okay. "It's not your fault."

He got halfway across the room when she looked up again and stopped him.

"I know that! You didn't kill him, but you promised to wake me up and you didn't, so it's *your* fault. Benjy's dead and it's all your fault!"

"No! Lanie, listen to me, it's no one's—"

"Look."

Before he could ask "look at what?", she stood up and came at him, holding the mirror out in front of her like a battering ram. Ryan took two steps back, suddenly afraid.

"Do you know why people cover mirrors when someone dies?" she asked, still coming at him. "It's so the spirit of the dead person won't be trapped in the glass. My grandmother told me that when my Uncle Kevin died, but I forgot. I forgot until Benjy. Do you believe it, that a soul can be trapped in a mirror? My grandmother believed it and she never lied. Do you believe it?"

She kept coming, and Ryan kept backing up until they were both in the hall and moving away from the nursery. He held both hands out in front of him, inches from the mirror she was holding out. If it touched him, he was afraid he'd start screaming and not be able to stop.

"Please, honey, just put that down, okay?"

It was dark in the hall, he hadn't bothered to turn on the overhead light, but Ryan could still see her eyes. They were pleading with him.

"But you believe it, don't you? Tell me you believe it."

They were passing their bedroom. "Yeah, okay, but

you're exhausted. Why don't you lay down for a bit, okay? Just for a little while. I'll wake you up in—"

Ryan stopped talking when he realized what he had said. The moved continued down the hall.

"You promised to wake me before, but you didn't. You didn't wake me, and he died, and the mirror was right there. But it's okay...it's okay because he didn't go away. He's here, Benjy's still here...in the mirror. Look. Look in the mirror, Ryan. LOOK IN IT!"

She took two quick steps, faster than Ryan expected, and thrust the mirror into his face.

It wasn't possible...couldn't be possible, but in the moment before his foot slipped off the top stair and he fell backwards into nothing, he thought he saw something...something small and blue that looked like a sleeping baby doll.

His eyes opened to a glowing, happy-faced moon smiling down on him from a blue ceiling, and the music box sound of "Twinkle, Twinkle Little Star" playing somewhere to his left.

Parts of him remembered, parts of him were fascinated.

He tried to sit up but his body wouldn't cooperate; it jerked and trembled, arms and legs flailing uncontrollably. When one arm struck something cold and hard, he yelped more in surprise than pain. The sound was strange and weak.

"I'm coming, I'm coming."

Her, it was her voice, and he felt his body relax against a soft, firm surface that crinkled under him. His head lolled sideways against a thin pillow and he saw metal rails.

Crib, no—*remember*—like a crib but different...a hospital bed. Yes, a hospital bed. Something had happened to him and he was in the hospital.

Falling. He remembered falling…seeing something in a mirror that made him jerk back...that made him fall back into nothing...falling…and falling until he hit something hard, and his neck….

Remember.

It made a wet sound when it snapped and the pain that followed flared like a bomb imploding...shrinking, compressing, dragging everything that he was, down into a darkness so deep that he couldn't see or breathe or—

He remembered and screamed, but the sound that came out of his mouth was a thin, wailing sob.

"It's okay! It's okay. Hush, now, I'm here."

Her face appeared above him, smiling down, talking softly as she wiped the tears from his face.

"Lanie, what happened? What's going on?" he tried to ask, but his words were gibberish, nonsense, noise.

"Shh, shh," she whispered. "It's okay. Did you have a bad dream? Hush now, it's okay."

"No, it's not!"

"Shh, baby, it's okay.

"What happened? Lanie, what's wrong?"

Another face suddenly appeared over him. It was older than *Hers* and the eyes glistened, but it was a nice face and parts of him knew it, had seen it before. It was like *Her* but different.

"Is he all right?"

He tried to reach for the older *Her*, but only managed to strike the bars.

Her laughed.

"See how excited he is? He knows you."

The *older Her* leaned closer.

"Do you really think so?" she asked.

Lanie brushed her hand over his face and he wriggled with pleasure. "Of course he does, the doctors don't know everything, do they, baby?"

He made a cooing sound.

"See, he's fine, but I bet he's wet. You know that always bothers him. Let me check."

Moving quickly, *Her* reached under the blanket that covered him and slipped two fingers under the leg of the thick padded thing wrapped around his bottom.

"Yup, he's soaked. Hand me another diaper and a wipe, will you, Helen?"

What happened to me?

His body twitched as *Her* pulled off the blanket and folded it over the rails at the foot of the bed.

"I thought I'd crochet him a blanket." The older *Her* looked away as *Her* pulled the cold wet thing off him, but didn't stop talking. "I was thinking two shades of blue might be nice. One light and one dark?"

"That would be great." *Her* touched the things between his legs with something cold that made him jump.

"It's okay, baby, shh, it's okay," the older *Her* said and put her hands on his chest. He could feel them, cold and hard against the thin shirt he wore. "Just be a good boy for Lanie, okay? God, he really hates this."

"No, he doesn't," *Her* said as she dropped the thick wet thing into something next to the bed that went *clunk*, "he just hates being wet, is all."

"My poor boy." The older *Her* pressed harder against his chest as he struggled. "I don't know why you insisted they remove the catheter. It was so much easier that way."

"You heard what the doctor said, there could be complications with catheters. Besides, I don't mind doing this for him."

Her smiled down at him.

"I know it's cold," *Her* told him, "but it will be all over in a minute. Hang in there, okay, buddy? Look out, baby, here comes the snowstorm!"

Her made a funny face and sprinkled something that took away the cold and felt good.

He stopped thrashing.

Thank you.

"See, he's fine. Okay, lift up," *Her* told him, but she didn't seem to mind when he didn't. *Her* just rolled him halfway over to slide a soft warm thing under him then rolled him back and snugged it down. "All done. Now, isn't that better?"

Yes. He smiled up at *Her*.

"You're welcome," *Her* said as she pulled the blanket back over him and tucked it in.

"But it's so much more work for you," the older *Her* said.

"No, it's not." *Her* leaned over and kissed his cheek.

Her scent—*soap and roses and coffee with cream*—lingered in the air and he pulled it deep into him. *He remembered.* "Okay, you're all clean, so why don't I go get your lunch, how's that?"

He gurgled and that made *Her* laugh.

"See?" *Her* said to the other one. "I told you he understands. You want to help me make his lunch or do you want stay and visit a little more?"

He looked up at the older *Her—she's my mother, I remember—* and was mesmerized by the way the wet in her eyes sparkled. Pretty, it was pretty.

"I can't do either today, I'm afraid. I only stopped by to see if…to see how he was doing. I promised to meet his dad downtown, he's still trying to talk me into taking that cruise and thinks he can bribe me with a Mediterranean buffet."

"A cruise, wow."

The older *Her* kept looking at him but the sparkles in her eyes had gone away and it wasn't pretty anymore. He looked away and noticed something bright and shiny and red tied to the bars across from his face. It was pretty but when he tried to lift his arm to touch it, the older *Her* put her hand on it and held it down. He looked up and the sparkles were back.

Pretty.

"I don't know," the older *Her* said. "The cruise is for two weeks. It's something we promised ourselves we'd do before the grand— before we got too old to enjoy it, but I don't want to be away that long, in case something happens."

He watched her come around the bed and hug the

older *Her*.

"Nothing's going to happen," she said. "Ryan's fine and he's going to stay that way. He's a fighter, you know that, and he going to keep fighting."

The sparkles ran down the lines in the older *Her's* face.

"But he'll never get better," she said, "he'll always be like this. My poor boy, maybe it would have been better if he—"

"Hush now," *Her* said, "don't even think that. He's here, that's all that matters."

The older *Her* nodded. "You're right."

"Okay, then. You go have the greatest lunch in the world and then call me tonight and let me know all about the cruise, okay?"

"Okay."

Her smiled down at him and winked before taking the *older Her's* hand. "Then it's settled. Come on, I'll walk you out and then get this guy his lunch."

He heard them walk away, then watched the man-in-the-moon watch him. Pictures started playing in his head, but only bits and pieces of them...

...the world tumbling, tumbling in front of him before it stopped, suddenly, and her—*Lanie*—running down the stairs toward him until...nothing...darkness...bits and pieces...then light and then dark and then...faces and crying and words like brain stem and traumatic and irreversible and...

He heard her coming back and smiled and the man in the moon smiled back.

"Here we are."

He managed to turn his head with only two tries and saw *Her* over the bars. *Her* had something long and white in her hands, and laughed when he squealed and babbled and squirmed.

"I knew you were hungry," *Her* said, and began untucking the blanket. "Do I know my boy or what?"

Lanie? What happened to me? "Lah lah gurgle squeal."

"Okay, okay, I'm hurrying, give me a minute. You know we have to flush the feeding tube first. Don't want my baby getting sick, do we?"

Lanie...please. "Lah lah geeeeee."

He felt a slight tug on his side and looked down to see her doing something to the clear tube that came out of his belly. It scared him, but then *Her* put the end of the long white thing into the tube and he felt his belly fill up with something warm. It felt good. It felt...happy.

"Is that good num-nums?" *Her* asked. "It should be, I put in some extra banana. Umm, yummy!"

Lanie, talk to me. "Lah lah taaa taa mmmm."

Her smiled at him. "I know, baby, I know. There, all gone. You're such a good boy."

There was another tug and *Her* took the long thing away and tucked the blanket back around him. When she was done, she leaned down and tapped the bright, shiny red thing next to his head and he turned.

The crib mirror.

"I know you're in there, baby. Come on, show me. Show mama you're there."

He watched the image in the mirror blur and suddenly he was looking out through eyes that weren't his at a face that was small and round and pale blue.

Benjy.

"There you are," *Her* said, and began unbuttoning her blouse. "Hi, baby. Hi, Benjy, are you ready for dessert? You're such a good boy, a strong boy and you'll never be sick again. Daddy didn't understand, but he does now, and together we're going to take good care of you for ever and ever."

When she finished unbuttoning her blouse, *Her* lowered the bars on the side of the bed and stretched out next to him. Pulling him close, she unsnapped one side of the nursing bra to release a breast swollen and heavy with milk and he felt his body twist and turn, trembling with excitement, his mouth making eager wet sucking sounds.

"Okay, okay, Mr. Greedy Gus." Cradling his head, she lifted her naked breast to his lips. "I love you, Benjy. We both love you so much."

Her skin was soft and warm against their cheek and the nipple tasted good, almost as good as the sweet thick milk that filled their mouth.

Shoved into a very small, very dark space, Ryan felt the body he shared with his dead son squirm with pleasure as they suckled.

But only he screamed.

Records of The Dead

John Linwood Grant

September 1974

NINE. The damaged reel. The celluloid has deteriorated, and for some minutes, all that is seen is a blur of figures. An unknown man mutters to the camera. At 0:07:32, the face of Emile Casson can be seen staring at the camera. His collar is loose, and he appears angry. This image continues to the end of the reel.

I can read lips. My aunt knows this, and she insists that I write down what I can determine from Nine for the twentieth time, as if it might have changed. It hasn't, obviously. The unknown man, from what I can get, is still complaining about being in the same room as "That Goddamn Frog." There is nothing useful on the reel, and she wheels herself out of the projection room without any sign of appreciation.

Another fruitless morning.

In the afternoon, while she sleeps, I go through the mail from the clipping agencies. An obituary covers the death of a man who once met the director, Emile Casson, in California. That would be in 1921, during Casson's abortive attempt to get into the West Coast industry. I already have that documented. The Frenchman's peripheral involvement in the communist movement, and his virtual blacklisting during the Red Scare, put paid to any plans. He came back to New York after three days.

The last envelope is from the Burgess Agency. It contains a photograph and a handwritten note.

Mrs. Westercott, this may interest you.

The photograph shows a group of men in black suits, and a wreath of lilies in the background. A funeral, or a wake. I turn it over, and see names scrawled in pale ink. Teddy Fleming, Joseph Karowski, Manny Goldschein, and a couple I can't read.

Joseph Karowski.

Oh my God.

The same hand that produced the accompanying note has added another line.

After Cedric Gibbons' funeral. Hollywood?

I should wake her up and tell her that we have a lead. Instead, I pour myself a sherry and wait, trying not to think of anything. I go to the shelves and consult the indexed notebooks which hold the most relevant details. Austin Cedric Gibbons, Art Director for MGM, eleven-time Oscar winner. Way out of Casson or Karowski's league; died the twenty-sixth of July, 1960.

After the funeral. This must have been a show of

respect – or a circle of old gossips gathering to remember imagined glories.

Karowski is second from the left, going to fat but looking well enough. His suit looks more expensive than the others. Fleming has his hand on Karowski's shoulder. Steadying, consoling, trying to remind him that the bar is open. I can't tell.

I've never heard of Goldschein, but I find Teddy Fleming. Theodore James Fleming. Worked as a sound recordist with Gibbons, but based on the East Coast. He seems to have been around in the industry through the crucial period in the mid-twenties. Another one who has passed – he died in '65, in New York, from liver failure. Maybe he came across Casson at some point.

Aunt Marian is asleep in her room. A powdered satin face mask keeps the sharp autumn light from her eyes, her gown spreading out on the bed around her, shroud-like. Wish-fulfillment on my part. Phoning the Burgess Agency, I get connected to a Henry Fields.

"We're interested," I say. "We need more about Teddy Fleming – addresses, relatives, that sort of thing. We'll pay double rates."

"I know someone, but they're not agency." His voice goes low for that part.

"Have them invoice Mrs. Westercott. She'll pay."

It's the one thing she does with any grace, opening her check book and giving that showy flourish of her pen.

I say nothing to Aunt Marian about the photograph. She has me watch Thirty-Two again, to try and identify the chinaware in the film. I check catalogs as she watches me from by the window, crouched in her wheelchair with her eyes half-closed. After an hour she snaps something derogatory, and wheels herself into the projection room that Uncle Hal had built in the sixties. Perhaps she'll fall asleep in there.

I had liked Uncle Hal. Forty years in accounting, much of it for the Astoria Studio, four blocks away. His reward was to fall off a stepladder whilst hanging a framed photograph in this room. A shattered hip and a broken rib followed by terminal pneumonia. He left behind a palatial Astoria flat, with a library and projection room, a large collection of memorabilia and film reels, and a widow. No kids, thank God. The thought of someone having to be her son or daughter appalls me.

And he left money. Real money. I imagine him in his office, manipulating figures, making those slight alterations which would ensure that Marian May Westercott could live the rest of her life without worrying. A gesture of accountancy, not of love.

Uncle Hal should be the one who haunts the flat. Instead, we have only Casson...

FOURTEEN. The man is in his sixties or seventies, and perhaps Italian —or Spanish. Mediterranean, certainly. His face is crumpled, as if a great hand has squeezed it until the eyes, nose, and mouth almost folded into each other. He speaks to the camera, showing a few rotting teeth. The table before him is spread with what seem to be small playing cards, laid out in a cruciform pattern. A caption appears: *Tarocco Siciliano*. We do not know what he is saying, but he points to various parts of the spread in turn. It seems he is asked a question, because he looks up suddenly and spits to one side. The film ends.

I turn over a page in my notebook, and scrawl *Miseria* again and again. It's the one card with which I am very familiar. The Chained Beggar.

When the postman calls on the third morning, he has a package for me. Miss Julia Williams. Confidential. Inside are names and addresses, newspaper clippings and brief notes. I spread them out on my desk. *Tarocco Siciliano.*

A photograph of Teddy Fleming with a woman too young to be his wife. Daughter, hopefully. Clippings about his work as a sound recordist, and yes, a mention of he and Karowski working together on a shelved series of cartoons. The production company went bust. It was for the Astoria Studio, and places them both in New York in 1926. The same time Karowski was working for Casson.

I settle on a single name and address. Diane Margut, née Fleming.

Aunt Marian is with her 'personal physician,' by which I mean a doctor who will take as much crap as my aunt wants to deliver, as long as his check arrives every month. Her liver rebels at the evening cocktails on which she insists, and her sight is failing.

I make a quiet phone call, and then shout through to the bedroom.

"I need to go to the drugstore, and the stationers."

A disinterested mutter gives me permission.

Uncle Hal's old Windsor sedan gets me to Diane Margut's place in Suffolk County. A solid suburban house. The woman sounded wary on the phone, but I explained that I was researching the history of the Astoria Studio. She agreed to see me.

Diane Margut is a slightly harassed looking blonde in her forties. She offers me a coffee, and we sit down in a very beige lounge.

"You say you're interested in my father, Miss Williams?" She sounds very Brooklyn.

"In the scene and the background. Particularly around the mid-twenties."

She sips her coffee, weighing me up. I mention some names, showing off my credentials.

"He must have known people like Goldschein and Karowski, as well." I throw this in whilst looking out of the window, making it the lightest of comments.

When I look back, she's frowning.

"You're not a reporter, are you?"

I squint as if surprised by the question. "Do I look like one?" I know that I look like a dowdy academic, getting middle-aged too early. Tweed and pearls; unpolished shoes; hair the color of mud, pushed back behind my glasses. No one has ever called me an attractive woman.

She looks awkward, and refills my coffee from the pot without asking.

"Sorry. It's just that Mr. Karowski... he and dad were friends. I call him Uncle Joe. He left the business in the forties, became very private. Still is."

My bone china cup is in danger of hitting the floor.

"I didn't realize he was alive."

"Oh yes. I had a birthday card from him a few months ago."

Time for a careful change of subject. We drift on to how her father got on with some of the names, whether or not he kept up his interest in film, and so on. After an hour, I put down my notebook and smile, thanking Diane for her time. As we head for the door, I pause.

"I don't suppose it would be possible to have a few words with Mr. Karowski? It would be great to add that personal feel to the book. You know how dry these things can get." A conspiratorial smile this time —the woman behind the academic.

"He's not on the phone. I guess I could send him a note, ask him."

I give her one of my aunt's cards, with my name written on it. "That would be terrific."

We part on agreeable terms, and I drive back the long way, an aimless route.

Emile Casson worked with very few people. Very few would work with him. Two names came up in what records we had: Louie Trent, a left-leaning drunkard who worked as his cameraman, and Joseph Karowski, a young Italian-Pole, his sound recordist when Casson experimented with sound systems, around 1925-1926.

Trent, like most of his contemporaries, was dead. 'Uncle Joe' was not.

ELEVEN. An empty can, marked 'Colored children from East Harlem, June 1925."

At dinner, I tell my aunt that I may have a link to Karowski. I don't tell her he's alive. She spits out a mouthful of roast chicken and cranes her head forward. Her thin, wrinkled neck reminds me of what we are eating.

"Why didn't you tell me earlier?" she snaps.

"It may not work out." I sound defensive. "The doctor says you're not meant to get unnecessarily excited."

She subsides, keen to be seen as the put-upon invalid.

"Um." After a few minutes of noisy chewing, she puts her knife and fork down. "I want to hear it again, tonight."

Uncle Hal left a lot of recordings, picked up during his times at the studios. Some are real collectors' items, going back to the early Vitaphone disks. The sixteen-inch monsters each hold eleven minutes of sound, the same length as a standard film reel. If you have the accompanying film, and can get them synchronized, you can live the twenties again. Should you want to.

I don't.

I take out the tape marked Casson Thirty-Seven. We never play the original disk, which is lodged in a safe deposit box at her bank. She's been obsessed with it since Uncle Hal died. Obsessed with Casson's work. No one has ever found the accompanying Film Thirty-Seven, or any of the other records which would have meshed with the film reels.

The original label on the record says 'Casson 37. 8/9. L'homme Italien. Sound – J L Karowski.' The cans holding Casson's silent film reels are marked in a similar manner, except that they end with 'Camera – L Trent' instead. Sometimes there's no title, but there is always a number.

FOURTEEN. The man with the cards makes gestures of protest. He takes the table by its edge and tips it over, the small, strangely painted cards fluttering in every direction. Some form of zoom lens is used – the focus blurs, and then holds on a single card on the floor. *Miseria.*

Uncle Hal found the record and the films in a disused warehouse next to the Astoria Studio lot, back in 1941. The industry had pretty much moved to California. The Army were taking the place over, and my uncle, along with a few friends, searched the corners for anything which had been missed. When I was older, Uncle Hal showed me what they'd found.

Seven films, all one reel long except for Seventeen and Thirty-Seven.

"See, Julia? They wouldn't let Casson on the lot, proper, but he had friends. They let him use Warehouse H and borrow equipment."

I was looking at a heap of dented film canisters, a wrecked projector, and other detritus.

"Why's this stuff important?" I asked. This was the early sixties. I was twenty-seven, unmarried, jobless, and studying French. I thought I was going to travel.

"Well, maybe it isn't. But it's all that remains of his work."

"So who was this Casson – some kind of misunderstood genius?"

"Just another oddball director. He wasn't the only one back then. Fought in the First World War, then came over here. Got himself pegged as a socialist agitator. The studios didn't like that."

"What happened to him?"

"Died in Spain. The Red Brigades."

"Huh."

We played pitch and catch the same day. He should have lived; she should have fallen from the stepladder. That's the thought in my head as she wheels her dry, shrunken body into the projection room. I place the record on the turntable.

The first four minutes and eleven seconds consist mostly of background hiss. The sound booth would have been well away from the camera, and the audio cable shielded, but you can hear the whir of the camera. Then a light voice, accented, which must be Casson...

Ce sera bientôt. It will be soon.

The microphone knocks against a hard surface.

He breathes badly. Oui, montre moi. Yes, show me.

At 0:6:27, a chair or something similar scrapes the floor. The next words are spoken very close to the microphone.

Au-dessus ou au-dessous, vous êtes entre les deux. Voyez-vous maintenant? Y a-t-il une clarté? Above or below, you are in between. Do you see now? Is there clarity?

A low moan, and the sound of ragged breathing. Another voice, very American, says "Hey, Emile, leave the guy some dignity, for Chrissake." I've always assumed that must be Louie Trent on the camera.

Tais-toi, il essaie de parler. Shut up, he's trying to speak. Mon Dieu, he sweats!

Footsteps – someone pacing.

Attends, c'est le moment?

There is a harsh gargle, like someone trying to cough up sputum or some obstacle, and...

Eleven minutes have passed. The record ends.

I could do a better transcription if I had the film, so I could at least see Casson's lips move. But there is no film Thirty-Seven. The record implies there are nine whole reels missing, destroyed, thrown away. Uncle Hal searched for Casson memorabilia until the pneumonia set in – a hobby, like looking for a stamp whose only real value is its rarity.

Aunt Marian turned that hobby into her life. At first, I thought her search for Casson and his work might be some sort of displaced grieving for my uncle. It wasn't. As the months ground by, I began to see only an aging woman with no friends and nothing better to do. I don't think anyone else really cares about an unsuccessful Commie film director who never amounted to anything.

"Did you catch anything new, Julia?"

"I have the Karowski rumors to follow."

She peers at me. She is a projector herself, her petty malice and selfishness playing over every wall of this place.

"I suppose so," she says, pursing wrinkled lips which gleam with Vaseline. I wonder that she has enough spittle in her to swallow.

We part. At least I have a private room. As I read some pathetic romance magazine, I decide to have Henry Fields look further into the Fleming connection. It will cost, but I'm not the one who's paying.

I've no reason to doubt Fleming's daughter. Karowski is alive, and the way she spoke of him, he's not that far away.

The only man who knows what the record represents.

THIRTY-TWO. A young woman takes a cup and saucer from someone off-camera (you see a man's hand, part of his sleeve). Casson sits by her, taking notes. He is a thin man in his thirties, a sliver of France with dark, slicked back hair. The china is ornately decorated with Zodiac signs. She tips the cup to let the last few drops of a dark liquid fall onto the ground, and then peers into the cup. She frowns, and shows it to the camera. Tealeaves.

We know that Casson was ejected from the Manhattan Psychiatric Center in 1925. He was filming on some kind of terminal ward there, ostensibly a film for teaching purposes. Something he did disturbed the doctors. Other than that, he failed to make the news, and his work was never shown in cinemas. Hardly surprising, if the surviving reels are typical.

He had no wife, no children, no known relatives. Inquiries in France have never yielded anything. But now I have some American leads, at least. The next week brings reports via Mr. Fields. Vague stories of sound recordists drinking together in the fifties, in East Harlem. A third man seems to have been part of the scene, but he died in 1961. Marco Fracassi. He had a music shop, which also repaired gramophones, off East 112nd Street. The shop is still going, apparently, so I need to pay a visit.

I drive along 2nd Avenue and park outside what looks like a respectable enough hotel, tipping the doorman to keep an eye on the Windsor. I'm modestly dressed and I have a small revolver in my bag – Uncle Hal taught me to shoot. I'm no good at it but can make plenty of noise.

They call it Italian Harlem, but the Greeks are moving in all over the place. I can't see much difference between them. Men smoking cigarettes by open windows eye me briefly, but apparently see nothing of interest. The old brownstones merge with derelict lots, a crisscross pattern of neglect, and I pass a Windsor much like my uncle's, its tires gone and the hood sprung. Two Italian kids are playing on it, jumping up and down. They shout abuse at me and laugh.

The Fracassi place is easy to find. Inside, it's dust and memories – racks of sheet music, a few instruments, and a bench heaped with broken recording equipment. A man in his forties is jabbing a screwdriver at the innards of a tape recorder. He looks up.

"Sì? Posso aiutarti?"

"Do you speak English?" My Italian's not bad, but it would be easier that way.

He puts the screwdriver down. "Yes, of course."

I can't imagine any pretense to use. "I'm looking into early sound recordists, the men who worked around the Astoria Studio. I understand the late Mr. Fracassi knew some of them, and I wondered if anyone here could help me?"

"Which men are these?" His tone is neither suspicious nor welcoming.

I pull out a copy of the photograph of Karowski and Fleming, which he takes, peering at it over his glasses. A faint smile forms on his lips.

"Sì. Teddy. He came here, and the other —Joe?"

"Joseph Karowski."

He nods and holds out his hand. "I am Cesare Fracassi. Marco's son."

"Julia Williams."

He takes me into the back room. A sink, a gas ring with a stove-top expresso maker, three chairs, and a pile of magazines. They're not music magazines. He covers them with his shop-coat in a swift, practiced movement.

Over espresso, he tells me about the fifties. There were four or five enthusiasts who would gather at the shop and then go drinking. Karowski was the odd one out. He didn't drink much, and there was talk. When I ask what kind of talk, he hesitates. I put a twenty-dollar bill on the unoccupied chair.

Cesare Fracassi has heard of Casson. Karowski's association with Casson was not in his favor, but Fleming had spoken up for his friend.

"What was so bad about Casson?"

"Only talk, you know. He had this thing —he asked questions, took people to film."

"He paid them?"

"Sì, but my father said they did not want to go back, ever. Always it was Fortuna, fate, what was in the cards, he wanted to know. Zingari matters - the stars, the cards, the tea-leaves..."

"Zingari? Gypsies?"

"Anyone who spoke of the future."

"Why?"

An expressive shrug. "And, signora, there was a death, my father once said. At the studio..."

I walk back to my car, struggling with a strange feeling. That single photograph from the agency has yielded more than the last six months' work. This is not my obsession, it's hers. Eighteen months of working for my aunt has improved my bank balance but dulled any real interest in film. She has that effect. Yet the last few days I have felt almost… excited.

TWENTY-NINE. Casson sits and stares at the camera

for eleven minutes. His eyes are wide, the pupils dilated. His hands are on his knees, motionless, and he blinks very little. His expression is intense. There is no indication of his purpose in the exercise.

Diane Margut telephones. 'Uncle Joe' will see me. I can go, no one else, and the address must be kept confidential. Otherwise, the meeting is off. The address is only a few blocks away from the Fracassis.

My aunt wheels herself into the room as the conversation ends.

"What was that?"

I place the phone down.

"That lead I was telling you about. Someone who knew Joseph Karowski vaguely. I could leave it, of course..."

"You must go," she says. "I won't have corners cut, you know that, Julia."

She looks like Casson in Twenty-Nine, apart from the tic in her left cheek. I am her camera.

"Of course, Aunt Marian."

SEVENTEEN. Two reels, clearly shot in sequence. The set is featureless —a corner of a warehouse or other abandoned commercial building. A tall, barefooted black woman, one eye milky (cataract?), shakes her head and draws items from an old carpet bag, long fingers folding various things into a piece of cloth. This takes some time. She ties the cloth up into the form of a bag, drips something onto it from a small bottle, and holds it up towards the camera. In the second reel, she stands there and speaks. Her lips say this: 'You won't find it. It ain't meant, and it sure ain't right.' Then she walks out of shot.

The sharp September wind reminds me of Aunt Marian's tongue, cutting with an indiscriminate malice. I drive west through the city in a sealed, finned coffin, over-eager to get answers.

Karowski lives in a brownstone spackled with bird droppings and graffiti. There are eight name slots by the buzzer, but only one has anything written on it. *Esposito.* Apparently that's the one. The lobby inside is in disrepair. There's an elevator, though, and it works.

The elevator opens onto to a corridor painted in relaxing greens. Two doors, neither marked with a name. The door to my right is slightly open, and I go for that one.

"Miss Williams." The voice is low, almost rumbling.

I twist round and see a man to my left. He's lost some of the weight, and gained almost fifteen years, but it's Joseph Karowski. I hold out my hand, but he waves it away, and shows me into what would once have been the other apartment on this floor. It is a treasure house. Racks of film reels in their original cans; shelves stacked with the sort of books Uncle Hal collected; old movie equipment, gleaming. A row of cinema seats has been bolted to the floor in front of a large screen. The seats look like originals from the early days.

"You kept up your interest," I say, impressed.

"In film, yes. Do sit down."

I edge my way into one of the seats, feeling the old plush under me. He stays on his feet, helped by a cane.

"This is about Emile Casson, isn't it?" He should have been in the movies, with that voice. "I know he's an obsession with your aunt, Mrs. Westercott, and I can't imagine you've sought me out to hear my stories of the film industry."

"They're all dead, Mr. Karowski. Everyone we can find who knew Casson even slightly."

"We get old."

"I didn't mean that, in itself, was strange. But, well... he was, wasn't he? The man himself."

The old man looks up at the ceiling, which is tiled with some sort of soundproofing. "Strange? What have you seen of his work?"

I pass him a list of the films Uncle Hal salvaged. He reads it, nods.

"I thought he'd destroyed Twenty-Nine. And you're better off missing out Eleven. That was the first one I worked on with him. We tried to use sound-on-film, but it didn't come out well. Emile became angry with the children—"

"He abused them?"

"He shouted a lot and asked them questions. Inappropriate questions."

"You mean about sex?" I'd never come across anything

suggesting Casson was that way inclined.

"About death, and what they thought it would be like. I kept away for a while after that. Went back around Seventeen. No sound, but Louie Trent and I were two of the only people who would work with him. I did everything else." His shoulders sag. "Hell, I was in my early twenties. Emile had dough— we didn't." He sits on the end of the row, stretches out one leg, wincing. "So, your aunt wants to know if she can fill in the gaps, I guess."

"That," I agree, "and more about the man."

"He burned most of his own work. Your uncle must have found a trash pile which everyone missed. Which one was it set your aunt on the trail?"

"It wasn't a film. It was this."

I reach into my shoulder bag and hold out the copied tape of Casson Thirty-Seven - Reel Eight. Karowski takes it from me. From the look on his face, he gains a few years, loses a few heartbeats.

"It was your work," I remind him.

"Yeah. The last film we made. We had the sound almost right, level and synchronization. I'd rigged up a series of pulleys, and..." He stops, and turns the record over in liver-spotted hands. "You've listened to it."

"We don't know what it means, or what was on the other eight records."

"You shouldn't even have this one. There was a runner – Jerry. He didn't just work for Emile. He did odd jobs everywhere around the studios." He paused. "I guess… yeah, he must have picked up one of the masters, assumed it should go to the plant to be dealt with. He wasn't bright. When it came back, he'd have left it in the warehouse."

"What was Film Thirty-Seven, Mr. Karowski?"

"Nothing, to most people. You have to know the history. Emile was, well, disturbed. He died in 1917, you know?"

I don't know what my expression says at that point, but the old man laughs.

"He wasn't a frikkin' zombie, no. I mean he died for a couple of minutes, in a field hospital during the war. After that, he had this thing, this idea that he needed to see what was coming, why he was still here. He wanted purpose."

"And that was what his films were about?"

"Yeah. I missed the early days, but he'd done them all —spiritualists, astrologers, so-called psychics, fortune tellers—"

"The tarot."

"Uh-huh. They say he even had some kind of hoodoo lady, in to be filmed."

"Seventeen," I confirm.

"That's the one." He eases his leg, which clearly pains him. "Then he got this idea that dying people saw more than they said, that they had some kind of insight."

"Manhattan Psychiatric Center."

"That was around the time I joined him again. He wanted me to lug gear into this hospital ward, and record what these dying joes had to say. It was a mess, cables and lunatics, attendants yelling —we couldn't get a decent sound level. One of them knocked the camera over, Louie got mad, Emile got mad. We were chucked out."

"So he was difficult to work with."

The smile on his face is unreadable. "Yeah, you could say. Always looking for something he couldn't find. But Jeez, did I learn a lot in the job." He frowns. "I don't want this out there. I'll buy what your aunt's got, and burn the lot. I'll give her a helluva price."

"She won't sell."

"Then say you found Joe Karowski, but he's lost his marbles."

What will I do if there is no Casson to trace, no endless cataloging and rummaging? No clipping agencies, no bored relatives. And no call to watch reel after reel, again and again. I ask him if I can have a drink, and he limps off. He brings back two stiff whiskeys. It's raw, burning my throat, but it's good. Better than my aunt's sweet, sickly sherry.

"Tell me what Thirty-Seven was. Then I'll decide. Is that fair?"

"Nothing's fair. But you seem on the level, and hell, you came this far. You want to see it?"

"What?" I choke whiskey back into the tumbler.

For a moment Joe Karowski is twenty-two or twenty-three years old, excited by his turntables, cables and cutting heads.

"I kept the last reel of Thirty-Seven, the one after your record. No sound, like I said. Only thing I have left of Emile's."

"Yes. I mean, yes, I want to see it."

He turns off most of the lights, and messes with a projector. For ten minutes he's a shadow, shuffling around the place in the half-dark. Used to this, I suppose. His cane taps against the hardwood floor. Tap, tap, as I finish my whiskey.

TWENTY-EIGHT. A group of people sit around a polished wooden table. The lights are very low. There are three men and five women. They're all smartly dressed. At one end of the table, a woman in her fifties, wearing some sort of elaborate turban, throws back her head, and her mouth opens. Something white and diaphanous begins to trail from her lips. Casson steps into the scene, agitated – angry? He pulls at the white matter, and flings it to the floor...

Karowski is by the projector, fitting a reel of film in there. "There was an old Italian guy who was dying. He lived not that far from Marco Fracassi, who--"

"I've met his son."

"Yeah, well, the son wouldn't know this bit."

"I'm sorry. Go on."

"So Emile has this idea. The dying guy has a daughter who doesn't think much of him, and they have no money. Zilch. Emile pays her so as he can film her father, Roberto something. Get this – Emile wanted to film the man dying. The actual moment. This Roberto doesn't know the time of day, even who he is; the daughter doesn't care. Louie says he'll operate the camera, but he doesn't like it."

"You took the man to the set in Warehouse H."

"We did. Emile says he's going to ask Roberto questions at the very end. It's like the Manhattan all over again, but controlled."

"That's... grotesque."

"Yeah. It was. Three of us, waiting, on a locked set. October 1926."

"What happened?"

"We did nothing for the first day except keep the guy clean and give him water. Emile gave him morphine if he seemed to be in pain, but not enough to knock him out..." He falters. "You can judge as much as you want. I don't suppose I've more than a year or two left in me. There was a Joe Karowski there, but I don't think I know him anymore."

"It's all right," I say softly.

He mutters something I don't catch, and starts the film.

THIRTY-SEVEN. The same set as Seventeen. The table used in Twenty-Eight can be seen shoved up against the back wall. It has what look like medical supplies on it. And a plate of sandwiches, one of them half-eaten. In the center of the scene is a pallet bed. The bed's occupant is hard to look at. A man, clearly old even before he developed whatever disease or condition reduced him to this gnarled, distorted figure.

"We shot seven reels with nothing much on them." Karowski clears his throat. "When Louie started on the eighth, things changed."

"That's the one on the record."

"Yeah. Emile was agitated. He paced a lot, and kept going to Roberto's side. He started asking questions. You can't hear most of them over the camera. He was whispering in the old guy's ear."

THIRTY-SEVEN. Casson enters the frame. He has a cup of water, which he puts to the man's lips. The water runs down and soaks the bed linen. Casson leans close, and seems to be speaking, but we can't see his lips. The figure on the bed has some kind of minor spasm, a clawed hand clutching the sheets. Casson is trembling. He takes hold of one thin shoulder, only the back of his head visible.

"Louie started swearing, saying he'd had enough. Emile kept muttering 'When?' and 'What do you see?' Over and over. I said we should give the guy another blast of morphine, let him go quietly, but Emile wasn't listening. Instead he pulls out this knife..."

THIRTY-SEVEN. The man on the bed —Roberto— stiffens. Casson is still leaning over him, blocking some of our view. The man's forehead glistens with sweat. His eyes, crusted around the lids, are very dark. The lens blurs and then focuses again, much closer to the dying man's face. Suddenly the man's eyes widen. His lips move, forming short sentences… and Casson moves back, disappearing from shot. As he does, we see the wound in Roberto's upper chest, the dark pulse of blood which runs from it... End of reel.

I realize I am shaking.

"He killed him. Casson killed him."

"Yes," says Karowski, his voice flat. "The guy was finished anyway, but Casson stuck him, to get his take."

"Those words, before the Italian dies—"

"I didn't get them on record. Louie grabbed what he could, disks and reels, and stormed off, cursing." He shudders. "I was too thrown to interfere. Of course, he forgot that the last reel was still in the camera. And he missed the master for your disk, I guess."

"Casson?"

"Emile was in a corner, staring into nothing. He didn't want to talk about it. Later, I helped him dump the body in the river. I was too shaken to argue."

"And after that?"

"The next day, he checked out of his hotel, and as far as I know, left the country. I never heard from him again. I 'borrowed' some of the sound gear for myself and got out of there. You know the rest."

He switches the lights back on and refills our glasses. We smoke a cigarette, and look at each other.

"I read lips," I say.

He shrugs, drawing on his cigarette, and then his eyes widen.

"So you..."

"I need to see it once more. Just once more."

He's unhappy about that, but he obliges. Afterwards he takes me through to a modest lounge, where he can sit on a sofa with his bad leg up. He wants to ask, but he doesn't want to. We sit in silence for three or four minutes.

"Okay," he says, straightening up. "Tell me."

"He talks about France —something about lost days, and a woman's name —Marguerite? He says 'Spain', then he says 'Madrid'. And, I think, 'March nine, 1937'."

Karowski looks angry. "You're playing me."

"No, honestly."

"It's Madrid. But you knew that, right?"

"No. I mean, I'm not even sure what I'm saying." The initial shock of what I've just seen has addled my brain, but things start to click. "Casson died in 1937, didn't he? That's a bit weird. I read he died at Guadalajara, with some International Brigade."

It was Casson's work that interested my aunt, not his end.

"Guadalajara's outside Madrid." Krakowski's voice is dull, a shocked rumble. "Emile was on the way to the front there, against the Italian fascists. He was shot in the chest by a sniper on the outskirts of the city, early on the ninth of March."

And now we both know.

Casson heard the date of his own death from the man he killed.

The old man and I have little more to say to each other. A record led me here, whipped on by an old woman with too much money and nothing better to do.

I stand up and shake his hand. This time he takes it, trembling with a question.

"Forget it all," I tell him. My decision's been made. "Mrs. Westercott will hear that Joseph Karowski remembers nothing. Film Thirty-Seven was nonsense, a failed film by a failed director."

"Thank you."

I find my own way out. On the street, kids are trashing a burnt-out Studebaker. I don't plan to visit East Harlem again. Back at the car, the same doorman grins at me. He has very blue, very Nordic eyes.

"I scored what I needed," I tell him, and drive away.

Aunt Marian will learn that the past is a dead end. And I don't imagine that her future holds a lot. I see her lying back on those lace-edged pillows for the last time, cheeks sunken and blue, disapproving of death like she disapproves of everything else. I should be horrified by what I've learned today, or full of more pointless questions. But as I drive home, I realize that I'm not.

I feel released.

As I turn the car towards Astoria, I wonder what my aunt will have to say in her final moments, what presentiments she might glimpse. There are many sharp knives in the apartment kitchen, the sort of knives a panicked burglar might grab…

I think I might like to be there at her end.

To read her lips.

UNDERGROUND

George Edwards Murray

The light of the Octorium was blinding. They had planned it that way. It contrasted with the dull orange of the torches that lined the stone w
Octorium, central in the vast sundial of the Reformatory, managed to glow so brightly, beautifully white, save for the roving silhouettes within. When Nikolai first came to the Reformatory it gave him a headache, but he was told that after six months it would subside. He was glad it still hurt a little.

Nikolai squinted as he ducked down to the Service Port and grabbed two trays. He had waited in line for twenty minutes. The only other Service Port, on the other side of the Pen, was closed. Andrei's body still lay in front of it. Nikolai walked back across the Pen, sure to smile and look to the beaming column and the hot-white windows through which hundreds of silhouettes passed in silent judgment. He got into the line for food and gave a tray to Gregor. Gregor let the tray dangle from one hand as he stared across the Pen at Andrei's body.

Nikolai nudged him. "Don't gawk. Things like this happen here."

Gregor turned back to Nikolai and said, "No, my friend. This happens nowhere."

"Well, it happens here."

Gregor's eyebrows danced and he said, in a variety of intonations, "*It* happens here. It *happens* here. It happens *here*," as they advanced toward the Food Port with the rest of the line. Nikolai kept his head down, subservient and compliant.

How much time, he thought, until the sentence is over? A year? Two? An hour? Only after madness sets in? And then would they tell him the reason for his incarceration? Had they even told Nadja?

In the Octorium a few shadows stopped and gazed. Whenever he and Nadja had been assigned to the Octorium for the day they had made a game of it, trying to find a handsome face on the Thief's Level, or a beard on the Juvenile Floor. And they would try to find a smile on the Traitor's level. That game had been the most difficult. It was why, now that he found himself on the other side of the glass, he smiled whenever he could. Anything to stand out. Anything to hint at reform.

The Reformatory was a prison in two parts. The first part, the structure itself; the pit of brick and mortar tunneling deep beneath the center of the city. The cylindrical prison comprised of the Octorium in the center, the open Pen around that, where the prisoners roamed most of the day. Spaced in the outermost ring were the dormitories of the condemned. Presumably there were also hallways beyond which attendants could roam and push through food and literature and medical aid.

The second part was the Shame. The Octorium: a dazzling column in the center of the Reformatory, like the axle of a wheel, covered in windows that blazed white, rendering the people inside a mob of faceless shadows. Each person in the city was expected to fulfill his or her civic duty, to wander the Octorium for at least one day a month, staring out into the mass of convicts as an anonymous, formless, specter. There were no locks in the Reformatory. No bars. The Octorium was enough. It was more humane, so the theory went. For one of those shadows was Nikolai's mother. Another, his father. All his past lovers. His neighbors, his teachers, his friends and enemies, all peering in to check his progress, to monitor his rehabilitation, to confirm that yes, Nikolai was reforming, yes, Nikolai was good. Nadja was perhaps there, and perhaps she was not, but would Nikolai ever take that risk? No, he would change, he would force himself to change, quietly struggling under the eye of the omnipotent *who knows?*

No one had ever escaped the Reformatory. No one ever wanted to. Who would escape the opportunity to become a better man? The reasoning was sound.

"Damn catastrophe," said Gregor, regarding Andrei's remains. The body lay on its back a quarter turn around the Pen, dripping through the iron-grate floor onto the thieves below, four feet of exposed intestine flopping to the side like a paralyzed limb. If Nikolai squinted, he could see the mushrooms dotting Andrei's organs like quaint villages on the side of a mountain.

Some men above and below stared through the grate floors and ceilings. It made Nikolai sick to look up or down for too long, to see through floor after floor of imprisoned men, shifting around like insects in a spider's web.

"Don't look," he said to Gregor. "It is disrespectful." His eyes flitted to the Octorium. Some more shadows had stopped to look, probably at Andrei, possibly at Nikolai. "We will take care of it after dinner."

"How do you think he got it?"

Nikolai bobbed his head to the Octorium. "You're here for Reform, Gregor. Leave medicine to the doctors."

"Who are you afraid of?" said Gregor, his mouth twisting into a bastard-smirk.

"I am only afraid of myself," said Nikolai, quoting from some pamphlet. "I am afraid of my own recidivism. Everything else is distraction."

Gregor groaned and banged his tray against his head. At the front of the line, one of the men started crying and shaking. He threw his tray to the side and walked briskly down the line, whimpering with his hand to his mouth. In the Octorium the shadows pointed and pressed their faceless heads to the glass. As the man entered his dormitory Nikolai saw the trio of mushrooms pushing through the skin of the man's wrist. He was tearing at his flesh before he closed the door.

Some men said it was in the food. Fungus thrives in moisture and what was wetter than the slop shoveled onto their trays each day? Those men took to gnawing on their pillows or shoes, retreating into hunger-madness before starving to death. Others said it was an affliction of touch, and they walked with their hands sucked inside their sleeves and hid in doorways and became specters, wasting away silently and without contact. Still others said it was a curse from God befitting enemies of the State.

For most, the end came when the mushrooms began to sprout in the brain. When Anatoli and Pavel had finished tearing each other apart there had been little left but blood and flesh and mushroom-spotted organs. Some, like Andrei, disassembled themselves. The peaceful remainder merely retreated into their dormitories and did not come out. Nikolai did not know what happened to those men. Nobody who witnessed those quiet deaths wanted to talk about it.

Gregor had told Nikolai, upon first hearing of the affliction, "It's the State that let it loose. They want to wipe us out with the damn things."

Nikolai did not believe such talk then nor did he believe it now, as he lay in his bed, one arm over his eyes, the dying candle slowly letting in the dark. It was not spread by food, for the sickness was random and sporadic, and even gripped those who elected to starve. It was not a disease of the touch, for Nikolai had handled each and every body, dragging them diligently to the Rubbish Portal like the upright citizen he was, and he had acquired nothing but a sense of righteousness.

And it was certainly not brought on by the State.

There was a knock, and when Nikolai cracked open

the door he was greeted by a mad eye darting in its socket.

"Nikolai," said the door.

"Yes, Gregor."

"Did you see them take Andrei away after we dragged him over to the Rubbish Port?"

"Yes." Like the Service Port and Medical Port and Food Port, the Rubbish Port was an iron door in the stone wall that only opened knee-high. Andrei had been pulled through by a group of anonymous hands.

"Did you notice anything?" Gregor asked.

"Notice what?"

"They wore gloves when they pulled him in."

"So?"

"They don't wear gloves when serving food or passing out books."

"So?"

"They were afraid to touch him."

"So?"

Gregor pounded on the door and rubbed the bridge of his nose with his fingertips.

"Nikolai," he said. "I'm talking about getting out of here."

Nikolai's chest froze and he looked to the Octorium. There they were, motionless black bodies and featureless heads, abyssal judges. And they had heard. They had heard and now the news would escape and climb all the way to the Emperor himself and the invisible ticker tracking his sentence would grind to a halt and spin back. And Nadja would see it all. Nikolai tried to slam the door, but Gregor stopped it with his foot.

"Listen to me," he said. "What happens if someone tries to slide out of a Rubbish Port?"

"Why would anyone try that?" said Nikolai, so that even those in the Octorium could hear.

"But what if someone did?"

"They'd get thrown back out. But this is not the place—"

"What if they can't throw you out? What happens if they're afraid to touch you?"

Nikolai shook his head. His mouth was dry. The musing was equivalent to drawing a plan, which was equivalent to doing the deed itself. How many months were being tacked on to his sentence as they spoke?

"Your mother might be in there, Gregor," said Nikolai, his eyes flickering to the Octorium.

"Mother's in the women's prison. You know that."

"Father, then."

Gregor laughed. "Good, I hope he's in there somewhere."

"Gregor, don't pull me into this. I'm here to serve my time."

"You're here because of a piece of shit that will die with the next revolution."

Nikolai gasped, more from fear of being caught than out of adulation for the Emperor, and some of the shadows in the Octorium shifted. One of them turned and Nikolai could see it was a woman with long hair and full breasts and his heart twitched and his breath caught in his mouth.

Gregor reached through the door and hit Nikolai, lightly, such that it could be interpreted as a friendly game from the viewpoint of the Octorium. Nikolai felt the malice in it.

"You're pathetic," Gregor said. "You can't think on your own. I bet you can't even love."

They were given books the next day. Despite himself, Nikolai had watched the hands that pushed them through the Service Port. Elegant and nude, with long fingers, skin so thin he could see the bones shifting beneath. They looked so fragile. After Nikolai handed the books out to his fellow inmates he locked himself in his dormitory and read for the rest of the day. He could not afford to be seen with Gregor, not for the moment.

The day's candle was burned to a nub and he was involved in the middle of *On Dissent: A Neutral and Balanced History*, written by the Emperor himself, when someone shrieked in the next dormitory over. Nikolai jumped and the book slid out of his hands and did a split on the floor, cracking the spine.

Another gurgling shriek accompanied the sound of breaking wood, of drawers tumbling to the ground and scattering papers. A neighboring tempest. Nikolai lay still. The storm did not abate, the pained growls growing louder, like an animal after a failed slaughter. Nikolai swung his feet over the bed and padded across the room towards the empty Pen. The din was excruciating, screaming so loud it seemed it would tear the vocal cords. Room 712. Dmitri. A boy of perpetually smooth chin, always shivering as if stranded on a mountain.

Nikolai rapped on Dmitri's door and called his name, but the screaming continued until it devolved into rasps and whimpers. Nikolai pressed the lever and pushed the door and, upon seeing the wretch before him, stumbled backward. The boy quivered on the floor, hands to his stomach, his glassy eyes fixed on the doorway, curly hair slicked down with sweat. His swollen belly rose out of his pajamas, pink like a sunset. He looked like a woman with child. His abdomen gurgled and occasionally swelled like it was breathing.

Nikolai stepped in and grabbed Dmitri's hand and said to him, "I'll get you over to the Medical Port."

Dmitri gagged and nodded. Careful not to touch the boy's stomach, Nikolai picked him up and started the journey to the other side of the Pen. A few of the homosexuals played cards in the sky while some thieves told quiet stories in the underworld. Both groups glanced at the pair as Nikolai staggered across the Pen.

"I'm going to die," slurred Dmitri.

"No, boy. They'll fix you right up," Nikolai said.

"They don't want me fixed."

"Of course they do. They built the Reformatory to fix you."

"I'm not talking about them." The boy gestured to his stomach. "I mean them." Nikolai looked down and bit his tongue. Dmitri's stomach bubbled like a cauldron as dozens of mushrooms strained to break free, jostling and pushing just beneath the skin.

"You know," said Dmitri, teeth gritted, stomach straining, "we had something like this back on the farm before we were relocated."

"You don't say."

"Yeah. Whole mess of mushrooms got up in the woodwork of the house and started eating it from the inside out. Papa figured it was because of the wet summer we had. They were everywhere. Popping out where wall met floor, or in door jambs. Sometimes they grew in our books." The boy grimaced and shifted, and his stomach made a growling sound.

"What did you do?" asked Nikolai.

"Papa reasoned that he should tear out all the infested boards and put in fresh ones."

"Did it work?"

Dmitri heaved and gagged. Little creeks of red began to form across his belly. "When he tried to remove them the mushrooms burst and got in the air and spread through the rest of the house and into the fields. They got into Papa's lungs and killed him. It's like they were waiting for us to try and take them out, just so they could spread."

Ahead, the door of the Medical Port slid up to reveal a forest of white-clad feet and beckoning gloves. Nikolai quickened his pace. Dmitri panted, and his stomach rumbled and shifted. Now the men below and above had ceased their activities and watched as Nikolai set Dmitri down. The first hand reached through the door, grasped the boy by the ankle, and began to pull him in.

Dmitri's eyes rolled back and he shook all over, and the hand that grasped him dropped his foot. The Medical Port slammed shut. The slits of red on Dmitri's belly widened into blazing fissures as his gut swelled and blood poured from his mouth.

Nikolai grabbed his hand, as if the comfort would halt the sickness, but Dmitri's belly pulsed and swelled and rose, skin splitting until it erupted. A cloud of moist red dust rose from the husk of the boy, coating both Nikolai and the walls —and all the men above and below, who began to flee in terror, swiping frantically at their clothes.

Nikolai only stood in place, skin sticky, stomach curling up into his throat. The body was barely visible in the carmine mist. The skin of Dmitri's chest spread out at his side in ragged swaths, and his ribs rose from his torso like stained talons. Inside his exposed abdomen, mushrooms clumped together in orbs the size of skulls, pushing organs to the side, straining against bone, leeching on flesh. They stank of decay. Nikolai collapsed to the floor, his knees splashing in muck, and was sick. When he was done, he turned away from the corpse and staggered, coughing, to the Cleaning Port. He pounded on the door and stripped, and as he waited for the cleansing water his skin burned from the light of the Octorium.

He did not sleep for hours, fearing he would have nightmares, but when he finally drifted away there instead came a dream of Nadja. It was primal and animalistic and wonderful. Somewhere in the vestiges of waking logic, Nikolai knew the State would disapprove, that the things he was doing to her were shameful, that women were vital to the preservation of the state and should not be touched in any way but for the production of children. But in the dream, her skin was hot, and he could taste her sweat and hear the sharp cry of his name as he reveled in the curves of her buttocks, the rhythmic bounce of her breasts, and he had her a thousand times, in a thousand ways, each time basking in her abject ecstasy, of which he was Lord, and she his worshipper, and he burned with love so deep it pained him, for there was no possession of her that was enough to overcome his desire.

Amid the carnality, the heaving, the bestial grunts, the singular thought rang out: I don't give a damn about your reason.

Nikolai's heart plunged and he awoke in darkness. Sweat ran down his face. Nadja was gone. His stomach writhed and he vomited on the floor. As he finished retching, the hot liquid on the floor, mired in darkness, squirmed into life. Shadows upon shadows, but nonetheless unmistakable: dozens of mushrooms writhed in the vomit, shaking their stalks like tails to propel themselves.

Nikolai yelped and flung open the drawer of his bedside table and fumbled for a match. He could hear them squealing, slithering over each other in the filth. They made a sound like mating birds, so loud, so unpredictable, so dangerous and organic. His fingers pinched a match and he struck it against his table, and when finally safe in the aura of light he saw only the splattered remnants of the day's meals. His heartbeat pulsed in his neck and ears, and for some shaking minutes he thought perhaps the things had scampered beneath his bed, until logic crept back into the room and the world was ordinary once more. Mushrooms did not crawl, Nadja was not in his arms, and the State was probably infallible.

In a few days the smell of Dmitri had faded into an earthy kind of musk but it never went away, no matter how long Nikolai stood in the spray of the Cleaning Port. It was soaked into his skin. The other inmates took circuitous routes around him. They backed into walls as he walked by. They read their books and played cards on the other side of the Pen. They were like becalmed ships, and he Apollo, threatening a thousand days of unbroken sun. His Goodness did not make up for being Different.

A week later as he stood in line for a meal, bleary-eyed and reeking, Gregor said, "What happened when you tried to put Dmitri through the Port?"

It was the first time anyone had asked. "Nothing," Nikolai said.

"Did the Med Team touch him?"

"Why don't you have a tray?"

Gregor grinned and held out his hands, fingers curved like claws. "I want them to put it right in my hands and I want them to watch me eat it like an animal."

"They won't serve you without a tray."

"So they'll have me starve?"

"Get a tray."

"No. I want to see what happens."

"Don't you care?" Nikolai asked. The Octorium hummed.

"What if I don't? What would they do? They didn't plan for me not to care." And when Nikolai looked away and stepped forward in line, Gregor asked, "What did Dmitri say to you?"

Nikolai put up a hand, and before Gregor could ask again, the air popped and hissed, and throughout the Reformatory resounded the stentorian voice of the Emperor.

"Salutations and good tidings to you all," he said, as walls shivered and grates flexed and men leapt up like dogs searching for their master.

"Impossible," said Gregor.

"There are pipes in the walls," said Nikolai, relieved to be free of the discussion of Dmitri. "He's speaking from the top of the Reformatory into a horn and the pipes carry the sound downward." He did not know if this was true, but it was better than assuming magic.

"My subjects," continued the Emperor. "It has been brought to my attention that there have been some concerns regarding the safety of your Reformatory. Despite what you may think you know, I promise there is no safer place in the city, and indeed the whole kingdom, than this place, here and now, deep below the surface of the earth. This is a place of order, not madness. Healing, not illness. Creation, not destruction. Your loved ones pass through this place every day in the hopes of witnessing your redemption. Do not disappoint them with your doubt and fear. Peace be with you, and may order and reason prevail."

The voice stopped as if it had been clipped, and the walls rumbled no more. Gregor leapt up and pointed to the various ports around the Pen. "Ha ha! They're scared now! The Emperor himself feels he needs to quell our fears! What do you think that means?"

"We shouldn't be thinking anything, Gregor." But somehow Nikolai could not look at the hopping, dancing maniac, could not look into his eyes and tell him absolutely that he was a fool. He could only think of Dmitri. For a moment, Nikolai felt like praying.

Gregor leaned so close his nose almost touched Nikolai's, and he said, "We shall coat ourselves in the blood of the next infected, and when they open the Medical Port we shall slide out untouched."

When Nikolai said nothing, Gregor straightened and looked down his nose. "Very well, if you don't want to see Nadja again, if you think you deserve to be here with the thieves and blasphemers and prostitutes, then you can sit here. As for me, I'm strolling out."

He took five steps before he started to shake.

Nobody from the State came to help after the slaughter. Ignored were the hurled pieces of flesh, the blood smeared all over the grates and walls and the Octorium itself, running down the glass in long crimson vines, on all floors from top to bottom, such that there was a hot drizzle for hours. The afflicted had torn through skin, through muscles, biting each other, twisting joints, pulling limbs out of sockets, cracking bones, flaying each other with butter knives. All at once, an explosion of red. As flesh was rent and organs ripped, a torrent of mushrooms fell and rolled across the floor and made a sound like thunder.

The ones who escaped the slaughter had taken shelter in their dormitories, and when it was over only Nikolai was left alive in the Pen, bizarrely untouched, soaked in blood, cowering next to the Rubbish Port.

When it was apparent no help would arrive, Nikolai stepped out slowly, as if emerging from a chrysalis. He walked across the grate, the iron sticking to his feet and leaving red grids upon the soles. The carnage was total and fearsome. Some victims were no longer men so much as leaking mounds of meat and bone. Severed fingers lay scattered across the floor and sometimes fell from the grate above. The air was humid with blood. Nikolai walked until he found Gregor. He had died with his mouth agape, hands clasped to retain his escaping entrails. A half-dozen mushrooms huddled together in his throat. Their aroma was different than Dmitri's—sweet and seductive, almost like wine. Nikolai's stomach twitched. He could feel the blood around him. Dizziness, a rush of a thousand thoughts, a pleading to understand. Worthless time passed, and Nikolai found himself on his bed, not caring that his sheets were moist and warm with blood. He could not clean this; could not clean away this violence. With the whole Reformatory mad, what point would there even be? And what would Nadja think of him, that he was grouped with such animals?

He had to leave. Here was where beasts were made, not cured. He would escape and throw himself at the mercy of the Emperor, make an appeal to order. Surely this violence could not live outside the Reformatory.

Surely its life was meant to begin and end here, in this place of madness.

Nikolai lay in bed and waited.

The Pen was still dripping with blood when he reopened his door. His bare feet made peeling noises as he walked to Gregor's body. He knelt and pulled Gregor's granite-cold hands aside and exposed the torn flesh. He glanced at the Octorium. Each window held within it a static silhouette. They all wanted to watch. Nikolai put his back to them, gritted his teeth, and plunged his hands deep within the wound, soaking his hands, the lumps of mushrooms slick beneath his fingertips, before pulling out and smearing liquid warmth on his face and arms.

Without turning back to the Octorium, Nikolai lifted Gregor and carried him to the nearest Rubbish Port, as if to dispose of the body. The metered echo of his footsteps in the slick emptiness was the music of order, of righteousness, of model citizenship. He placed Gregor's body at the Rubbish Port and crouched and banged on the door with a coated fist. Beyond the wall there was a shuffling of feet and some murmuring. For a moment Nikolai feared they would not dare open the Port, dreading the red haze that still hung within the Reformatory.

Eventually the iron flap slid open and four gloved hands, awash in alabaster light, grabbed the corpse by the foot and began to tug it through the Port. Nikolai's legs quaked, and the transgression suddenly seemed impossible. The shame welled up in his body, the piercing glare of his mother and father and all his peers just behind him. He thought to sit down and weep, but Gregor was now through the port up to his waist, and the sweat from Nikolai's brow made simmering lines down his face, and he thought of Nadja, perfect, pure, surely waiting, and then Gregor was through to his neck, and in a burst of speed Nikolai dove through the Port.

He tucked and rolled and found himself in a marble hallway. As he skidded to a halt, he marveled at the torches that lined the walls. Great iron things, their starlight flames each taller than a man. It was like being back in the Octorium. Like being back in a normal life.

And like demons, his captors stood over him —men and women with long blond hair and white masks, and coveralls spattered with blood. They stared at his dripping face and arms, stammering, and when Nikolai leapt up and swiped his hands across their faces, they cried out in fear and shrank away, praying. Nikolai laughed. The power was good, in that the power was goodness, in that Nikolai was a beam of light in darkness, passing through this purgatory a new man. Emboldened, he reached into Gregor and plucked a dozen mushrooms, and as the guards frantically wiped away the blood Nikolai ran through the curving hallway. Ecstatic, loosed, unbound. Soon he was sprinting up a flight of stairs and then he was on the floor of thieves, ports snapping past in blurs. He made almost a full revolution before he came to another set of stairs and ascended once more.

Torches whipped by in flashes as Nikolai flew ever

toward the surface and reason and his beloved. Some more demons appeared now, trying to halt his descent, bound head-to-toe in protective leather, as were books, only without wisdom, without insight, and Nikolai cast the mushrooms from his hands like an aspersion of holy water. They scattered and he laughed, for in his pocket he had grenades unlike anything with which the State could contend. It gave nightmares to demons and spooks and all manner of foolish things that had haunted him in times before. Times no longer. He let a few more mushrooms fall behind him.

At last he reached the exit, a towering door of gold, upon which was etched the visage of the Emperor, frowning as the sun shone from behind his throne. Nikolai grabbed a brass handle and dragged the door open and stepped into the night of the city.

It was like breathing for the first time.

The streets were dark. His toes were cold on the cobblestone, and somewhere in the distance a horse trotted before the rumbling wheels of a carriage. Behind, the Reformatory was a mere copper door set within the base of a statue of the Emperor sitting on his throne. The figure glowered in moonlight.

Exhausted, exhilarated, Nikolai sat on the ground and let the cool of night cradle his thoughts. From the top of the statue an alarm bell sounded. It was the first time it had been used. The garrison would come soon. Could he find Nadja before then? Nikolai was not even sure where she would be.

His throat hurt. He doubled over and coughed so hard his eyes bulged and his throat became tight with some obstruction. He coughed again and a pulsating mushroom fell into his open hand. Nikolai's skin flushed with terror, then a strange peace washed over him as the thing unfurled. Nikolai chuckled and threw it into the dark. He did not see where it landed. And from the Reformatory came a sound like a rush of water, and a thousand voices calling for him to listen to reason.

Lydia

Cindy O'Quinn

"Did I ever tell you about the time I walked into your room?"

Lydia stared dead ahead and did not acknowledge her sister's presence in the room, much less the question she had asked.

Rose continued. "I was thirteen, so that would have made you nine, almost ten. I remember, because it was the year after Mom almost killed Dad.

"Anyway, I walked into that pitiful little room of yours. Remember, you had the one at the end of the hall? The paint on the walls was horribly cracked, and regardless of repainting, the cracks came back like dark veins, bleeding through under thin skin. I don't even think it was a bedroom at all, more like a storage closet, but you were so excited to have your own room when we moved into that old house.

"I walked in, not all the way, but just inside the door, and there you were on the floor, your stubby little index finger in a wad of your ginger hair, twirling it round and round. It was a nervous habit, one that you held onto for years. And you had these makeshift dolls, fucking hideous monsters would be closer to the truth, and you were talking to them. They were lined up in a row, at least three of them, and you were whispering so soft and sweet to them, like they were precious little angels. Do you want to know what else you did? You leaned over real close and put your ear next to one of the dolls' mouths. That image haunts me to this day; it's burned into me, and I'll not soon forget it. I get chills thinking about that grotesque thing possibly murmuring to you, speaking some angel or demon language that only you, its creator, could understand. Did they speak to you? Did they call out your name when they grew lonesome without you near?

"I left your room without saying a word, because I was afraid. Afraid of you, Lydia, my little sister, the one I was supposed to protect and look after. I watched you all the time after that. It's hard to believe, but you never knew it, you never felt me near. Maybe you did. I watched as you gathered parts to make more of your little followers, or whatever they were. Rubber arms tossed from passing car windows along the road, decapitated plastic heads that were shaved and no longer wanted, left in the park. You hit the jackpot at the town dump. Entire dolls sometimes, but you still rearranged them with other parts. Old marbles for eyes, buttons for ears, scissors, and even a machete for an arm. All held together with string, electrical tape, and school glue. And they were never complete until you painted their nails black like your own. In the end, you had six little ones as your captive audience. More than just a tidbit creepy, sis.

"We never really talked about religion; it was another one of those things that I just assumed. I mean, we each wore the tiny wooden cross necklaces on leather cords; I thought you knew what that represented. Do you remember that Christmas when the Baptist church ladies brought those and other gifts for us? I don't think Mom would have accepted the presents from them had we not been peeking in from the kitchen. I'm not sure why, but it was as if she thought the gifts were poisoned by those women. I don't mean literally, but they weren't given with the best of intentions or something. Hell, I'm not sure what I mean. I do know that within a few months, one-by-one, those gifts disappeared. All but the necklaces around our necks.

"Do you remember how Dad cried when Mom made him leave? It wasn't long after she'd nearly killed him. I wondered if maybe you knew why she wanted him dead. I didn't know a man could cry like that. I had never seen it before, and I haven't since. He cried himself a river, and then he got drunk and almost drowned in it. How twisted is that? Our dad drowning in a river of tears, or a bathtub. Whatever. People don't stay together forever anymore, not husbands and wives anyway. For years I blamed Mom for making Dad leave. I knew there couldn't be a reason good enough for her to split up our family. I hated her for not telling me. I convinced myself there wasn't a reason, she was just being a bitch, a ding dang bitch. Remember, we used to say ding dang to everything? We were happy then, ding dang it!

"Surely you remember Mom losing her mind. What a

fine and dandy time that was. It was just enough to bring the church ladies back here to have another lookie-loo. They certainly got more than they came for when Mom told them that their snooping hadn't worked when they had been sent by our dear old dad, and it sure as hell wasn't going to work now that he was gone.

"Lydia, that interaction between Mom and the church ladies confused me for a good while, but it eventually came to me. Dad had found religion, and those gifts were from him. That's why Mom wanted rid of them, and she would have done away with every last one, had we both not kept those crosses around our necks all the time. I tried to get all the answers out of her, but her end was so near, it was useless. Her eyes were glazed over like one of your zombie dolls. And then, poof —Mom was gone too.

"I was eighteen, so of course I was given guardianship over my little sister. Oh, how sweet it was in the beginning. You loved me then. Just me taking care of my fragile younger sister. Fragile or not, those hideous creations of yours had to go. What would people have thought? That you were weird, and I couldn't have that. The good people in the neighborhood wouldn't have donated to weird, but they certainly donated to orphans. That's what we were, you know? Everyone in the neighborhood, as well as the church ladies, had a field day doting over us. And the donations seemed endless. All good things eventually end, or whatever the hell that saying is.

"You grew up and wanted to leave. Leave me. The fragile little girl, who'd grown up talking to angels that were made from her love and plastic parts that no one else wanted. Ungrateful! You were so ungrateful. If you only knew what I did for you. I kept Dad happy, I kept him from visiting your pitiful little room late at night. And when Mom went crazy, I kept you safe from catching her madness. It was contagious as hell. I bet you didn't know that."

Lydia sat stiff, ankles permanently crossed, hands folded neatly in her lap. A rusted zipper served as her no longer speaking mouth, mismatched marbles where eyes used to be. Dozens of smelly cardboard pine trees hung in her hair and on her clothes, held in place with clothes pins, a failing effort to mask the rot. Rose added a fresh coat of black polish to her sister's yellowed nails to match her own.

ANGELMUTTER

David Surface

You can't kidnap your own baby, can you? That was the question on Maya's mind as she steered her car through the dark over the serpentine twists and turns of 31-E.

It had all started when Kaitlyn wouldn't stop crying. Maya had tried everything: the bottle, the pacifier, picking her up and carrying her around their cramped little apartment until the muscles in her back ached. The desperation had started to rise, the one she knew would turn into anger, until she remembered the car—the baby always fell asleep in the car. Maya had wrapped her up in a soft blue blanket, gently lifted her into the infant carrier, and brought it out to the back seat of the old Camry. She was just going to drive around the block a few times, but there were too many stop signs, and Kaitlyn had kept squirming and complaining, so Maya took the next exit onto the highway, she took it. Soon Kaitlyn had stopped complaining, and Maya was flying along in blessed silence, feeling the steady hum of the highway in her bones.

As the lights of the town disappeared behind her, a thick and heavy darkness seemed to swallow the little car, turning the windshield in front of her into a mirror. She could see the bones of her face lit up from below by the green dashboard lights, and suddenly she was back on one of those wild rides from not so long ago, the air filled with sweet smoke, loud music, and the laughter of friends, the silver metallic taste of vodka warm in her throat. She reached out automatically to turn on the radio, then she stopped, remembering the baby asleep in the back seat.

The glowing numbers on the dashboard said 11:40. She pictured Brad's red, angry face, and the feeling of peace vanished. Ever since Kaitlyn was born, Brad had treated her like a different person, hovering over her, judging her every move. She knew that all this caution and watchfulness was not for her sake. When he'd made her quit her job at the record store so she could stay home and take care of their daughter, he'd said, *You're a mother now,* and it sounded like a prison sentence.

Still, there were good moments, like those nights when Kaitlyn finally stopped crying and Maya would walk the floor, holding their two heads close together, so close that she believed she could feel her daughter's brain working, feel her young thoughts blinking on-and-off inside her little skull like fireflies.

When Maya glanced down again at the clock and saw the time, 12:00 AM, she felt a pang of alarm. Brad's shift was over, and he'd be home soon. Before Kaitlyn, he used to stay out till two or three in the morning, drinking with his friends. Now he came home early every night to check up on Kaitlyn, and on her. Had the baby been fed? How long had she slept? Why the hell did she let the baby sleep so much during the daytime?

Maya tried to explain that she was exhausted and needed to sleep, which was true. She also told Brad she slept when the baby slept, which was *not*. She meant to, but the moment she saw that soft, steady breathing take over and sweet silence fill the apartment, Maya would feel a surge of energy in her veins like the one she used to feel on those nights when she and Brad would share a few lines of blow and stay up all night, talking, listening to loud music, and fucking till dawn. Now whenever she found herself alone in the late hours, awake and alive, she felt a ghost of that same rush, that same kind of trembling on the edge of something incredible just about to happen. Then Kaitlyn would wake up crying again, and that feeling of freedom would vanish.

12:45 AM. She pictured Brad pulling into their driveway, wondering why the hell her car wasn't there, then entering the apartment and walking from room to room, calling her name. She remembered the last time he'd come home and found her gone. She'd left the baby for a few minutes to walk to the Quick Mart for a six-pack. Kaitlyn had kept her on her feet all night, crying for hours, and she was damned if she was going to go without a couple of beers after all that. So she'd waited till Kaitlyn cried herself to sleep, then slipped out the door and walked fast along the railroad tracks to the store. It was only a hundred yards away, not far at all, but there was a crowd at the register, stoned college kids, so it took her longer than she'd anticipated. By the time she got back to the apartment, there was Brad's old red truck parked in the gravel lot, home from work an hour early. He'd made Maya step inside the bathroom with him and shut the door before he hit her—he said it wasn't something a baby girl should see.

Maya didn't realize how far she'd gone until the sign for Smith's Grove rose up in her headlights and sped away behind her. She was in Barren County, almost seventy miles from home. What would happen if she just kept going? What would Brad do? What *could* he do? They weren't divorced, not yet. Kaitlyn was still her child. She couldn't be charged with a crime, no matter how late she stayed out or how far she drove. She could do whatever she wanted.

You are the most selfish little bitch in the whole world.

It was her mother's voice, cold and cutting as the edge of a knife. When Maya was seventeen, her mother had pretended to be her older sister for almost a year, and made her play along. Maya's father had left, and her mother was afraid that any new man would be frightened off by a woman with a teenage daughter. Once when Maya slipped up in public and called her *Mom*, her mother had struck her across the mouth. The man she was with had turned pale and vanished.

See what you did? her mother had hissed at her in that terrible voice. *You are the most selfish little bitch.*

A wave of nausea and exhaustion washed through her and the road in front went black for a moment. Quickly, she pulled the car over to the side of the road and sat there, taking deep, shaky breaths, the engine idling. How far from home was she? How many nights since she'd slept? The scene in front of her, the long grey road and the black trees on either side, flickered like a lightbulb that was about to go out. She would never make it back home this way.

Digging deep into her purse, she dragged out the plastic baggie with five or six black capsules rattling inside, took one out and broke it open. She shook the white powder onto the back of her left hand, lifted it to her nose and snorted it fast, feeling the bitter burn trickle down the back of her throat, then the rush of power that seemed to rise from the soles of her feet all the way up to her brain. Black Beauties. She'd found them in a drawer a few months earlier, souvenirs from another life. Everyone else took what they needed. Why shouldn't she? Didn't she deserve that?

A choked cry from the backseat drove her heart into her throat. She twisted around and saw Kaitlyn writhing fitfully in the car seat, her tiny fists balled up. *"Shit,"* Maya hissed. Why hadn't she brought a pacifier or a bottle of formula?

You wouldn't need a bottle, Brad had told her, if she would only do *what comes naturally.* Maya had tried *what comes naturally* and had hated it. That pinching greedy mouth, her nipple cut and bruised between boney gums. *Never again,* she'd thought. Now, alone on a dark highway with a crying, hungry infant, she almost regretted her choice.

It was the idea of another creature, another human being *feeding* on her...there was just something inherently disgusting about it to her. More than disgusting; frightening. That was how she'd felt with that small, pinching mouth latched onto her—frightened. She knew it wasn't how a mother was supposed to feel, but she couldn't help it. Her own mother had surely never done that for her.

When Maya was eighteen, her mother had disappeared, taking the money she had been saving for college. She had fallen apart for a while after that. That was when Brad had found her. She'd sworn to him and to herself that she would never be that kind of mother. Her child deserved better.

A loud scream from the back seat brought Maya back to the present. Her first reaction was fright, followed by irritation, then guilt and a low-burning resentment. *Why can't you just go to sleep?*

Kaitlyn was screaming full throttle now, the shrillness ricocheting off the car windows, drilling into her ears. Maya looked at the clock—almost 2 AM. She tried to judge the time it would take to get back home, but her mind wasn't working. She peered ahead through the dirty windshield, looking for a road sign or some source of light. Service station markets sold formula, didn't they? For people like her. Of course they did.

Maya reached around to touch Kaitlyn's head. The skin beneath her hand was scorching hot.

Twisting around to the back seat, Maya felt a jolt of fear. Kaitlyn's face was burning bright red, and between her cries, Maya could hear a harsh, rasping sound.

Throwing the car into drive, she pulled back out onto the highway, tires spitting dirt and gravel. A hospital. There had to be a hospital somewhere, an emergency room open all night. But she didn't know this part of the country, so she just kept driving deeper and deeper into the night, searching for some kind of light, while Kaitlyn's harsh cries filled her ears.

Her heart, still pounding from the Black Beauties, felt like it was going to explode.

She could see it now, the police finding her car crumpled against a tree, or lost in the middle of a cornfield, flashlights bobbing and weaving through the darkness, stabbing through the driver's window and finding her body slumped against the steering wheel. Would there still be a faint cry in the back seat? She could see the ruined car door being pried open, strange arms reaching in and pulling the baby free, lifting her to safety. If it was going to happen, Maya thought, let it happen like that.

When a light rose up out of the darkness ahead of her, a sob of relief burst from her throat. A low cinderblock building came into view with a single light burning at the end of a high wooden pole, two old-fashioned gas pumps rusting at the corner of a cracked asphalt lot. Maya pulled into the lot and saw that one side of the building was open, hubcaps and fenders on the rear wall, coiled rubber hoses hanging from the ceiling like black jungle vines.

Maya got out, ran to the edge of the light and stopped. There was a man inside; huge, bearded, and shirtless, working on a large tire that he held between his knees.

"Please..." Maya said, "Is there a hospital around here? My baby...she's sick..."

The man's eyes flicked up at her face for a second, then back down at his work. Maya watched him take a swab at the end of a long wooden dowel, dip it into a bucket of thick black liquid, then rub it slowly over the inside of the tire.

"Please," She spoke louder, wondering if the man was deaf. "My baby is sick. She's really sick..."

Putting the tire down, the man glared at her, stood up,

and disappeared without a word through a small door in the back wall. A moment later, a woman with a gaunt, weathered face appeared in the doorway. She stared cautiously at Maya, unsmiling. "Where's the baby?" she asked in a flat, hard-sounding voice.

"She's in the car..." Maya looked away, afraid to face the judgement in the woman's eyes. *What kind of mother leaves her sick child in the back seat of a car?* The woman said nothing, but followed Maya out to her car. Maya unsnapped the car seat straps and picked Kaitlyn up. Her eyes were glazed and half-closed, and her breaths were now coming in harsh, irregular rasps.

"Please," Maya said, "Is there a doctor here? Anybody?"

The woman stared down at the baby in Maya's arms. "Wait here," she said, in the same flat voice. Then she turned and walked back through the door in the rear wall and closed it behind her.

The garage was full of the stink of oil and gasoline, so Maya stepped outside to wait in the open air. The woman was going to call somebody. A doctor, or maybe someone who knew where to find one. She wouldn't just leave her here like this. She was going to help her. She had to.

Kaitlyn was almost completely silent now, still

burning hot in Maya's arms. Maya lifted her head and stared into the single light burning high above her, at the halo of bugs whirling and pinging around the white hot bulb. How had she gotten here? Why was this happening to her? Her back was aching, and her arms had started to tremble. She knew she was being tested. She'd failed every test till now. She was not going to fail this one.

The light above her shrank smaller and smaller to a pinpoint and began to blink on-and-off. A heaviness seemed to rise up from the ground through the soles of her feet and through her whole body, threatening to pull her down. She had to stay awake now. She had to.

Putting Kaitlyn back in the car seat, she dug the plastic bag out of her purse again, broke open another black capsule and sniffed the bitter white powder from the back of her hand. She held her breath and shut her eyes tight against the terrifying galloping of her heart.

The sound of gravel popping and crunching under four wheels made her open her eyes to the glare of headlights swinging toward her. Once the car had stopped, the driver left the headlights on, so Maya had to lift one hand above her eyes to see the small figure getting out and walking toward her out of the glare. When the figure came closer, she could see a small woman with close-cropped gray hair. The woman wore faded blue jeans and a white cotton shirt, and peered at Maya intently through large, thick lenses.

"You the one with the baby?" the small woman said.

"Yes…are you a doctor?"

The small woman scowled and shook her head. "Registered nurse. Where's your baby?"

Maya led the woman to the car where Kaitlyn lay quietly in the back seat. The woman scowled disapprovingly, reached down and touched the baby's head, and her scowl softened to a look of concern. "How long's she been like this?"

"I don't know," Maya said, "a few hours. She was fine before..."

The woman knelt down beside the car, touched the baby's chest and stomach, leaned closer and put her face against Kaitlyn's to feel her breath, then laid her head against her tiny chest for a long while. Maya stood and watched, feeling stupid and useless.

When the woman finally stood up, she sighed, then looked Maya in the eye.

"What's your name, sweetheart?"

"Maya."

"My name's Cora. Maya, your daughter has an infection. It's serious. Where's your home?"

"Owensboro..." Maya could barely get the name out.

"Owensboro..." the woman scowled, glancing back down at the baby lying still in the back seat.

"There's a hospital in Franklin..." Maya said. Cora shook her head slowly.

"That's too far. It'll take too long to get there."

Maya listened hard, trying to understand. When she realized what the woman was saying, her whole body began to tremble. "No! Please...you've got to help her!"

The woman sighed again; her lips set grimly. "I can try to make her comfortable..."

"No!" Maya cried out, "She was fine this morning...she was fine..." She repeated it over and over again, as if the words could change what the woman was telling her, change what was happening. Then the light was growing smaller again, dwindling down to a tiny point that dimmed and flickered out.

When Maya could see again, she was looking up into Cora's face, so close that she could see her own, reflected and distorted in the woman's thick glasses.

"You better lie still a while," Cora said. "How long since you slept?"

"My baby...where's my baby?"

"She's right here."

Maya reached out and held onto the woman's wrist. "Please. Don't let my baby die. Please...Don't let her die."

The older woman slowly removed her glasses and rubbed her eyes. She seemed weary; as weary as Maya felt. She looked away into the darkness for a long time, as if she was trying to decide something. When she put her glasses back on and regarded Maya again, there was something different about her, something softer and more open.

"Do you think you can come with me somewhere right now?" the woman asked. "Do you feel strong enough to do that?"

A few minutes later, Maya was sitting in the passenger seat of Cora's car, holding her daughter tightly in her lap. They drove past a few old, weathered houses that quickly disappeared behind them, and soon they were in the old, dark country again. Maya didn't ask where she was being taken; she knew somehow that she was not supposed to ask.

It was Cora who broke the silence. "How did you come here? I mean, how was it you came to be here tonight?"

"I don't know. My baby wouldn't sleep. She wouldn't stop crying. So I just put her in the car and started driving..."

"And you ended up here." The older woman nodded to herself as if Maya had just explained something important.

Maya looked down at Kaitlyn's face. In the dim light from the dashboard, it looked drained of color, ghostly. When she realized she couldn't feel Kaitlyn breathing, Maya almost cried out, then she saw the baby's mouth twitch and watched a tremor run through her tiny body. When Maya could speak again, she asked, "Where are we going? I thought you said there was no hospital near here."

The older woman said nothing. They rode in silence for a while. Finally, she nodded at something outside the window.

"Here we are."

Maya looked outside and saw what looked like a huge barn door made of old gray wood and rusty metal. When they drove closer, she could see that the door was built right into the side of a hill, like one of those old-fashioned icehouses, although she'd never seen one this large before. There was a huge metal bolt across the door, holding it shut.

The woman turned the ignition off but didn't get out. They sat there in the terrible silence for a long time before Cora spoke.

"Maya...I have to ask you some questions. First, I

need you to promise me something. You need to promise me that you'll answer them truthfully." Cora turned her gaze away from the giant door outside and looked at Maya. "...Because I think maybe that's something you've had some trouble with. I mean, it's been hard for you at times. Am I right?"

Maya couldn't speak. She nodded once. Cora continued.

"So, it's really important for you to be honest with me now. Can you do that?"

Maya nodded again.

"Alright then," Cora said, "Do you have any people out there? I mean, people who depend on you?"

Maya thought of Brad sitting alone in their apartment, watching the clock and getting drunker, and the hell that was waiting for her there.

"No," she said.

"No father? Or mother?"

I don't know, was what Maya almost said. But instead she shook her head again.

"No."

Cora continued to study her face. Then she sighed again. "Well... come on, then." Cora got out of the car and walked around to open the passenger door. Maya got out carefully, still holding her daughter.

She could see now that they were standing in a kind of circular clearing. The sky was a black bowl of stars over her head. Walls of rough-hewn rock surrounded them—a quarry. She knew then that whatever was behind that giant door hadn't been dug out of the earth, but out of solid rock.

When they were closer to the big door, Cora stopped and turned to face Maya. She laid her hand again on Kaitlyn's head, then her chest. She looked back at the big door behind them, then turned and looked into Maya's eyes.

"Maya…How strong a woman are you? Because you're going to need that now."

Maya didn't know how to answer. The older woman studied her face for a while. Then, seeming to have found whatever she was looking for, she walked over to the big door and dragged back the thick metal bolt. Maya felt a damp, chill breeze as the big door swung open. Clutching her daughter closer to her chest, she followed Cora into the dark.

For a long time, Maya could see nothing. She didn't understand how the older woman could see where she was going, but she stayed close to her, following the sound of her footsteps on the rough rock floor.

Before long, the chill seemed to fade, and the air around them became warmer. A heavy animal smell she couldn't identify filled her nostrils, along with a sweet cloying scent that reminded her of funeral flowers.

Maya could hear other noises: soft shuffling and sliding sounds in the dark, and what sounded like faint, guttural animal voices echoing around her. The sounds were closer now, coming from directly in front. She felt Cora's hand on her arm.

"Stop. Just stand right here."

There was a quick scratching noise, then a small bright flame sputtering to life. Cora was holding an old kerosene lantern, adjusting the flame, then lifting it higher into the air, shining the pale light ahead of her.

At first, Maya didn't understand what she was seeing. It came to her piece by piece—pale flesh, arms and legs, hundreds of bodies entwined and moving both separately and together, twisting and heaving gently like flotsam on the surface of the ocean, but vertical, reaching up into the darkness. It was the limbs rubbing and sliding together that made the rustling, slippery sound of skin-on-skin. The low animal noises she'd heard before were coming from them too. Maya thought of animals feeding in a barnyard.

Cora lifted the lantern higher. Maya followed the light with her eyes. Once again, she couldn't believe what she was seeing. A large round orb the size of a boulder, glistening wet and black with a cold glint of light at its center. The orb blinked.

Maya screamed, a short, dry scream that caught in her throat. She could see the other eye now, equally huge, a jagged mouth like the entrance to a dark, wet pit. A face.

Maya felt a gush of warm liquid soaking her jeans, running down her leg. Her mouth moved to make a word she couldn't say. Cora's hand was on her shoulder now, squeezing firmly, holding her down. "It's alright," she whispered, "It's alright. She won't hurt you."

What is it? were the words Maya was trying to say, but all that came out was a choking sound. Cora seemed to understand and spoke in a hushed, calming voice.

"She came here a long time ago. My grandmother told me *her* grandmother remembered it. Said she fell from the sky. People here were all German back then...they called her Angelmutter."

A wet, ripping sound came from above, and Maya saw what looked like sheets of wet, wrinkled membrane unfolding from behind the immense thing in front of her. It took her a moment to realize that what she was seeing were wings.

"She was hurt. She came in here to die. Some people tried to help her. They brought her things, but none of them helped. Then they finally figured out what she needed..."

The hundreds of bodies clinging to the front of the huge thing stirred and shifted, their faces all turned inward toward the orb. That was when Maya recognized the wet, animal noises she couldn't identify before. They were the sounds of sucking.

"She doesn't want anything from us," the older woman continued, reverently, "She's not like you and me. All she wants is to give. It's what she was made for. It's what keeps her alive."

Maya stared at the mass of naked white bodies shifting and churning like a whole colony of larvae devouring a dead bird, swarming over its breast between outspread, motionless wings.

"Who are they?" Maya finally managed to say.

"They're all the ones who need her. The sick, the dying. She won't let them die. They know that. As long as they stay here with her like this, they'll never die. That's why they're here. That's why you're here, too."

Maya tore her eyes away from the sight in front of her and looked at Cora. The older woman's face was illuminated by the soft kerosene light.

"I knew it the minute I saw you," Cora said. "You need something. Something you can't find anyplace else. That's right, isn't it?"

Maya looked up at the wall of pale bodies in front of her. A ripple seemed to pass through them like grass in the wind. She felt her whole body begin to tremble again.

"Don't be afraid, sweetheart, just do it. Do it now."

Maya looked down at her daughter's face, all the color drained from it in the dim lamplight. Then she stepped closer to the thing in front of her, the trembling in her body growing. By the time she was holding Kaitlyn out in front of her, she was shaking so hard she was afraid she might drop her. She watched, transfixed, as her daughter was taken in and merged with the rest, like a single drop taken in by a deep body of water. Far above in the dark, Maya heard a long, sibilant hiss that sounded like a sigh.

From the darkness behind her, Cora spoke again. "Now you."

Maya didn't understand.

"You know it's true, don't you, sweetheart?" Cora said. "I knew it the minute I saw your face. It's your heart. You won't make it home."

Maya stood there, trying to understand what the older woman was telling her. When she did, she felt the earth fall away beneath her feet. It was true. She would never make it. She'd always known this, ever since she was born. There was a weakness inside of her that no earthly thing could repair. Not her mother, not Brad. Not even Kaitlyn. She tried to look inside herself, but the only thing there was an emptiness waiting to be filled.

Tears running down her face, Maya turned to face the

wall of writhing white bodies and began to unbutton her shirt and jeans. Then she was stepping out of her clothes and climbing upward into that living tangle of arms and legs and beating hearts, trying to find her place among them, searching for what she needed to stay alive.

"For Every Sin, an Absolution"

Kristi DeMeester

I am fifteen the first time my mother pays for me to see the octopus. Inside those yellowing tents with their black-stitched tears we are not supposed to see, my mother pushes coins toward the mustached attendant who looks at her breasts and then at mine. Smiling, he tears off two tickets and points in a vague direction through the crowd. "You'll be in time to see the escape. If you hurry, you'll be able to watch it eat. An entire rat today," he says, but my mother does not lift her eyes to his, and she pushes me forward so that my skirts tangle against my boots, and I stumble. The attendant laughs, and I know his eyes are on my bottom. I straighten, and Mother and I find our way to the center tent where there is a detailed illustration of an octopus in a large, glass container with a filigreed copper top that resembles a cake dome I once saw in a bakery when I was a girl.

We settle ourselves into our seats, and Mother goes very still, her hands folded on her lap and resembling marble or porcelain or any other thing through which blood does not flow, and when the assistants wheel the octopus's dome onstage, Mother leans over and breathes into my ear, so low, so quiet, that I have to shake my head because I cannot hear her, and she repeats herself again, and then again, and over and over until it is impossible not to understand what it is she's said.

"He is your father."

Inside the dome, the octopus clings to the sides; pushes itself away from all those eyes that would demand something of it, that would ask it to be something it was not, and I follow its dim grey-and-brown form as it circles through the water. It is not beautiful in its skin, but in its movement, it is heart-achingly lovely. I am not beautiful, and neither is Mother, but I do not move with grace in the way the octopus does. Over my tongue, I roll those two syllables—*fa-ther*—until they lack any meaning at all.

At school, there are girls who explain in breathless tones what it means to have a husband, how a baby squirms its way into your belly through him, and then out again in a bright mess of blood and pain, but there is a promise of comfort and companionship in a husband and a baby, and I wonder if the octopus promised those things to my mother. If, in those tentacled arms, she imagined a future that was more than dishes and laundry and breathing up into the dark and counting backward from two hundred to keep her heart from falling out of her with a wet slop.

We watch as the octopus squeezes itself in and out of various small places as the crowd applauds politely. If the octopus sees my mother sitting there among all those blank faces, it does not betray itself. It is tired, and there is a job to do. My mother has withdrawn her handkerchief. She crumples it in her fist, and her cheeks are flushed, but she does not cry.

There are questions I want to ask her, my lips burning with the terrible weight of them, but the attendants on stage are in the height of their performance, the octopus spread wide like a star as it covers the glass, and my mother has gone still as death, the color drained from her lips. I swallow down ten years of girlhood taunting of how I had no father, and that he hadn't died in the war after all, but that it was likely my mother was a whore who had never learned how to sponge, and I was a smeared mistake.

If there had once been a father in my life, I had never known him, and Mother had never spoken a word of who the man was. When I asked, she turned her eyes away and said that it had been a long time ago, and the hurt inside of her was still sharp and to please not ask her again. I did not want to cause pain for my sweet, quiet mother—who sometimes forgot who she was and had to spend mornings in bed, a damp cloth over her eyes—and so eventually, I stopped asking.

Onstage, the octopus rolls one great, translucent eye toward the audience, the unnatural pupil seeming to rove from face to face as if taking measure of those who've come to see it—a memorization in banality. When the eye passes over me, I feel nothing, but there's no sadness in it. I have not known him. There's nothing to mourn in that ambivalent stare, and if Mother stiffens beside me, it does not matter, because the octopus is looking elsewhere, and the attendants are scuffling about, their gloved hands concealing a small box cloaked in what is supposed to look like black velvet but isn't. Inside, something breathes and shifts, and I close my eyes because I do not want to see; I close my eyes because there is the taste of death and fear already thick around those seated, and we all take a collective breath, waiting for the moment to come.

But the exhalation does not come, and I peer through my lashes, willing my heart to slow, telling myself that there will be no blood, no ropy tangle of muscles exposed to the air, and when I finally allow myself to look, the rat is swimming in the dome, his claws scrabbling at the edges without catching purchase, and the octopus is tucked into a corner, his tentacles drawn beneath him.

"Oh." Mother's voice is breathy and high, and she twists again at the handkerchief. I can feel the attendants growing nervous, their smiles cracking under the strain as they tap at the glass, as they dip their hands into the water to shove the rat toward the octopus, but it ignores their silent pleas, the threat trembling in their fingertips. The rat is flailing now, his legs beginning to tire so that he has to lift his nose higher and higher, and the crowd shifts uncomfortably, a muttering starting up from somewhere in the back. We have come here to watch a feeding, not to see an animal drown. There's a difference in that sort of violence. We are not *those* kinds of people.

"*Oh*," Mother says again, and the attendants move quickly, their smiles and waving hands a distraction as another scoops the rat from the dome to deposit him back into the box. There is an exclamation and a blur of hurried words—something about the show concluding and how we'd be granted an extended ticket to return to see a feeding if we'd just step this way—and through all of it, the octopus watches the audience rise and flutter about, all of them remembering that there were things to do before they came here.

Mother does not move at first. I don't expect her to, and I stay seated with her, and the attendants ignore us. There is the rat and the octopus and so many other people to contend with, and so they do not see when my mother reaches for the dome, her hands trembling, and the octopus reaches back.

Before the attendants can cover the dome, Mother and I watch as the octopus curls a tentacle upward and seemingly into itself. When the tentacle comes away, floating for the briefest moment before vanishing into the maw at the center of the octopus's body—eaten as the rat should have been—Mother stands.

"Please," Mother says, but the octopus moves no longer. The glass dome vanishes behind more black cloth, and Mother is walking quickly toward the opening in the tent, so I have to hurry to catch up to her. For the rest of the night, she does not speak to me no matter what questions I ask, or how I lift my voice until I am shouting. She only turns away, her hair swept over her face, as I demand to know how an octopus could be the father of a girl; as I ask why she took me to see such a thing only to leave with no explanation.

There are still accusations lying rough across my lips when I drift into sleep. I dream of dark water and the tight, panicked sensation of drowning, but the octopus is not there, and I cry out for him in the way a child would cry after a fall, but I am alone in all that water and there is nothing warm to grasp, and I wake, gasping beneath dim sunlight.

Mother stands at my door, her fingers curled against the frame, and her eyes are wet. "Breakfast," she says, then turns away, and a deep hurt flowers in my belly. There is pain in her past I cannot understand, and yesterday was a confusion, another episode like the days when she forgets her name and remains motionless in bed.

We do not speak of that day ever again.

Mother's last breath comes when I am twenty-two. I am not there when she takes it. It is a neighbor who finds her. Popping by to see if they could share a cup of tea only to discover Mother's body spread over the floor, her dress peeled open from the throat as if she'd been trying to tear it off of herself, her shawl cast away, and her lips bloodied.

They do not tell me about what's missing from my mother's remains when I go to see the body—those doctors with their grave faces and smiles that do not reach their eyes—and I am forced to look at my mother's hands, forced to see the missing ring finger; the loose, jagged skin.

"What is this?" I ask, and the doctors only shake their heads.

"She may have cut it and fallen and not been able to call out. While cooking, perhaps?" The doctor is heavily mustached, so that when he offers an actual smile, I cannot see his teeth.

"This is not a cut," I say. I am not stupid, but still these doctors smack their lips and tell me how sorry they are for my loss and usher me from the room. I do not see my mother's body again, and my mouth tastes of iron and salt, and my hands shake with the transparency of their lie. It is only when skin tears that it appears in such a way, but there is no one else to question, so I go quietly back to my mother's house to clean up what remains. I look for her finger, but I do not find it, and I imagine terrible things: the blood on her lips and what secret was traced in that crimson bloom.

I bury her in a closed casket and tell myself it was not my fault, but they are empty reassurances, and in the night I think of her teeth closing over that finger, how she would have bitten down to take herself apart and then gobbled down what came away. I blink against the thought, light a candle and stare into its dim light, but the vision will not leave me.

A fortnight passes, and the house is emptied of its furniture, the floors swept and scrubbed, and cobwebs brushed from the corners. I cannot abide the silence, cannot continue waiting for my mother's footstep to sound just behind me, and so I lock the house as I leave, intent to walk until my muscles ache and my fingers are numb with the cold, and I've forgotten that she has vanished from this world.

I do not know how long or how far I have walked when I find the tents. They are still yellowed, still stitched together with dark thread, but there are no crowds, no children chasing after each other, their voices rising into excited shrieks, no attendants milling about trying to entice passersby into coming inside to see something extraordinary, to break away from the drab world they know and to enter into a world of fantasy. Here, there is only wind and the whipping snap of the tents and what feels like a silence greater than the one I've left behind in my mother's empty house.

My skirts are heavy with a chilled damp, and I am tired in a way that has leaked into my blood; it courses through me in dulled throbs. I make my way through the tents, looking for a scrap of color or a blur of movement, but if there is anything living in this place, it is hidden away. I shiver, and draw my shawl closer, my boots scraping against the hard earth as I make my way further into the great mass of tents.

The signs indicating what marvel lies within are gone, and I stop at the entrance of each opening to peer inside. Most hold nothing more than a few chairs and the deep smell of animal sweat and refuse, but ahead, almost in the center of the tents, is a lone placard. It boasts a dark swirl of text and an illustration I cannot make out from such a distance, but my skin crawls, and I think I know what I will see drawn there. I close my eyes and remember, inching forward, and, when I open my eyes, I see the long, curling tentacles; that great single eye open to stare out into an infinite, blanked out world.

I tell myself it is not the same place my mother brought me to all those years ago. I tell myself it would be best to turn and leave these tents to crumble into the dust. In the deepest parts of my mind, I believe neither of those things. I part the opening of the tent and step inside.

The chairs are as I remember them. Set in a semicircle around the small, raised dais and close enough together to make it seem as if there is no separation between the bodies, but one continuous mass that goes on and on, their eyes forever watching. I do not look up to see if there is anything on the stage. Not yet. If I do, I will understand that it—that *he*—has been here all this time, waiting, and such knowledge would unravel all that is still keeping me sane.

It was a story. She was confused and tired. This is the glass memory I have constructed for myself about that day. The one that became truth because I willed it to be. But I am here, in this tent, and I know that when I raise my eyes, I will see that same dome, the water perhaps murky and scummed against the glass, those tentacles shifting and moving in shadowed, graceful arcs.

And so, I look. And I see.

The dome is there, the copper top streaked in patina, but the glass is clear and the water clean as if someone had placed the dome on the small stage just moments before I entered the tent. Inside, the octopus has stretched itself wide, and it floats, ambivalent to my presence, and I remember again the heat of my mother's whisper. *He is your father.*

Suddenly, the tent is stifling, and I pull at my shawl, at the collar of my dress, but then stop, my fingers trembling as I recall my mother's dress, how it had been torn open at the throat, and I bring my hands together and press them palm-to-palm as if in prayer. But this is no holy place; this earth is not consecrated ground.

"You are not the same. You are not," I say, and the octopus rolls an eye towards me, and I flinch under the heavy gaze.

Slowly, the creature draws into itself, the tentacles curling upward as they did before, and it is so hot, and my lungs try to draw in air, but the air is damp, and I am choking, reeling forward so that I fall prostrate beneath the dome. The octopus shifts so that I am looking up into that maw as it feeds, tentacle after tentacle vanishing until the thrashing in the water is frenzied, the octopus jerking through this violence against itself, and I feel the heat deep in my belly. Remembering my mother's missing finger, I fear I will be sick, that I will vanish in this place, this father-creature devouring its own body above me.

I wonder if perhaps she thought it was a kind of offering. If, remembering that day I saw the octopus the first time, she imagined it would call him back to her, if spilling her blood and reabsorbing what she'd lost, would enable his return.

I tremble, my mouth forming words I can no longer identify, and the churning water slows until it is once again quiet in the tent.

I repeat myself again and again until I remember what it is I'm saying. "I'm sorry."

The octopus only watches, the damaged tentacles floating beside it, and then it opens its mouth once more, and before everything falls away, before the world blinks out, I see the pointed tip of a finger emerge from within.

"You found her," I say, and then there is only darkness.

When I wake it is to the sound of coarse voices and rough hands against my cheeks, my arms, and then my body is weightless as someone lifts me upward. "S'all right now, Miss. Can you hear me?" My head lolls backward, and a female voice shouts.

"Mind her neck, John. She'll be sore, I expect. What she was doing out walking this time of night in the middle of nothing, I'll never understand."

He turns then, and I look out over a wide, moonlit expanse of rough field. There are no tents. No glass dome. No octopus.

"There she is, then. We'll have you warmed up in a bit, Miss." The man is silver-haired but clean-shaven, and he smiles down at me with tobacco-stained teeth. "You get lost out here, love? Is that it?"

"There were tents," I say, and my voice is thick and stupid, and I wish to be away from here. From this man and this woman I do not know, and from this place that still holds the smell of decay and animals.

"What's that, Miss? Tents, you say? Nothing out here but grass and sheep."

The woman appears, her head wrapped in a heavy scarf, and she clucks her tongue. "Poor dear. Half addled with cold."

I do not speak further, but keep my tongue still and

let the pair fuss over me. Their home is warm and filled with the scent of stew that they ladle into thick bowls and spoon into my mouth. They assume I became lost in the fields, and I do not correct them, and only when I can tell them my name, where I'm from, do they agree to let me leave—chaperoned, of course—and return to Mother's empty house.

"If it hadn't been for Bennie, we mightn't have found you. Whistled and whistled, but he wouldn't leave your side, so I had to go hunting for him. It's the creatures that have a sense of things that are wrong, isn't it?" the man says as he walks beside me, and I smile back at him and force myself to nod.

"The creatures. Yes," I say, and hope he cannot see how my shoulders have begun to shake.

"Take care of yourself, Miss," the man says when we are on my mother's doorstep, and he presses a hand to my wrist. "Out there, in the dark, the earth can look mighty strange."

I lift my hand in a wave and wait for him to vanish around the bend, and then I go inside and lock the door behind me. I wait for sleep, but it does not come. The inside of that house sounds like a glass dome filled with water or like fingers tapping against wood.

When the sun rises—the rooms filled with grayed light—I leave my mother's house. I will sell it, and there will be another family who fills it. Another mother and father and child who will live and sleep and dream inside those rooms, and perhaps they will hear the water and wonder what it could mean, but the water will not be meant for them, and so they will continue on under its sound, and eventually, they will forget to hear it.

I go back to my own little house, with its small herb garden, and its tiny bedroom, and its smells of clean air and rosemary. I open the windows and stare out into the sky and wait, but there are no sounds other than wind and birdcalls and the slow, creeping sound of things growing.

I stare at my fingers.

I tell myself I am not hungry.

I tell myself I am not like my father.

BIOGRAPHIES

THE EDITORS

Christopher Golden is the *New York Times* bestselling, Bram Stoker Award-winning author of such novels as *Ararat, The Pandora Room, Snowblind, Of Saints and Shadows,* and *Wildwood Road.* With Mike Mignola, he is the co-creator of two cult favorite comic book series, *Baltimore* and *Joe Golem: Occult Detective.* As an editor, he has worked on the short story anthologies *Seize the Night, Dark Cities,* and *The New Dead,* among others, and he has also written and co-written comic books, video games, screenplays, and a network television pilot. Golden co-hosts the podcasts *Three Guys with Beards* and *Defenders Dialogue.* In 2015 he founded the popular Merrimack Valley Halloween Book Festival. He was born and raised in Massachusetts, where he still lives with his family. His work has been nominated for the British Fantasy Award, the Eisner Award, and multiple Shirley Jackson Awards. For the Bram Stoker Awards, Golden has been nominated eight times in eight different categories. His original novels have been published in more than fifteen languages in countries around the world. Please visit him at www.christophergolden.com

James A. Moore is the bestselling and award-winning author of over forty-five novels, thrillers, dark fantasy and horror alike, including the critically acclaimed *Fireworks, The Seven Forges* series, *Blood Red,* the *Serenity Falls* trilogy (featuring his recurring anti-hero, Jonathan Crowley) and his most recent novels, *The Tides of War series (The Last Sacrifice, Fallen Gods* and *Gates of the Dead) Boomtown, and Avengers: Infinity.* In addition to writing multiple short stories, he has also edited, with Christopher Golden and Tim Lebbon, the *British Invasion* anthology for Cemetery Dance Publications. Along with Christopher Golden and Jonathan Maberry he is co-host of the *Three Guys With Beards* podcast.

The author cut his teeth in the industry writing for Marvel Comics and authoring over twenty role-playing supplements for White Wolf Games, including *Berlin by Night, Land of 1,000,000 Dreams* and *The Get of Fenris* tribe book for *Vampire: The Masquerade* and *Werewolf: The Apocalypse,* among others. He also penned the White Wolf novels *Vampire: House of Secrets* and *Werewolf: Hellstorm.*

Moore's first short story collection, *Slices,* sold out before ever seeing print.

Jim also teaches seminars and classes, once again with Christopher Golden, under the heading of The River City Writers. They can be found easily enough on Facebook. More information about the author can be found at his website: jamesamoorebooks.com.

THE AUTHORS

Andrew Bourelle is the author of the novel *Heavy Metal* and coauthor with James Patterson of *Texas Ranger*. His work has been published in *The Best American Mystery Stories*, *Florida Review*, *The Molotov Cocktail*, *Mystery Tribune*, *Pulp Adventures*, *Swords & Steam Short Stories*, *Weirdbook Magazine*, and other journals and anthologies. He is on twitter at @AndrewBourelle.

Jeffrey B. Burton was born in Long Beach, California, grew up in Saint Paul, Minnesota, and received his B.A. in Journalism at the University of Minnesota. Novels in Burton's Agent Drew Cady mystery series include *The Chessman*, *The Lynchpin*, and *The Eulogist*. His short stories have appeared in dozens of magazines. Burton is a member of the Mystery Writers of America, International Thriller Writers, and the Horror Writers Association. He lives in Saint Paul with his wife, daughter, and an irate Pomeranian named Lucy.

Winner of both a Bram Stoker and World Fantasy Award, **P.D. Cacek** has written over a hundred short stories, six plays, and six published novels. Her most recent novel, SECOND LIVES, published by Flame Tree Publishing, is currently available from Amazon.com. She is currently working on a new novel, SECOND CHANCES. Cacek holds a bachelor's degree in English/Creative Writing Option from the University of California at Long Beach and has been a guest lecturer at the Odyssey Writing Camp. A native Westerner, Cacek now lives in Phoenixville, PA. When not writing, she can often be found either with a group of costumed storytellers called *The Patient Creatures* (www.creatureseast.com), or haunting local cemeteries looking for inspiration.

Kristi DeMeester is the author of *Beneath*, a novel published by Word Horde Publications, and *Everything That's Underneath*, a short fiction collection from Apex Books. Her short fiction has appeared in approximately forty magazines, including Ellen Datlow's *The Year's Best Horror* Volume 9 and 11, Stephen Jones' *Best New Horror, Year's Best Weird Fiction* Volumes 1, 3, and 5 in addition to publications such as *Pseudopod* , *Black Static, Fairy Tale Review* , and several others. In her spare time, she alternates between telling people how to pronounce her last name and how to spell her first. Find her online at www.kristidemeester.com.

M. M. De Voe is a Manhattan-based writer whose short fiction has won many literary prizes. She wrote the book for a sci-fi musical with Bill Moulton, R/Evolution, which premiered Off Broadway in 2014. She founded the literary nonprofit, Pen Parentis, in 2013, providing resources to writers who are also parents (penparentis.org). Anthologized alongside Joyce Carol Oates and Margaret Atwood and nominated for three Pushcart Prizes, some recent placements include Black Static (winner of Campaign for Real Fear), Santa Barbara Review, Tales from the Canyons of the Damned, Bellevue Review, and Daily Science Fiction. She is the recipient of multiple grants including the Manhattan Community Arts Fund, Fund for Creative Communities, and Arch and Bruce Brown Foundation Grant for Historical Fiction with Gay Positive Characters. She was a Columbia University MFA Writing Fellow. Follow on Twitter @mmdevoe. Like on Facebook at www.facebook.com/mmdevoe. www.mmdevoe.com

John Linwood Grant is a professional writer/editor from Yorkshire who lives with a pack of lurchers and a beard. Widely published in anthologies and magazines, he writes contemporary weird fiction, plus stories of murder, madness and the supernatural for his 'Tales of the Last Edwardian' series, including the 1920s conjure-woman Mamma Lucy. His latest novel *The Assassin's Coin* (from IFD) features the unstoppable Mr. Edwin Dry, as does the new collection *A Persistence of Geraniums* (Ulthar). He is editor of *Occult Detective Quarterly*, and anthologies such as 'ODQ Presents' and 'Hell's Empire'. Feel free to bother him on Facebook, and at his popular website greydogtales.com.

Amanda Helms is a science-fiction and fantasy writer whose work has appeared in *The Cackle of Cthulhu* anthology, *Daily Science Fiction, Cast of Wonders,* and elsewhere. Amanda blogs infrequently at amandahelms.com and tweets with a smidgen more frequency @amandaghelms. She and her husband live in Colorado with their increasingly lazy Boxer mix.

Liam Hogan is an Oxford Physics graduate and award-winning London-based writer. His short story "Ana" appeared in Best of British Science Fiction 2016 (NewCon Press) and "The Dance of a Thousand Cuts" appears in Best of British Fantasy, 2018. More at http://happyendingnotguaranteed.blogspot.co.uk or tweet @LiamJHogan.

Sarah L. Johnson lives in Calgary where she is a curly hair gladiator, ultramarathoner, and indie bookstore events wrangler. Her horror fiction has appeared in Shock Totem, Crossed Genres, Year's Best Hardcore Horror Vol. 2, and the Bram Stoker Award nominated Dark Visions 1. She's also the author of Suicide Stitch: Eleven Tales (EMP Publishing) and Infractus (Coffin Hop Press).

Eóin Murphy has been writing since that time he wasn't allowed to go see The Monster Squad in the cinema and decided to write his own version. He lives in Northern Ireland with his wonderful wife and fantastic son. Eóin's work has previously been published in local small press publications including The Incubator Journal and Phantasmagoria. This appearance in The Twisted Book of Shadows represents his first major sale and he is quite excited about this development. Eóin is currently working on his second novel, a supernatural thriller set in post-Brexit Northern Ireland. Eóin can be found lurking on Twitter at @RageMonki

George Edwards Murray is a horror and fantasy writer from Maine. He has been published in Daily Science Fiction, Bourbon Penn, and other venues for strange tales. See more of his work at www.elegantapocalypse.com.
Cindy O'Quinn is an Appalachian writer from West Virginia, who now lives, writes, & homesteads on the old Tessier Homestead in northern Maine. She is the author of *Dark Cloud on Naked Creek*, and the poetry collection, *Return to Graveyard Dust*, which made it to the 2017 HWA Preliminary Ballot. Her work has been published in the HWA Poetry Showcase Vol V, Nothing's Sacred Vol 4 & 5, Sanitarium Magazine, The 2017 & 2019 Rhysling Anthologies, & many others. Member of HWA, NESW, NEHW, SFPA, Horror Writers of Maine, & Weird Poets Society. Follow her on Facebook @CindyOQuinnWriter, Twitter @COQuinnWrites, and Instagram cindy.oquinn.

Rohit Sawant's fiction has appeared in *Weirdbook*, *CultureCult Magazine* and can be found in *Transcendent*, *On Fire*, *Sherlock Holmes: Adventures in the Realms of H.G. Wells* and other anthologies. He lives in Mumbai, India. When he isn't working as a VFX professional, he likes to draw portraits and cook. His favorite Batman is Kevin Conroy. You can find him at rohitsawantfiction.wordpress.com and @iamrohitsawant on twitter.

David Surface lives in the Hudson River Valley of New York. His stories have appeared in *Shadows & Tall Trees, Supernatural Tales, Nightscript, Morpheus Tales, The Tenth Black Book of Horror,* and have been anthologized in *Darkest Minds* from Dark Minds Press, and *Ghost Highways* from Midnight Street Press. A story co-authored with Julia Rust, 'TallDarkAnd', appears in the Swan River Press anthology, *Uncertainties III.* He is a regular contributor to *Black Static Magazine* where his column 'One Good Story' appears. His stories have received long-list Honorable Mentions in Ellen Datlow's *Best Horror of the Year, Volumes 7 and 8, SFEditors Picks*, and have been nominated for the Pushcart Prize in fiction. You can visit him online at davidsurfacewriter.wordpress.com

Melissa Swensen is a horror writer from Sacramento, California. At present she finds herself in a state of metamorphoses, some old, rotten pieces of her have fallen away and strange new appendages are growing. Impossible to say how she'll end up. Or where. Her work has appeared in *The Molotov Cocktail*, *The Literary Hatchet*, and in the anthology *Strange California*. You can connect with her on Twitter @honeygloom.

Sara Tantlinger resides outside of Pittsburgh on a hill in the woods. She is the Bram Stoker Award-winning author of *The Devil's Dreamland: Poetry Inspired by H.H. Holmes*. She is a poetry editor for the *Oddville Press*, a member of the SFPA, and an active member of the HWA. Currently, Sara is editing *Not All Monsters,* an anthology that will be comprised entirely of women who write speculative fiction. The anthology is set for a 2020 release with StrangeHouse Books. She can be found lurking in graveyards or at saratantlinger.com and @SaraJane524 on Twitter.

Surrounded by gnomes, gargoyles and poisonous plants, **KT Wagner** writes Gothic horror and op/ed pieces in the garden of her Maple Ridge, British Columbia home. She enjoys daydreaming and is a collector of strange plants, weird trivia, and obscure tomes. In her spare time, she organizes writer events and works to create literary community. KT graduated from Simon Fraser University's Writers Studio in 2015 (Southbank 2013). A number of her short stories are published in magazines and anthologies. She's currently working on a fantasy-horror novel. KT can be found online at @KT_Wagner, and at www.northernlightsgothic.com.

Trisha J. Wooldridge writes grown-up horror short stories and weird poetry—some even winning awards! Her recent publications include stories and poems in *Gothic Fantasy Supernatural Horror*, *The HWA Poetry Showcase Volume 5*, *Pseudopod* podcast, and *Wicked Weird*. As child-friendly T.J. Wooldridge, she's published three spooky kids' novels, poetry in The Jimmy Fund charity anthology *Now I Lay Me Down To Sleep*, and will be in the upcoming *New Scary Stories to Tell in the Dark* (HarperCollins 2020). She's a member of SCBWI, HWA, New England Horror Writers, New England Speculative Writers, and Broad Universe. Join her adventures at www.anovelfriend.com.

Jason A. Wyckoff is the author of two short story collections published by Tartarus Press, *Black Horse and other Strange Stories* (2012) and *The Hidden Back Room* (2016). His work has appeared in numerous anthologies, as well as the journals Nightscript, Weirdbook, and Turn to Ash. He lives in Columbus, Ohio. Married; four cats (on average). You can find him online at jasonawyckoff.weebly.com.

CPSIA information can be obtained
at www.ICGtesting.com
Printed in the USA
FSHW022159151019
63066FS

9 781949 140095